M000289375

BLACK GHOST

BLACK GHOST

GHOST

FREDDIE VILLACCI, JR.

BLACK GHOST

Copyright © 2020 by Freddie Villacci, JR
Invincible Beauty Publishing

First Edition

ISBN: 978-1-7352247-0-1 Paperback
        978-1-7352247-2-5 Hardcover
        978-1-7352247-1-8 Ebook

No part of this book may be reproduced in any form or by any electronic or
mechanical means, including information storage and retrieval systems, without
written permission from the author, except for the use of brief quotations in a book
review.

This is a work of fiction. Names, characters, businesses, places, events and incidents
are either the products of the author's imagination or used in a fictitious manner.
Any resemblance to actual persons, living or dead, or actual events is purely
coincidental.

Cover design: ebooklaunch.com
Interior design: Erik Gevers

One last job and he's done for good...
until two rookie agents ruin it all.

Cunning
    Resourceful
        Seemingly supernatural

Bic Green is a world-class contract killer. Tormented by his demons and a life steeped in blood, he clings to absolution from his evils by channeling his funds toward his goddaughter, Gracie, for her quest to cure cancer.

When a shadowy Congressman gives him 21 days to assassinate America's ten wealthiest citizens, Bic has a choice, maintain his code of never killing innocent people or take the eight-figure payout and fully fund Gracie's research. Bic plans each murder meticulously, creating elaborate ways to make each billionaire's death look accidental. Nobody suspects a thing.

But after two rookie FBI agents, the headstrong Mack Maddox and his troubled partner Caroline Foxx, stumble on an unsuspected clue, they quickly begin to unravel the insidious plot. With billionaires dropping like flies and their superiors ordering them to stand down, they push forward until they find themselves deep in the crosshairs of the Black Ghost.

With no time left, terrifying questions stir within Bic's psyche. Is he a killer using Gracie as an excuse for his ritualistic murders? Even more importantly, if he can't stop himself, who can?

If you're a fan of fast-paced thrillers filled to the brim with action and suspense, then you won't want to miss the page-turning debut novel in the *Black Ghost* series. Grab your copy today!

Dedicated to my wife, Jennifer,
Having the strength of your unconditional love
has given me the courage to take on
failure and always continue to
try just one more time.
I love you.

To my son, Vincent,
You are my creative inspiration.

1

The ex-Ranger scanned the surroundings then lowered his rifle and beckoned. Congressmen John Alfred Tidwell stepped out of the helicopter, ducking while hunching his shoulders against the harsh bite of the unseasonably cold Wasatch mountain winds. The distinguished looking forty-year-old stood nine thousand feet above sea-level on a Black Ops landing platform carved into the side of Mount Nebo. Despite taking a deep breath, the crisp air barely filled his lungs. Regardless, he took a second and savored a long view of massive towering jagged rock peaks capped by pure white snow. He snapped out of the tranquil moment and pulled his Burberry long coat tight. Time to take care of business.

Snow crunched under Congressman Tidwell's shoes as he walked briskly past the three other helicopters that had landed on the bank of pads. This particular secret installation was an artifact of the cold war, tucked away in the middle of nowhere. Under the platform was a network of tunnels leading to defunct secret laboratories and high-level interrogation chambers. Most importantly, the decommissioned black ops site was spy-proof. It had to be considering what he was about to propose as a solution to everything that had gone wrong.

He fished out his access card.

"Senator." His escort took the card and swiped it through the scanner. The large metal doors slid to the side.

"Wait here. I'll be back." Tidwell took his card back.

"Sir, I don't think that's a good idea."

"I don't pay you to think, leave that to me."

The soldier nodded, then after only a moment's hesitation offered his side arm to the senator. "Sir, I won't be able to do my job from out here."

Tidwell ignored the gesture and entered the facility alone.

As he walked through the empty halls, each step echoing off the walls, he worked the problem in his head. He had been responsible to have the US government agree to fund a quarter of a trillion dollar joint venture with a Russian conglomerate to pump oil and natural gas out of Siberia to include an unprecedented delivery system of four thousand miles of pipeline to four ports along the Black Sea and the Pacific. The whole thing had fallen apart on the floor of the house and now he was left holding the bag of broken promises with a bunch of former KGB and current Russian mafia members.

Tidwell stopped in front of a nondescript door–formerly an interrogation chamber–and stared at his shaking hand.

"Steady, John. Steady." He took a deep breath.

A slow smile crept across his face before entering the room. Stale air that smelled of fresh cigar smoke and decade old pain wafted out.

"Gentlemen," he said as he walked into a room with a naked bulb dangling over a rectangular steel table.

Tidwell felt the razor-sharp stares of his partners. Gary Bryson, a bald, heavyset yes man of a Senator in his mid-fifties sat to the right. To the left, Phil Utah–the Deputy Director of the CIA–had a strong build with a long, sun beaten face, droopy blue eyes, and bushy brown mustache. And sitting opposite Tidwell at the entrance was Anthony Parelli, the source of the cigar smoke and organized crime's most sophisticated high-end player in the US. Tidwell's eyes lingered for a moment on Parelli's hands. His knuckles and fingers were calloused and scarred from literally fighting his way to the top. Tidwell hid a shudder by pulling out the seat closest to the door and settling in it.

All three men stared at him, silently, though Parelli rhythmically tapped his fingertips against the steel table.

"I can't believe this happened," Senator Bryson broke the silence, his jowls bouncing as he spoke. "Three years ago you got us in bed with the Russian mob, convincing us to give them millions of dollars to bribe almost everyone in mother Russia."

"I promised to deliver, and I didn't. That's on me." Tidwell leaned forward, comfortably propping his elbows on the table, not yet ready to play his ace.

"Cut the crap, John–," Agent Utah spoke with a slight drawl. "The Russians are swarming around like mad hornets." He leaned forward almost barking at Tidwell. "They have a 'scorched earth' policy.

They'll kill us, our families, other loved ones. That's what's on you."

Senator Bryson became somber, "what do you mean kill us? Just have them arrested!"

Agent Utah shook his head, "you kidding? There's thousands of 'em and you'll never get close to the shot callers. Once they decide to, they'll gut us like pigs and we won't be able to stop them."

Parelli never looked at either of the two other men. He just stared intently at Tidwell, not twitching a muscle.

Still relaxed, Tidwell placed a flash drive on the table, "I have a way to save this deal."

"Here it comes." Agent Utah pulled out his Sig Sauer 357 caliber pistol and slammed it on the table, "Don't you ask me for more money, John. Bribing the Russian mob after a failed deal doesn't work. They just keep coming at you for more money till you're broke then kill you anyway."

"We're so screwed." Senator Bryson spoke quietly to himself, his sweat mixing with nervous tears.

"Enough," Parelli said, slapping a meaty hand against the cold table. The bang echoed for a heartbeat in the room and all eyes turned to him. The dark-haired mobster casually pulled a new cigar out of the inner pocket of his tan Armani suit.

In an oddly disjointed moment, Tidwell marveled that the man looked so young, despite being over 50 and a smoker. He had brought Parelli in as a consultant to help Utah and Bryson connect with the right people in Russia, and Parelli had quickly become a full partner.

Parelli rotated the stogie over the flame of his custom butane lighter, slowly puffing it to life.

"Dang it, Parelli. You got somethin' to say, say it." Utah said.

Anthony Parelli puffed out a smoke ring, then narrowed his eyes and spoke in a low, steady, and above all, calculated, voice. "We all have a lot of dough tied up in this deal. If the reputable Congressman from California has a solution other than my boys going to war with the Russians—I'd like to hear it. And he does have a solution." Parelli then scowled at Agent Utah, "And, Phil, you pull a gun again and I'll feed your balls to my Rottweiler."

Agent Utah holstered his weapon and signaled to Tidwell to give him the room. "By all means, Houdini, share with us how you're going to make a quarter of a trillion dollars appear in the government piggy bank from nowhere in twenty-one days."

3

Tidwell glared at the men, his eyes drilled out any illusion of an easy fix. The commitment he needed from these men had escalated far beyond the pale, the next twenty-one days were going to be a nefarious cocktail of all seven of the deadly sins.

2

U.S. Senator Gary Bryson waited anxiously on the steps of the downtown L.A. courthouse. Shading his eyes from the sunny day, he looked furtively around him as politicians jawed about issues to hovering journalists eager to land the next big story and businessmen rushed from one appointment to another to make their next buck.

Bryson paused at the courthouse entranceway, eyes darting here and there, as if assessing where some danger might lurk within this otherwise normal day. Then, with a deep breath, he darted down the steps, avoiding eye contact with everyone.

Ten feet from the street, Bryson noticed a black town car pulling up to the curb. He didn't recognize the car at first and froze. The tinted glass lowered.

"Senator," said his assistant with a grin. "You'll be late for your meeting."

Breathing a relieved sigh, Bryson got in.

The town car pulled into traffic, weaving through the downtown streets as the senator distractedly checked his phone, ignoring his assistant droning on about the afternoon schedule. They turned south on Vermont, headed toward the 10.

"Sir, is everything all right?" William asked.

The senator's phone rang, and he jumped. He checked the caller ID and swallowed hard as sweat began beading on his brow.

"Sir? Are you–?"

Bryson shushed William then barked at the driver, "Head down to 8th Street, now!"

Disheveled and breathing heavily, Bryson glanced behind himself every few steps as he hurriedly made his way through the massive parking garage.

He pulled out his cell phone and frantically thumbed through his contacts, looking for a number. Tires screeched and he dropped his phone. Bending over to retrieve it, he felt like every lunch from the past two weeks was about to come up. Gulping, he caught his breath, then sprinted for the elevator.

Pick up please God pick up...

"What do you want, Bryson?" said the voice on the other end.

"Bubba, I'm on my way to my attorney—they're coming for me. There's only one way they're going to let me out."

"What?"

"I have no choice."

"You're overreactin', Gary. That might not be the best idea."

"Overreacting? Bubba, this is way beyond government contracts. Way past white collar." Bryson paused to catch his breath, then continued, "Marty has to get me out of this mess. I can't even trust my people. I'm on an island all by myself."

"What do I keep tellin' ya, Gary? Don't get mixed in these kinds of projects—they'll bury you."

"I didn't realize," he said with a whimper.

"Don't start whining to me, Gary. Man up and tell me, what'd you get yourself into this time?"

"It's big... real big. And bad."

"Just lay it on me."

"Murder. Assassination. A lot of innocent people are going to die. Women too." His voice trembled with emotion. "They're being clever about it, though. No one will figure it out until it's too late."

"What are you talking about?"

"They're bringing in a specialist. Do you have any idea what that means? A specialist?"

"A specialist?"

"A profess—" He darted his gaze around and lowered his voice. "A professional killer. This is big, Bubba. I've seen the list! Rock stars, all of them. And all killed to fund—"

"Now take it easy, Gary. I'm sure no one's going to die."

"I—dear God, is this line secure? I've said too much, haven't I?"

"Stop with the ridiculous conspiracy crap. Do I know these people?"

"Of course you know them. Everybody does."

"Just calm down, Gary, and give me some names."

"Not now. I'm almost to my attorney's office. I'll call after I get there."

Gary Bryson rushed out of the elevator into the elaborate law office of Feldbrook, Little, Korman, and Kahn. He gasped, relieved to see nothing out of the ordinary... just the soft smile of the pretty young receptionist in a thankfully empty reception area.

With only a nod at the receptionist, Bryson walked down the long corridor to Marty's fancy corner office. *My retainer helped pay for this corner office,* Gary thought. *You better help me fix this.* He barged into the office without a knock.

He knew a dead man when he saw one.

Marty Kahn had taken a bullet to the forehead. Blood flowed down his face, over his expensive white shirt and Burberry tie.

Frantic, Bryson picked up the phone and dialed 911. As he did so, a man stepped out of the shadowy corner of the room. He jabbed and struck Bryson twice in the nose. Calloused knuckles smashed into the senator's nose and blood erupted from his nostrils as the phone went flying. Bryson reeled back, clasping his hands over his face. "What the hell??" He didn't get a chance to say anything more, interrupted by a meaty fist slamming into his temple. He crashed to the floor, stunned, and bleeding profusely. As he stared up at the attacker, he managed to gasp, "It'll never pass."

The man responded by pulling out a Ruger 22 from a concealed holster under his jacket and firing two silenced shots to the senator's head.

3

Rookie agent Caroline Foxx walked through a long hallway in the Los Angeles FBI field office with two cups of coffee in hand. Her destination was the rookie cave, down a long stairwell and into the agency's bowels, at the far end of the basement. She stopped before the door to the stairwell to do a last-minute check of her appearance in the polished marble wall. She turned sideways once, then back again, frowning. Her athletic body accentuated an otherwise plain conservative grey dress-suit. This had been her compromise; she expected her male counterparts to take her number-two ranking at Quantico seriously, otherwise it would have been ripped jeans and a T-shirt for Caroline Foxx.

She entered a small, cramped room loaded with state-of-the-art surveillance equipment. Sitting in one of the only two chairs, Mack Maddox idly popped sunflower seeds as he read a book on trading stock options. His gun and ID badge lay casually tossed on the table, and he had swapped dress shoes for his old pair of flip flops. He was so focused on what he was reading that he didn't even notice her enter the room. She cleared her throat.

"Oh! Hey. Did you crush the coffee beans by hand?" Mack looked up from his book, his blue eyes gleaming with confidence. "In Brazil?"

"Out of uniform already, I see?" Caroline returned fire, handing Mack a coffee. "Figure out how to make your first million yet?"

"Yeah. Avoid government work."

Caroline got comfortable. It would be a long surveillance. Then again, from everything she had ever heard, they all were.

"A hundred violent crimes will be committed this week alone in LA, and they have us caged in this hole listening to this buffoon."

Mack took another swig of coffee. He didn't need to respond. She knew he felt the same way. Neither one of them had joined the FBI to waste away on special task forces doing meaningless surveillance work on American politicians.

Caroline remembered the line of crap Assistant Director Bender had fed her. How it was a *privilege* to be assigned actual fieldwork right out of the Academy. How valuable her contribution was to the Bureau. How it would serve national security. Yadda yadda yadda.

She and Mack knew the job had been created for one reason: to get dirt on politicians that would be used during election years. They weren't protecting America, they were two mindless cogs in the vicious machinery of party politics–all at the taxpayer's expense.

"Seriously, though," Caroline said, "do you have any idea how many teenage girls are trapped in sex trafficking, hundreds, maybe thousands right here in LA alone?"

He was lost in a daydream, his coffee cup frozen at his lips. "Hm?"

"Did you hear anything I said?"

"Sorry, I got lost there for a minute."

"No kidding." She looked at the monitor. An audio signal had registered not more than fifteen minutes ago. "What did I miss?"

"What do you mean?"

She pointed to the monitor. "Bubba got a call?"

He looked up and noticed the signal. "Dammit!" He fumbled over the laptop keys to replay the call.

"Probably another sex call," said Caroline.

"That's usually an after-dinner thing."

"Bet you a Snickers bar it is."

"You're on."

Caroline crossed her fingers hoping she could count on Bubba Taylor to entertain them with what she referred to as his "community outreach." Since the assignment had begun, they hadn't heard any conversations even remotely related to selling nuclear secrets to North Korea, which was the reason they were tapping the lobbyist's telephone lines to begin with.

She quickly logged onto the system from her laptop, then signaled to Mack, who was just fitting in an earpiece. He adjusted the earpiece and nodded.

They listened quietly for over a minute.

Caroline gave Mack a quizzical glance.

He smirked and said, "It's his girlfriend."

"I can*not* believe this gross old man. Anyway, you owe me a Snickers."

"Not yet. Crap, he's having better success than yesterday."

Caroline wrinkled her nose in silence.

"What's wrong?" he asked, as he listened to the senator getting off. "You can't tell me this bothers you anymore than–"

"No. It's just that I didn't quit my dad's firm to spy on fat cat lobbyists. If we don't get a real assignment pretty soon, I'm seriously going to punch somebody in the face."

Mack nodded. "I feel you. I could be working on Wall Street making millions, driving a Ferrari, banging a different supermodel every week."

"A man with lofty ideals, I see. They're not as fun as you'd think."

"Ferraris or supermodels?"

Caroline pursed her lips and twitched an eyebrow at him. "What's that pig doing now? I can't bear to listen."

Mack blushed a little. "Um, ah, let's just say she's got a new toy... she's calling it her little Bubba."

Caroline pulled her hair back into a ponytail and secured it with a hair tie. "Cheaters are horrible people," she grumbled. "Serve him right if we called his wife–see how he'd like it if she left his ass and took half. Living in this basement and gathering dirt on gross old perverts is *not* what I signed up for. The honeymoon is over." She paused and looked at him. "Maxwell? Hey, Caroline to Maxwell? You listening?"

"Huh? Yeah, sorry. Honeymoon."

There was a call-waiting click on the line. Taylor cursed expressively and flipped the call over.

"Pick up," said Mack, motioning to her earpiece. "Another call coming in."

"Ugh. Don't tell me, a threesome."

Mack stared at the table, his fingers dancing on his knee.

"*What do you want, Bryson?*" Bubba Taylor asked.

Caroline jammed away at the keyboard while listening; she looked to Mack excitedly. "This call originates in LA."

The call ended and Caroline snatched her gun and badge off the table. "Stay on the line in case he calls back. I've got the location of the cell–I can get there in five. Text me if the cell location changes."

"Are you crazy? We can't just go into the field."

"I'll just be passing through!" Caroline said as she ran out the door.

4

Fluorescent lights flickered overhead, illuminating an abandoned storage facility on Chicago's South Side. The space was so long out of commercial use that the air had lost the chemical factory smell and was just musty now. A map of America was taped to the far wall with different U.S. cities circled, dates written next to them, and an assortment of other notes scribbled in the margins. Composite sketches of an African-American man covered the remaining walls, ranging from versions of the man in his early twenties right through to his late sixties. The room reeked of an obsessive, life-long manhunt. Hanging incongruously in the center of the space was a well-used punching bag.

A skinny, forty-something man squirmed against the wall, staring bug-eyed at the man looming over him. Bic Green, three times as massive as the unfortunate squirmer and a good eight inches taller, stared through *Terminator*-style sunglasses at a worn-down photograph of the same dude plastered all over the wall. The photo was old; and the young man's face was obscured, but not the eyes–they were deep, intense, and memorably piercing.

"I'm not interested in you," Bic said in a deep, unexpectedly soft voice. His eyes never left the photo; containing his rage almost left him shaking.

"Good to hear, my brother," the man said cautiously, releasing the breath he hadn't realized he was holding.

"I'm interested in a man you knew."

"Just give me a name, and I'll tell you the dude's Social Security number, where his momma's crib is, and who he buys his rocks from."

Bic looked over to the punching bag.

The sight of the name scrawled on the bag in faded black marker sent Bic back to his darkest place; all he could hear was a repeating, horrific hollow thud from an iron skillet connecting to a skull.

Bic grabbed the man by the throat, still looking at the bag, still hearing the thud, repeated like a skipping record and jarring him each time with the sense-memory of pain.

Trying to breathe, the punk squinted at the heavy bag, "Clarence?" he barely spoke.

"Clarence Green. Where is he?"

"I don't know."

The noises in his head faded. Bic released the man's throat then gestured to the sketches on the wall.

"Come on, man," said the punk, "some old black dude in a pencil drawing?" Then he added, sarcastically. "Sure, yeah, I know him. He's down on MLK Boulevard panning for his next dime bag."

With surprising speed, Bic punched the man in the gut. The impact sent the man into the wall.

"There's no way a scumbag like you didn't cross his path."

"You have any idea how many old, washed-up brothers I've sold dope to?"

"Not sold to," Bic growled impatiently. "Someone you would have worked with."

The man whimpered, laboring to catch his breath. "You've got me all mixed up, man. I never had me a partner. Only thing a partner will do in my business is get you shot in the back."

"He would have come to Atlanta about nine years ago. You know the story; brutal addict turned into a ruthless drug kingpin."

That struck a nerve with the man. He swallowed hard. Bic reeled back like he was going to strike the punk again.

"Arright, arright! Don't hit me again! Listen, man, you don't want to find that guy. He's probably dead, the way he was going. But if he ain't, trust me when I tell you, you don't want to cross that man."

Bic pointed to the sketches. "Which one does he look like?"

The man looked at each image, uncertain. But his eyes bulged in appreciable fear when his gaze finally returned to Bic's face. "Look man, don't hit me when I say this."

"Say it."

The punk winced as if about to be struck. "He looks like you!"

Bic grabbed the man by the collars and threw him against the wall.

"Where is he now?"

"*Argh*, man! Listen, man, rumor had it he was high as a kite 24/7 and was obsessed with that crazy-ass black magic stuff–killin' animals and Lord Jesus only knows what other type of messed up voodoo crap. You just know instinctively not to mess with that type of man, ya feel me?" The pusher fell silent for a moment, as if waiting for a response. He squirmed uncomfortably. "Listen, as fast as he took over the city, he left. Never heard from him again. He lit out like a ghost."

Like a ghost.

Bic's phone buzzed. He looked at the pusher, then motioned him to leave. The erstwhile captive didn't need to be told twice. He hopped up like a rabbit, opened the garage door, and scurried away.

Bic opened the file attached to the blank message. It was a list of ten names, with a million-dollar figure next to each name and a dossier of each person, packed full of faces, info, locations, and backgrounds.

He deleted the message once he had the data, wondering if his new employers could secure their information as well as required, or if they were just too powerful to care.

Not that it mattered. The rage was swelling within him once again.

5

Caroline woke with a start, her brow beaded with sweat, her breath caught in her throat. Panic froze the scream on her lips, paralyzing her.

That dream again.

She lay in bed next to Ashton in the master suite of his Malibu beachfront mansion, the silk sheets clinging to her clammy skin, soaked with sweat. She had woken up just past midnight Saturday morning, thankful for one small comfort–that the nightmare, riddled as it was with guilt and despair, didn't rouse her with a scream. She didn't want to have to explain it to him. Motes of the dream floated before her: a young girl raped, tortured, murdered, all while Caroline watched, helplessly rooted to her spot. The faceless man finished, laughed, and walked past her and out of sight. And when she turned her head back to the battered body, she saw the dead, pleading eyes and the purple handprints staining her body.

She feared the dream. The guilt from it had driven her to walk away from her past life. It had worked. The new job was a distraction until earlier this evening when she walked in on two dead bodies. That scene had brought it all back.

Carefully she squirmed out of bed, trying not to wake the soundly-sleeping man beside her. The heady smell of sex still lingered in the room and he would be in his deepest sleep, but still, she didn't want to have to make excuses so she took care.

The crashing waves outside provided excellent cover as she slipped from the bed and tiptoed around the room, collecting her clothes. As she dressed, she glanced at the handcuffs, broken lamp, and a black leather flogger on his nightstand.

Usually these kinds of nights were a release, a way to get out her

17

frustrations and keep the dark thoughts–and the dreams–at bay. She always felt embarrassed by her behavior in the light of innocent morning. She didn't blame Ashton for what she felt. She had been seeing the successful CEO for a couple months now and had just realized what their relationship was built on: a business transaction of wants. Their lovemaking sessions were nothing more than gentle butchery. That just wasn't who she was.

Or was it? Was a lawyer who released a child killer entitled to love?

She wouldn't get the answer here. She left quickly, vowing–as she had many times before–that she would make penance for what she had done.

6

Later that night, Caroline drove around in her car, slowly patrolling the streets of one of the seediest parts of LA. The dry, desert smell of the Santa Ana winds masked the lingering smell of humanity trapped in the streets. She hadn't done this in quite some time. The guilt hadn't been this bad since she left her father's law firm and joined the FBI.

Doubts plagued her like the devil winds fanning a brushfire. Had she made a mistake becoming an FBI agent? Did she think she'd be able to handle seeing dead bodies? Clearly, she couldn't, seeing Bryson and his attorney lying there in pools of blood, brain matter scattered everywhere, had brought the nightmares back. What to do now? If she didn't make things right, her past error was almost certainly going to destroy her now as it did then.

She looked from street corner to street corner. Gang signs were tagged on every conceivable surface. The thought came to her: *Make it right again.* She tapped the steering wheel anxiously, hunting for her release.

"Ah, hello..." she said under her breath.

In front of a convenience store with bars on the windows, a group of men–boys, really–stood in a circle, surrounding a young woman. The girl didn't seem in danger, but it was well after midnight. A couple of the men had bottles covered in brown paper bags, and the group was passing around a joint.

One of the men turned and picked up the girl. She immediately pried herself away, but the man was persistent in grabbing at her.

Caroline pulled over and jumped out of her vehicle. "Take your hands off her," she yelled, sprinting toward the group.

"Who's this snow bunny?" the tall muscular man with dreads

asked.

Caroline barged into the middle of the group toward the girl. "Are you okay?"

"Huh?" said the girl. "What's up with you, lady?"

Caroline grabbed her arm, "Come on. I'll take you home."

The girl pulled her arm away. "Get

off me, cavegirl. You trippin'?"

Caroline looked at the four men glaring at her. They could easily jump her, but she held her ground. "This is no place for a young girl. Trust me, I know."

"I'm safer with my two brothers and cousin than with you, ya dumb b."

Embarrassment heated the tips of her ears, clouding out the jeers of the group.

"Sorry, I didn't know you were all family. Just make sure you stay safe, okay?" Caroline said, slinking away, her heart pounding and sinking fast.

7

At 8:00 AM sharp on Saturday morning, Caroline sat facing Harold Bender, Assistant Director of the FBI's LA field operations, in his office, alone. Under the pretense of silencing her phone, she discreetly typed "WHERE R U?!" to Mack. She then returned her attention to A.D. Bender, who silently read their case report.

Bender closed the manila folder and leaned back in his leather chair, which squeaked quietly with the motion. The permanent scowl the Assistant Director wore contrasted sharply with the smiling man in the framed presidential photo-ops behind him.

"I'm impressed by this file," he said, looking at her frankly across the expanse of his oak desk.

"Thank you, sir."

Bender took a sip of his coffee, letting the silence stretch between them. This was a test. He was waiting her out, knowing she was going to ask to be included. Rookies always filled in the silence.

She wasted no time in stating confidently, "Sir, I think my partner and I should be assigned to this case."

"What partner?" He looked at her and smiled indulgently. "Listen, I realize you feel you're ready to take on this case. But you'll have to sit this one out."

"Sir, with all due respect—"

"This is a high-profile murder, Agent Foxx. This isn't some senator's wank-off calls."

Caroline gritted her teeth.

"There'll be plenty of other opportunities, once you're a little less green."

Controlling her irritation, she pressed on. "I understand, sir. But

21

we're the right agents for this. We found it. I mean, if it wasn't for us—"

"You caught the tail end of a telephone call, agent. You did your job. Now let those with proper experience handle it. That is how it works. You do your job, then the next person does their job. The matter's closed. Now, if you don't mind, I have another appointment."

He rose to walk her to the door. "I admire your tenacity, Agent Foxx. Keep it up. Seriously. You'll go a long way in the agency." He opened his office door and extended an arm to usher her out.

She grimaced darkly and hoped it came off as a smile. She was about to make a final plea to Bender when she saw Mack, who smiled broadly and thrust his hand out to Bender as he strode up to the door.

"Agent Maddox, so glad you could finally join us," Bender said.

"I know, sir, and I apologize. I was researching the case further this morning and lost track of time. I get like that sometimes when I'm chasing information." He held up a file. "If I may?"

Bender's eyes flickered to the paperwork Mack held up but he didn't take the bait, ignoring the file instead. "We just finished up here."

"No worries, sir. I just wanted to update you. We found a link between Taylor and Bryson—something beyond campaign contributions."

Not budging from his door, Bender responded, "They're known to be friends."

"Yes, of course. But we uncovered an off-the-books series of overseas financial transactions. These two had more going on, and Agent Foxx and I think that might be why Bryson called him yesterday. I passed it along to your team. Your next case brief will have this info. Just wanted to keep you up to speed so your team didn't know before you."

Bender exhaled sharply through his nose and held out his arm to usher the agents in.

Caroline shot Mack a dagger-filled glare as the two junior agents followed the A.D. back into his office.

Bender sighed. "Have you considered the possibility that the attack might have been directed at the lawyer? Bryson may have just been an innocent victim."

Mack held his ground. "You don't believe that, do you, sir?"

"You heard the tapes," Caroline added. "They clearly reveal that Bryson was into something that he thought would get him killed."

"And here he's dead," Bender said curtly. "No, I don't believe the lawyer was the target. At least not the sole one."

"There's something out there linking Taylor to Bryson," Mack said, pressing his point home, "and potentially the murderer's identity, in those off-book transactions."

Bender glared at Mack. "And you think you're the perfect person to dig it out, Maddox, is that it?"

"Are you kidding? Too much pressure. But hey, anything we can do to help the team."

The Assistant Director looked back into the file and thought for a long moment. "Alright. You both can provide logistical support. But only research. You'll be aiding Agents Moretto and Jackson in navigating the political nonsense. They'll be doing the field work. *All of it.* Understood?"

Mack stood up, not even bothering to conceal a rakish grin. "We won't let you down, sir."

"Don't."

8

Caroline followed Mack out of the office, shutting the door quietly behind her. The mid-morning sunlight beamed in through the glass windows running the length of the hall. They walked past Bender's assistant, Alexis, a hot twenty-something Californian beauty. Caroline caught the smile Mack gave her.

"No," she said.

"What?"

"Alexis?"

"So?"

"That's why you were late."

"I don't kiss and tell." His lips twitched in a slight smile.

"You don't need to. Her shirt's practically on backwards."

As they approached the elevators, she said, "I work that bastard for twenty minutes and he doesn't budge. You walk in late reeking of his assistant's perfume and he puts us on the case."

"Still jealous about me finishing number one at Quantico."

"Bite me."

"Would you rather I didn't get us on it?"

Caroline glared at Mack. "You did it on purpose. The way you handled that undermined our partnership and teamwork."

"You're paranoid."

"No, no, I get it now. I'm an idiot."

The elevator doors opened.

"Our ride's here."

"You let me go in there and fall on the knife with Bender. Then you come in like Braveheart. Just one problem with that."

"What?"

"A real man *leads* the charge."

25

Mack looked uncomfortable, and finally sighed. "I'm sorry, Caroline. I had no idea about the off-book deals until an hour ago."

"I knew it. You weren't late this morning. You were early." Caroline thought for a moment and then put two and two together. "You disgusting little man-whore."

Mack grinned a Cheshire-cat grin. "You won't believe what that girl will do for little Mackie boy here. I got Alexis to give me the file she was putting together for Bender's noon brief."

"You basically gave him information he already had to get us on this case?"

"Yep."

He shrugged. "It had to happen this way. Neither one of us could stand being in that basement any longer."

The reality dawned on her, and she couldn't help feel relief. "You'll forgive me if I don't high-five you at the moment."

"When you said 'bite me', exactly where we talking about?"

"With *that* mouth? I'd rather dive into an alligator pond."

9

Bic Green waited in line at Gunthorpe's butcher shop on Chicago's South Side. Honking horns and other traffic sounds rose each time a customer entered or left the shop, but Bic only briefly noticed. He was growing impatient. He needed to be at Midway Airport in two hours, and this morning the blasted butcher was as slow as Christmas.

He had no problem seeing all seven heads between him and the meat case. His immense size meant he nearly always stood out, a disadvantage that he worked hard to overcome in his business. Dressed in old blue jeans, a dark navy T-shirt, an oversized Chicago Bears jacket, a ball-cap, and sunglasses, he looked like many of the loyal Bears fans residing on the South Side. And then there was his very dark skin. In the U.S., his complexion was distinctive; he was more often taken for African than African-American.

The minutes kept slicing away with loud ticks from the overhead clock. Bic had returned to Gunthorpe's exactly twenty-six times, once for every job he had taken over the past thirty-four years. He had bought a lot of pork chops here, and had put them all to good use.

Starting with Vietnam, he had taken well over three hundred lives during his career, but he couldn't recall one of his victims' faces. Every time he pulled the trigger, snapped a neck, or slit a throat, the only face he ever saw was that of his father Clarence Green. Fifty years later, the pain, anger, and violence still washed through him.

The butcher behind the counter rang the bell and said, "Next."

Bic realized with a start he was up.

"What'll it be?" the butcher asked.

Bic shook his head and scanned the glass, seeing rib-eyes, T-bones, chicken, ground beef, and ribs all piled neatly. He looked again, but didn't see what he needed.

"We're ten deep here," the butcher said impatiently.

"I don't see any pork chops."

The butcher pointed toward an empty tray. "Big sale, we're all out. What else can I getchya?"

"How about in the back freezer?"

"We only sell what's cut from the night before. No exceptions."

Bic's body temperature rose, his thoughts roiling with fury and irritation. He needed those chops and would do anything–even kill everyone in the store with his bare hands–to get them.

He looked at his watch. He now had an hour and a half to get to the airport. He took in a deep breath and gathered his thoughts. He had never done a job without getting pork chops from this shop. And they had to be from here, from this shop.

Time to break rule number one, he thought.

He looked down into the counter glass and stared at the reflection of his large, square face. He removed the gargoyle glasses resting on his thick nose. The next thing the butcher saw, he would remember for the rest of his life–a rare experience, as no one else who had admired Bic's gaze before this had ever lived to talk about it.

Bic looked up, and his eyes met the butcher's. The man's face went ashen.

"Son," Bic said gently, "I need ten individually-wrapped pork chops." He replaced his sunglasses, then leaned over the counter toward the butcher. He whispered, "I don't want any trouble, but I'm not leaving without those chops–*so just go in the back and get them.*"

The butcher nodded, spun around, and hurried into the back freezer.

10

Congressman John Tidwell stared at the front page of the morning paper in his plush San Francisco congressional office. The cover story was "AIRPLANE HIJACKED BY TERRORISTS" with a picture of the wreckage below the title, and assorted bloody victims. But it was the slug at the bottom of the page that disgusted him most: "CONGRESS UNANIMOUSLY PASSES $250BN EMERGENCY AIRLINE SECURITY BILL."

Those terrorists had effectively hijacked his quarter of a trillion dollars. He had worked for two years securing those funds for a joint venture with Russia to extract oil and natural gas from the frozen heart of Siberia, which included an unprecedented 4,000 miles of pipeline to four ports along the Black Sea and the Pacific. Two years–down the toilet a month before his budget would have been pushed through.

As consolation for screwing him over, colleagues from both sides of the aisle promised him that when the budget committee reported the next fiscal financial projection, his bill would be the first to benefit from any revenue increase. With only twenty-two days until the committee's next meeting, he had to deliver on the promise he had made to his Russian business interests–not to mention the Russian mob.

It was time for Plan B.

Sarah, Tidwell's assistant, entered his office and said tentatively, "Sir, there's a man here who says he has to see you,"

"You know what to do," Tidwell barked at the girl. "Set him up with one of the staff."

"I tried, but he insists on seeing you. He claims he's one of your partners," she hesitated.

A skinny twenty-year-old white kid wearing baggy jeans, a flat-billed baseball cap, and a perpetual annoying smirk sauntered into the office and plopped himself into a chair opposite Tidwell's desk. "I told you, *amiga,*" he said. "I only need two minutes of the good congressman's time."

"Sarah, call security."

The assistant left the office as if shot from a cannon.

"Today's not the day for some righteous speech," Tidwell growled. "Leave now, or security will have you arrested."

"That's funny" he smirked. "As I said. I'm one of your new partners. Gentry Jacobson, Senator."

Tidwell was not at all amused.

The kid continued, "You hired me to make a list."

This hit a nerve with Tidwell, but he covered it. "I have no idea what you're talking about!"

"That's the thing about outsourcing. Does 12K to hack into a list of people's personal information and create detailed profiles about ten people–ten *important* people–ring a bell?"

Tidwell held his ground. "That sounds illegal."

This amused Gentry, who said, "Legal, illegal–it's all a gray area nowadays. I think public opinion is more dangerous than a Judge's opinion." The man continued, groping Tidwell's 19th Century carved, walnut Swiss Black Forest desk clock, "The pay seemed fair–initially, but I couldn't help notice the people on the list were worth over half a trillion dollars. So, I did a little digging. I couldn't help myself. I get bored. It's kind of a genius problem.

"I learned that someone was paid two-point-five million to perform a service related to that list. Imagine my surprise when, after a little more digging, I learned what that service was. Congressman Tidwell, that's quite a dangerous cookie jar you've got your hand in."

"I think you've made a mistake, I have no idea what you're talking about."

Gentry pulled out his phone. "Really? Then you won't mind me sending this list to, say, CNN and Fox for the public to see? You know, as a scorecard of sorts? To track those still standing–"

"What do you want?" Tidwell demanded.

The young man smirked, "A quarter of a mil. That should be no biggie for a public servant like you to raise–considering how good you've gotten at raising money recently."

At this point, Sarah returned with a uniformed security guard in tow.

"Perfect timing," said Gentry.

"It's ok," said the congressman. "It's under control. Sarah, would you excuse us?"

When they were alone, Gentry stood up. "They sure love you here, don't they?"

"You're making a big mistake," Tidwell said.

"Twelve hours, Mr. Congressman."

He walked out of the room with Tidwell's clock in hand.

11

The bar's 70s rock-n-roll motif wasn't what Caroline had expected as she and Mack entered Chico's Pub to meet their new partners at around nine. What should have been a sad joint that smelled of beer and stale dreams was actually a pretty hopping bar with a great energy to it. Mack bobbed his head up and down to the music and pointed to the ceiling. "Now this is the stuff."

Caroline watched him indifferently, her head tilted.

"Not a Creedence fan, huh?"

"Nope."

Two bartenders poured drinks behind an old oak bar-top inlaid with several original rock album covers.

"My dad has this album," Mack said, pointing to a Pink Floyd album. "The original in the gatefold sleeve, not this cheap-ass knockoff." He pointed to another. "He has that one, too."

Caroline nodded distractedly, then asked, "How's he doing?"

"He's had a good couple of months. He's been keeping up with his meds." Mack obviously didn't want to talk about it.

"I think it's great you call him every day. Reminds me of how my dad and I used to be." Caroline looked off. "I miss that."

A loud, taunting voice caught Caroline's attention. To her right, a completely mismatched pair of men—a tall, athletic, well-dressed black man in his thirties wearing a sport coat, and an older, out-of-shape white man dressed like an old-school Italian wise guy—waved her over from where they played darts. The older man had just planted his latest missile in the barroom wall, a good two feet left of the dartboard, and cursed the game out like any good goombah.

Mack nodded to the bartender. "Two Coronas with limes, please," he said, then motioned with his chin to a high-top table next to a

33

pillar in the middle of the room. "That one's free."

As Mack reached into his pocket for his wallet, the loud man from the darts game approached them. "Put your cash away," he said, forcefully wedging himself between Mack and Caroline and putting one of his burly, hairy arms around each of them. He reeked of cheap cologne and didn't win any style awards in his overlarge Hawaiian shirt, fringed at the neck with curly black chest hair.

"Some girls have all the luck," said Caroline, shaking him off like a loose cape.

Mack extended his hand. "You must be the infamous Nick Moretto."

The man smiled. "How'd you guess?"

"Saw the gold chain, the shirt, and the accent straight out of a tin can. You're either auditioning for a summer stock production of *Goodfellas* or a narc."

The beefy Moretto threw his head back in a wet laugh, then jabbed a thumb into his chest. "Nah, the real deal here, all the way."

The man turned to his friend, who had appeared at his side. "This here is my partner, Tom Jackson."

"TJ," said the man. "Good to meet you."

"Caroline Foxx," said Caroline. She put her hand past Moretto and shook TJ's hand.

"Pleasure's all mine."

Moretto ignored the snub. "This bar makes a margarita that'll knock you on your ass," he said, then motioned to the bartender. "My good man, four of your finest margaritas." He looked to Caroline. "Unless you wanna just stick to the two Coronas?"

"A margarita will be fine," she said dryly.

"Good choice," said Moretto. "It'll loosen you up a bit. No offense."

"Excuse me?"

"I'm just sayin'. You look a little tightly wound."

"And you look like you're half a mozzarella stick away from an infarct."

He threw his head back again. "Funny! I like that."

Moretto led everyone back to the dartboard. "Partners for teams— you guys know how to play cricket, right?" He threw three darts into the twenty before Mack or Caroline could respond.

Caroline tugged at Mack's sleeve. "Is Pillsbury Corleone here really going to hustle us?"

Moretto wrote 'A TEAM' in chalk on the scoreboard. Underneath he wrote 'B TEAM.'

"B Team, you're up," Moretto smirked as he handed the darts to Caroline.

Caroline honed in as she got ready to throw her first dart. Moretto tried to distract her by growling, "You're swimming with the sharks now. You never know what might be lurking in the depths." He sang the theme from *JAWS*. "Duhh-dun... duhhh dun..." He threw his head back with a guffaw.

Caroline narrowed her eyes and whipped the first dart into the fourteen, followed quickly by the nine, then one in the seven. "The sharks will probably take down an old elephant seal before me. I'm not too worried."

TJ laughed as he slapped Moretto on the back. "She got you on that one, partner."

Moretto smiled in appreciation before responding, "The wise old seal never gets eaten, honey; only those young ones who don't see the teeth before the jaws come down."

Caroline handed her darts to Moretto. "I'm pretty sure the fat, slow, oily ones get it first."

"Nice shootin'. I see pressure's really not your thing."

"It's darts," she replied.

"Free lesson number one, rooks. You rattle easy. Never let anything get under your skin." He pointed to his head. "Lose this in the field and you wind up dead."

"We appreciate the advice," Mack said to Moretto, "We're both eager to prove ourselves."

"See this guy?" Moretto grabbed TJ's shoulder and shook it back and forth. "I love him because he can handle pressure. In our business, there's nothing more important."

Mack raised his glass and offered a loud toast. "Here's to getting to work then, and learning from two pros. I can promise one thing: we will bust our asses and not let you down."

"Mack," said TJ, "you might consider politics cuz you sure can kiss butt. Especially fat hairy Italian butt."

"Hey, I lost two pounds last week," Moretto complained, holding his belly. He nudged Mack with his elbow. "I lost my wallet."

12

Chicago Midway Airport thrummed with the usual vibrant mix of businesspeople, vacationers, and last-minute travelers–and Bic Green was in the thick of it. With his bag slung over his shoulder, he slowly negotiated the throngs of people, attempting to blend in.

As he approached the gate, he saw a six-year-old boy fall hard. The boy began to cry, but his sister went to comfort him.

The scene sent Bic's mind back to the day he had first met Chandra as he distractedly navigated the airport to his gate.

Bic Green, seven years old, spent his first day in foster care hiding in a dark closet, crying.

His new foster mother had yelled at him to stop whining about his mom, to stop grieving over this woman who had been everything to him. At some point, the door opened a crack, and Bic pressed himself into the corner of the closet. A little girl peeked inside, leading with a flashlight.

"Whatchu doin' in here?"

"Nothin'."

"Are you hurt?"

"No."

"Then why you cryin'?"

"I dunno."

The girl's tongue darted out and felt for the corners of her mouth while Bic got his sobs under control.

"I want to play in here with you," she said.

Bic scooted over and allowed her to crawl in beside him.

"This will be our hideout from the bad guys," she said.

"Ok."

"Did they take your mom away too?"

"No," said Bic. "She dead."

She rested her chin on the head of the flashlight. "Is that why you was cryin'?"

The boy shrugged.

"My name's Chandra. What's yours?"

"Bic."

"Bic?"

"Uh huh."

"What kinda name's Bic?"

He shrugged again.

"Is it ok if I be your friend?"

"I dunno."

"You don't wanna be here?"

A frown tugged at the boy's mouth, and his eyes began to well up, and he shook his head.

"You don't have nobody, right?"

He shook his head.

"I don't either–but you got me, and if I got you, then we do have somebody, right? So that's why we're going to stick together." She shined the light in his face. "Deal?"

She reached out to shake on it. Bic hesitated for a second, then lunged past her hand and hugged her so tight he was afraid he might have hurt or scared her.

He'd learn soon enough that Chandra didn't hurt or scare easily.

"This place isn't so bad." Chandra said. "We just need to do what the lady says, okay?"

The gate attendant called for boarding, interrupting his reminiscence, and Bic boarded the plane, still thinking of Chandra as he watched the two children embark. He would have to put her out of his mind for the time being. She was the kindest, most caring and gentlest person he had ever known…

She had no place where he was going.

13

Don't Stop Believing played in the bar, to a chorus of half-drunk patrons joining in. Forty-five minutes after the dart game, the four FBI agents were gathered around a high-top table, ignoring the festivities, focused on talking to each other.

"Okay, so we catch this bottom-dwelling drug dealer named Skinny P on the same day he's needed as a key witness for the Benedetto trial." Moretto sipped at the beginning of the group's third round.

"That was a huge drug ring case," Mack said. "I remember seeing it in the news every day." He noticed Caroline growing uncomfortable, her expression pained. Sure, Moretto was a chatterbox, and maybe these margaritas were a little potent. But at least she could feign interest in the name of camaraderie.

"Yeah," said Moretto. "Big-time. So anyway, we got this guy, and we were both excited. We cut it so close we had to bring him directly to the courthouse to testify. TJ just happened to conveniently have his favorite suit in the trunk. So, he convinces me to let him change into his suit at a gas station."

Moretto took another swig of his drink, belched weakly, and continued. "So, we're driving to the courthouse. TJ has the sun visor down, and he's fixing his curls like he's getting ready to walk down the red carpet at the Oscars. Then we get there, and I'm telling you there had to be a hundred reporters waiting for us. A hundred. Cameramen from all the major networks are there, live.

"TJ looks me dead in the eye and says, 'Let me walk him in.' 'Sure,' I say, knowing the camera adds ten pounds, right? So, he springs out of the car and gets this crab and starts hustling him into the courthouse. As they're walking, TJ's directly behind him with the guy's hands cuffed behind his back. All of a sudden, for no reason, Skinny P grabs TJ's coat sleeve and falls to the ground, like dead weight." Moretto's voice broke off to sloppy, hysterical laughter. "When–when he fell, he tore the whole sleeve of TJ's jacket off. The cameras started flashing and there was Mr. GQ over here for his first model shoot, missing one arm of his jacket."

Everyone laughed–though Caroline less so.

He paused to compose himself. "So yeah, cameras were flashing everywhere, plus video, and TJ's so pissed he just yanks the guy back up by his collar and marches him in. But Skinny P gets the last laugh. The next day on the front page of the *LA Times*, there's this picture of TJ with his sleeve missing from his jacket."

"Wait," said Mack. "I think I remember that!"

TJ grinned as he raised his glass. "Here's to unintended fame. Sometimes we have to take what we can get."

After the laughter died down, Moretto looked over the rim of his glass directly at Caroline. "Too bad it was all for nothing, huh, Agent Foxx? The biggest drug dealer in LA got off on a technicality."

"My dad was just doing his job," Caroline shot back.

"What would you call someone who, if paid enough money, would help bad people get away with any crime they committed. I'd call them a lowlife scum sucking parasite!"

Caroline popped out of her seat and her drink went sailing to the side. "Say one more thing about my father, and I'll kick you so hard they'll have to surgically remove your nuts from your throat." The drink smashed on the floor.

Moretto smirked calmly, unfazed by the tense situation. "Well, if you don't like my story, why don't you tell us one? Like how the hell you got Bender to assign you to this case?" Moretto turned his head and coughed the word "blowjob" out into his hand.

Caroline's face glowed hot red.

TJ interjected holding up a hand. "Alright, Moretto, that's enough. Easy does it. Please don't take him too seriously, agent Foxx. This is just like Sunday dinner at his house. He and his siblings argue like cats and dogs about anything. He's from a messed-up situation. That's just what they do." There was only one thing Mack could say that would diffuse the bomb. "Actually, I slept with Bender's assistant."

Moretto slapped the table triumphantly. "I knew someone was banging someone."

"It doesn't matter how we got on. What matters is stopping the next murder from happening," Caroline said calmly, burning into Mack with her green eyes.

Moretto leaned in. "Slow your roll. Right now, we're all in wait-and-see mode."

"*Wait-and-see mode?* What's that? Your personal slogan?"

TJ responded, "With no evidence at the scene, no motive, and very few leads, we don't have much choice."

"What about Bubba Taylor?" Mack asked.

"It's a dead end, kids, trust me," said Moretto. Even if we could waterboard that bottom-feeding turd, he won't say a word." He slunk off his chair. "I gotta take a squirt. Willingness to take things past words shows you got some *cojones*. I like that. Just make sure you think before you act. Some people hit back twice as hard."

14

M ack trailed behind Caroline as they walked through the crowded parking lot.

Mack stopped her. "What the hell was that with Moretto back there?"

"He's a pig. Just leave it alone."

"Nah, nah. It's more than that. There's obviously some bad blood between you two. Is it because of your father? If it helps, you know I don't judge you for something your dad did."

"What if I did the same thing he did, but even worse? How 'bout then? Would you judge me?"

He paused. "I'd try to see it from your point of view."

"Gee, thanks. And where the hell do you get off telling them about you and Alexis?"

"I had to say something. He accused you of—" he cut himself off to lower his voice. "Of blowing someone to get the job."

"Playing my white knight doesn't do me any favors"

"Are you serious? Did you hear yourself in there? If I hadn't stepped in, I think you might have tried to dropkick Moretto. Look. I just defused a tense situation. What's wrong with that?"

"I don't need you to. I can take care of myself. Besides," Caroline jumped to a more pressing thought, "Those bozos are just sitting on their hands."

"Cut them some slack, will you? They just got started; they need something to go on."

"Like what, another body? Is that what we do now? Take our time until someone else is murdered?" Before Mack could respond, she added, "I can't let that happen, not again."

"You're acting crazy."

"No, crazy is waiting for a murder to happen as a clue to stop a murder."

"Whatever you're thinking of doing will get us tossed off this case," Mack said sternly. He caught something in Caroline's steely determined gaze. "While we're on the subject, what *are* you thinking of doing?"

"Bubba Taylor's hiding something," Caroline responded. "We need to find out what." She looked back toward the bar entrance. "How did they not find one lead from Taylor? Did they even listen to that conversation with Bryson? Incompetent buffoons."

Mack ran a hand through his hair. "Why don't we brainstorm this? Figure out our next move?"

"Not tonight. It'll be an early morning," she said, pulling out her phone. "I'm calling a cab."

"Let me give you a ride."

"No, I'm good," she answered flatly, walking away.

15

Waves crashed softly in the distance, as the surf lapped against the beach, calming, rhythmic, and peaceful in the cloudless night. Caroline stood in the Malibu beach house driveway for several minutes, thinking, letting the scent of the ocean fill her with every breath. The glistening moonlight, illuminating the beautiful homes, felt like it was shining a mocking spotlight on her romantic life as she considered the reasons she was once again surrendering to this.

This wasn't who she was; this wasn't where she should be. Ashton represented a distraction from the darkest time in her life, only since last night it had the reverse effect. Not since she saw those two men, beaten, dead... so like little–

No, Caroline thought. She couldn't dwell on that, on *her*. She needed to make things better.

Seeing Ashton was a terrible idea. These ultra-successful CEO types only longed to gather, gain, and hoard. How could she think this was good for her? And yet the guilt galvanized her, too. Preventing further murders helped mitigate the guilt–but the stress was already getting in the way. Was he just using her, or was she just using him? Did it even matter? She needed this.

She let herself in and found Ashton working at his dining room table, his papers spread all over. He was so focused he hadn't even heard the door open or felt her eyes on him.

Finally, tired of being ignored, she said, "You should lock your doors. Lots of naughty people out there."

"What are you doing here?" he asked coldly, barely looking up.

His callous indifference stung; she covered it with an excuse. "I left my necklace here last night."

Caroline walked past him, giving Ashton a sideways glimpse of her body. "I have to finish this up," he said. "But if you're here for more than your necklace, you know where to go."

She sat half-naked in Ashton's playroom, lacing up leather boots with ridiculous six-inch heels, when she balked–she needed to say no to this. Things were too complicated. The need to deal with her guilt sexually was strong, almost compulsive, but there had to be a better way. Honest healing over catharsis? Could affection win over desire? She looked around the room, at the S&M gear in every corner, and realized she was just another one of these toys to Ashton. Was that the type of woman she was, just a toy for a powerful man? Something to use then throw away, like...

And suddenly Caroline's mind was made up.

Ashton walked into the room with his shirt already unbuttoned and hanging open while his fingers worked the clasp on his belt. "I only have a moment before I have to get back to the launch reports, but–" His face fell as he found Caroline dressed in her work clothes, slipping her shoes back on, and his excitement quickly turned to disappointment.

"What are you doing?" he asked.

"I don't want this anymore. I have to go," she said, pushing past him.

Ashton appeared surprised by her actions, but just as she had expected, he didn't try to stop her. He was too self-involved to care about anything but himself–and too weak to fight for what wasn't given to him freely.

16

Phil Utah, a twenty-six-year veteran with the DEA, grumbled and spat as he surveyed the small rental house. Two men–hired guns, not law enforcement–flanked him. Both of them were former military and, like so many of the private contractors Utah hired, perfectly comfortable with wet-work. Utah's piercing blue eyes, alternating between binoculars and plain sight, missed nothing.

A strongly-built man with a long weather-beaten face and bushy brown mustache, Utah fumed at how badly things were going. Today was the day the bill was going to be passed, and he had been promised enough money to do whatever he wanted once that happened. All he had to do was be Congressman John Tidwell's muscle. As John had explained it to him three years ago, he would be dealing with powerful underworld types to get this deal done, and he needed Utah to show these men he couldn't be pushed around. The work sounded straightforward, if not easy. And it was, at first. But things started growing complicated fast as Utah had been called upon to put out more and more fires.

Like this hacker the late Senator Gary Bryson had hired, who was now blackmailing Tidwell. But this was the least of Utah's worries. He knew, thanks to an informant, that the Russians had 'cleaning' crews in place should Tidwell's deal go south–as it was looking like it might. These crews were instructed to kill, not just Utah and his partners, but also the families of everyone involved. It was typical Russian mob mentality to pursue a scorched earth policy and kill everyone.

He wondered if killing Tidwell himself would placate the Russians. If so, he would do the bastard at the first chance and go back to his day job running the San Diego DEA field office. But until then, he had no choice but to obey. Too much money had been sunk into this.

No matter how crazy this plan became, he would see it through.

Utah signaled the two armed men to approach the house when he spied the hacker through the large living room window. The kid was on his couch playing some shoot-'em-up video game on a large flat screen TV. *Idiotic ass,* thought Utah. *He probably thinks this is all a game.*

Utah ducked down out of sight. "I'll go through the back door." Pointing to one of the men, he said, "You catch him if he goes through the front." Pointing to the other, he said, "You be our eyes." Utah inserted his radio earpiece and started to move in.

Jacobson continued to play his video game, oblivious to Utah or his men. Suddenly the game froze and Jacobson tossed the controller onto the coffee table, yelling "Piece of junk!"

He leaned down from the ratty beige couch to the coffee table and snorted a line of coke next to his laptop and the desk clock he had taken from Tidwell's office. As he rose, he caught a glimpse of the man looking through the bay window.

Jacobson dropped instantly to the floor. He crawled quickly to the back door, but froze when he saw the doorknob turning. Now in survival mode, the kid ran back through the living room, then up the stairs to the second floor. At the top of the stairs, he stopped and turned, nearly panicking–his laptop!

He ran back down the stairs as Utah and the other two men entered the house. Grabbing his laptop, Jacobson sprinted back up the stairs, praying that he hadn't been seen. And praying the drop from the second story wasn't an ankle-breaker.

Thirty minutes later, Jacobson exited a public city bus, walked up to an old pay phone, and made a call.

A male voice answered. "Yeah?"

"I hear you're the man who likes to put politicians out of business."

"That I am," the man replied.

"Well then," said the hacker, "I've got something for you that will bring the whole effin' house down."

17

Caroline wiped sweat from the Mississippi humidity off the back of her neck as she scoffed inwardly at the lavishly decorated living room of Bubba Taylor's antebellum mansion. It confirmed her suspicions: political lobbying was a legal racket, plain and simple.

"Tell me," said Taylor, "how you folks enjoying beautiful Natchez, Mississippi?"

"It's beautiful alright," said Mack.

Sometimes Caroline swore that Mack could start a friendly conversation with anyone. She was sure that if he was being mugged, he'd end up in the bar having a drink with the mugger instead. Of course, then Mack'd bust him, but still…

"You folks wanna see somethin', you come down to the river bluffs at dusk. You ain't seen a sunset till you seen a Mississippi River sunset."

Caroline was growing tired of the travel pitch, so she interrupted Mack's and Bubba's pleasantries. "We'd like to chat with you, if you don't mind, about your relationship with Gary Bryson."

"Well," said Taylor, easing himself into a fat, leather chair, "I already spoke with a whole slew of officers and agents. Hell, everyone and their grandmother has been by to see me."

"Then two more shouldn't be a problem," said Caroline coolly.

Taylor sighed, "Alright, Agent… Foxx, is it? What can I do ya for?"

"For one thing, you were the last person he spoke with."

Taylor shook his head slowly, as if denying a memory. "Shame. I helped the man get elected, twice. Lord knows when we'll get another friend of the people back in office. Politics is so infected lately, it'll be hard to replace what he could do for those of us who care about

America."

"The day he died, you told investigators you didn't know why he called you," said Mack.

"Sure enough didn't."

"Why do you *think* he called you?"

Mack leaned back, watching Taylor's expression carefully, cataloging each little twitch of the eye or pursing of the lips.

Taylor shrugged. "To complain about something. He was a very nervous man."

"So, what did the two of you talk about?"

Bubba smiled as he steepled his fingers in front of his chin. "I can't say I rightly recall, Agent."

"Interesting. Personally, I would remember the conversation if a US senator called me. Wouldn't you Mack? Yeah, I thought so. Are you sure you can't recall anything, Mr. Taylor?"

"Baseball. We talked about Baseball."

Caroline lowered her head. "Baseball."

"Mmm hm. I'm positive we talked ball. Any other questions?"

Mack, satisfied he had Bubba's measure, cleared his throat. "We've discovered a number of financial irregularities involving you and the Senator."

Taylor held up a hand. "I know where you're going with this and I'm gonna hafta stop you there. You can discuss anything else you like on that front with my attorney." He sipped his iced tea.

Caroline pushed on. "Before the senator was murdered, you told the police he was on his way to see *his* attorney. You also said you advised him not to do that, why?"

Taylor hesitated. "I don't remember."

"So, it was a little more than baseball."

"Sorry, sweetheart. I just can't remember."

Caroline pulled some transcripts from her briefcase. "Hang on... let's see... here it is. You told Bryson right before he was murdered, 'That might not be the best idea.' I'm just curious why you would give that advice? For that matter, how can you give that advice if you didn't know why he called?"

"You're playin' with my words, darlin'."

"I'm quoting you verbatim."

The man rose. "I think this interview's over."

Caroline persisted. "If you're feeling guilty about the senator's murder, just get it off your chest. It's going to come out anyway."

Taylor's wife poked her head into the room. "You alright, darling?"

"Just fine, honey," Taylor smiled as he lifted his glass, "Great batch of tea."

Taylor's wife smiled and left the room.

"Mr. Taylor," said Caroline, "does your sweet wife know about little Bubba?"

"Ex-*scyooze* me?"

Mack put his hand up. "Um, what my partner means is—"

"What I mean is we know you can lead us to who killed Bryson, you tell us now you have a chance not to be locked up for the rest of your life.

Taylor's face reddened to a burn.

"Tell us who you are protecting, or you're going to be getting it from a big Bubba in prison," Caroline said matter-of-factly.

"Ahh, poppycock!" Taylor said, "you both need to get your prissified California assess out of my house before I call your boss's boss and get you fired."

Bubba Taylor left the room, muttering curses under his breath.

Caroline looked at Mack. "Too forward?"

Mack grinned in return. "Nope. I think that was just forward enough."

18

S he needed it bad.

She was sure Bubba had incriminating emails on his computer. She needed to see them.

Caroline stared at the screen of her laptop; cool caution and furious zeal were warring for dominance over her conscience. Her finger hovered over the enter key.

Then a voice in her head spoke plainly. It said: *This is wrong.*

It was right. Yes, this was against the law. Yes, this was unethical, and an absolute career-ender for a Federal agent.

Hadn't Hoover himself done stuff like this? Wasn't it all in the name of the greater good? Because roads paved with good intentions *never* went anywhere bad… She sighed and rubbed her brow.

Of course, she knew she could accomplish all this on the up and up. Two words: administrative subpoena. But the red tape. And Taylor would be notified. And Taylor had some pull, politically speaking. He could—and certainly would—counter with a hit that had the potential of ruining her: one phone call to some media outlet during a slow news cycle.

Do the American people know their tax money is paying the salary of a woman who once let a child-raping murderer shamble free? Coming soon to a neighborhood near you and your sister, courtesy of Caroline Foxx, superhumanitarian!

Caroline's phone rang. She knew who it was. She took a long breath, and answered. "Mack, hey. Just taking a walk. Be back at the hotel in a bit."

"All right. Just wanted to make sure you weren't doing something stupid, like casing out Taylor's house," he joked.

You know me so well. Caroline glanced around the lobby, wondering if Mack was watching her. "That's funny. I'll see you in a bit."

Caroline hung up, hating herself for lying to Mack. She felt sick at the thought of losing her partner's trust. But she wasn't going to wait for another murder for their next clue.

On Gmail's login page, with Taylor's Gmail address already typed in as the user ID, she pressed enter requesting to have the verification code to obtain a new password texted to Taylor's cell phone.

Her heart quickened and a hot flash rushed into her neck as she masked her caller ID and texted Taylor this message:

This is a message from the Google Accounts Security Center. There has been unauthorized activity on your account.
Please reply with your verification code.

Within ten seconds, Taylor texted the verification code to her. She entered it into his account and created a new password.

On Taylor's email page, she went to the search bar and typed in 'Gary Bryson'.

A single email came up.

The email was addressed to the senator, and in the body was: *Gentry Jacobson will be a good contact for that type of work.*

What does that mean? Caroline thought. She scanned for the email that Bryson had sent to Taylor to see what his question was. She came up with nothing.

Not wanting to be detected, Caroline logged out then sent a follow up text to Taylor:

Your temporary password had been set to UkM633E99%kgTN8. Please log in immediately and change your password.

Three hours later, she and Mack were on an airplane back to LA. Once Mack had dozed off, she popped open her laptop.

Who are you, Gentry? she thought, opening the FBI database and searching for the name.

A file popped up. Gentry Jacobson was a known hacker with a rap sheet full of minor cybercrimes.

"Gotcha," she said, as she stared at a photo of a young man who had "computer geek" written all over him.

No APBs, she thought. An APB would get back to Bender. And Bender would ask for cause.

Thankfully, she could perform a search and surveillance on Jacobson and justify it as an "assessment"–the FBI's catch-all term for, well, doing what she was doing. As long as she had authorization to investigate Bubba Taylor, she had authorization to look at anyone she deemed relevant to the case. What's more, she could do it for thirty days without reporting it to Bender.

Before thirty days was up, she would either find the smoking gun or close the assessment.

19

Downtown Bigfork's cozy Main Street teemed with mom-and-pop shops, places that had been in business forever and were truly family-owned and operated. Children happily ran around while parents shopped or sipped coffees, and the whole area had a feeling of normalcy and nostalgia hard to find in most cities. Bic could almost smell apple pie and the American dream in the air.

He stood outside The Corner, an appropriately named corner coffee shop, sipping his black and two sugars while watching Larry and Sharon Tukenson window shop. They usually had one bodyguard with them, but today two G-man types trailed behind them, glancing over everything at least twice.

Bic blew on his coffee, assuming the role of the man passing through. The early afternoon sun now highlighted the pure white veins of snow climbing their way from the massive base of the mountain to its white cap–a stunning, serene sight.

The Tukensons entered the nearby flower shop. Both G-men paused outside, scanning to see if anyone was coming before they followed. Once everyone was in, Bic made his move.

He sauntered into the shop, noting Sharon and Larry waiting at the counter. The two bodyguards turned to Bic, but he quickly bent over to inspect a white bucket of long-stemmed red roses on the floor.

He could feel the bodyguard's eyes on him, but when the florist came out from the back with a grandiose centerpiece arrangement of wildflowers, Sharon's excited remark on how they would be "perfect for each table" pulled the guard's attention away.

Staring at the roses, Bic recalled returning from Vietnam with a dozen and seeing Chandra, the only family he knew, hooked up to all sorts of machines. Her cheeks were sunken and when she wasn't focusing on someone it was like her eyes were empty. All that was left was a wisp of the woman she had been when he'd left. Chandra, age twenty-seven, diagnosed with soft tissue sarcoma, wheezed as the choking tumors ran away with her lungs; and her life.

The two had grown up together–without parents, with very little food, never a present from their foster family on Christmas or a birthday–but none of that mattered. They had the love that they shared ever since the day she had pulled him out of that closet as a little boy.

She was his big sister, and she meant everything to him.

Chandra had convinced him to leave the Chicago projects to join the Marine Corps. He had lied about his age and escaped the projects, escaped hell, because of her. After training for several months he'd been sent off to Vietnam.

The jungles gave vent to the deep dark rage his father had given him. He possessed a godlike ability to kill Viet Cong.

Chandra's cancer had metastasized. Each day there was less of her. Medicaid wouldn't pay for any procedure with a less-than-favorable chance of saving her.

Bic hadn't felt so helpless since he watched his mama die.

But that was the day he met Chandra's four-year-old daughter, Gracie, for the first time. When he held that little child in his arms and looked into her big brown eyes, he swore that he would do whatever was needed to get Chandra the $100,000 she needed.

He couldn't even get a loan for that much, despite his military standing–and the job he had taken at a local factory wouldn't begin to pay for the treatment. Not knowing what to do, he contacted his buddy Tony from his old platoon, told him about Chandra, and asked for his help.

Tony arranged a deal that paid Bic the hundred grand upfront. Within two weeks, he found himself on an apparent suicide mission in the jungles of Colombia. His first contract kill was to take out a heavily-guarded drug kingpin.

Bic snapped out of his reverie as he walked toward Larry and Sharon with a single red rose in hand. Bic reached into his coat pocket just feet away from the two. Neither of them noticed, but one of the bodyguards did. He rushed toward Bic, but stopped abruptly once Bic got out his wallet and placed the rose on the counter.

Bic paid for the flower and left. After exiting the shop, he pulled out his phone and confirmed he had synced his phone with Larry's, and would be able to track his first target's location from here on in.

20

Gentry Jacobson sat at the desk in his lavish downtown San Francisco hotel room, his fingers dancing across his laptop as he encrypted the list he had created for Tidwell onto a flash drive. With each keystroke, he reveled in masterminding Tidwell's downfall. He glanced briefly at his GoPro-style video camera, then suddenly felt sluggish. He took a hit of coke already lined up off the desk. A rush of speed raced through him. "Yeah. Time for some hacker vengeance mofo." He was invincible now and got back to work.

Two hours later, Jacobson heard a knock on his hotel room door. After he verified the man's identity through the peephole, Jacobson invited Anthony Parelli into the room. Parelli, a dark-haired, physically imposing, well-dressed mobster in his late fifties, didn't look a day over forty thanks to his smooth olive skin.

Parelli entered the room slowly, vigilantly. Though one of today's most sophisticated high-level dealmakers in the criminal underworld, Parelli never forgot his roots as a Brooklyn enforcer; and he never lost his instincts. He specialized in making multi-million-dollar deals by getting politicians in his back pocket. He had learned years ago how profitable dirty politicians were, and how accessible the world's biggest money pot was: the US tax dollar. The beauty of it was that there was no accountability. Take 50 million dollars from someone on the street, there's all-out war, with death and destruction everywhere before the dust finally settles. But take 50 million dollars from the government and nothing happens, except another cause is created, and then they take their own 50 million.

Jacobson welcomed Parelli into the suite, hastily locking the door behind him.

Parelli's dark, shark-like eyes and broad, Italian-suit-covered shoulders would intimidate any sane man, but Gentry felt no fear; they were on the same team, after all. The coke lined up on the coffee table, which Parelli glanced at with brief disgust, made Gentry feel unbeatable.

"It keeps me plugged in for hours—nothing else does the trick," the hacker explained.

"You got what I've come for?" Parelli's heavy New York accent emphasized his desire to get right down to business.

Jacobson tossed the flash drive to Parelli.

"Is this everything?" Parelli asked.

"Yup. Every file, name, date, photo, and account number." The hacker smiled wryly. "I hope you burn that dirtbag Tidwell at the stake."

Parelli smirked as he pulled out a little device and plugged the drive into its port.

"It's encrypted, but as soon as I have the money, you get the key to unlock its secrets."

Parelli fiddled on his phone for a moment. When he was done, he put the phone in his pocket and there was an instant knock at the door. "That'll be your payment," he said.

Triumphant, Jacobson rushed to answer the door. His arrogance turned to utter terror once he recognized the bushy mustache on the other side. It was the man who had broken into his house.

Phil Utah shoved Jacobson back into the room and quickly locked the door behind him.

The hacker looked around in a panic.

"Huh," said Parelli. "You two know each other?"

"If anything happens to me," said Jacobson, "the names will get out. The last thing you want is a bunch of loose ends."

Both men stared at the hacker.

"Son, I couldn't have said it better myself." said Utah, stepping forward, gun raised.

The hacker held up his hands. "Now hang on just a second. I want you guys to say hi to my YouTube subscribers."

"Huh?" said Utah.

"Say cheese to the world, guys." The hacker nodded toward the GoPro camera concealed in the corner of the room.

The men turned their gazes to the camera, then back to Jacobson.

"Don't believe me? Turn on the TV."

Utah turned on the flat-screen TV on top of the long dresser and saw himself. He turned to the camera and back again to be sure.

Jacobson stumbled over to his laptop. "You old timers just don't get it. This is the real power in today's world, and guess what, you can tell that donkey Tidwell the price just went up to a million."

The hacker stared at the two men, sure he had outplayed them, until the TV screen dissolved to black. Jacobson's hacker mind was about to shift into automatic troubleshooter mode, when the TV became clear again. There now was the image of John Alfred Tidwell streamed live on the screen, his expression congested with fury.

The kid immediately tried to counter, typing commands to regain control, but it was hopeless–the hacker had been hacked. His laptop screen went black. The processor was fried.

Jacobson stood frozen with horror, trying avoiding Tidwell's gaze on the TV screen.

Utah holstered his gun and motioned to the flash drive. "This everything?"

"Don't think for a second I haven't made a backup plan," said Jacobson fearfully. "If you kill me, it will all come out."

"What do you have, son?" said Parelli. "Names on a list? Earlier today, we leaked a story with a bunch of names, some on the list, but with others mixed in–all the names, their companies, their net worth. A *Forbes* fluff piece that people will eat up. Whatever you have will only be adding to the white noise. In other words, you lose."

"You look a little sick, son," Utah said with a dead stare. "Why don't you take a nice hit to shore up that courage?"

Jacobson thought for a moment as he eyed the little pile of coke on the desk, then buried his face in it and took a big snort.

"Atta boy," Utah said, "now lay on the floor."

Parelli donned a pair of thick, puffy snow gloves, then grabbed the hacker, pinning his arms to his sides. Jacobson struggled in coke-fueled terror but couldn't break free from the man's iron grip.

Utah pulled a bag of white powder out of a small leather case. He added the white powder to the pile on the desk and cut the two substances together with a credit card. He then pulled out a large prepared syringe and walked over to the hacker.

"What are you doing?" Jacobson screamed, struggling anew to break Parelli's grip.

"You need to be careful whose office you barge into," Utah said.

He pulled the hacker's T-shirt up. The hacker yelled, "Please, no," but pinned down by a man twice his size, it was no use. Utah plunged the large needle into his chest and emptied its contents.

Gentry Jacobson felt an agonizing ball of fire surge through chest. His heart pumped furiously. Something inside him squeezed...

Parelli released Jacobson's motionless arms and grabbed the flash drive from the table, putting it in his pocket.

Utah took out some super glue, cleaned the little drop of blood off the hacker's chest with an alcohol wipe, blew it dry, then dabbed a tiny drop of glue onto the needle hole, sealing it shut. Parelli briefly inspected the work.

"You think he was bluffing?" Utah asked as he stood.

"No, but neither was I. I'll have my people shopping around. We'll flush out any other cockroaches connected to this schmuck," Parelli replied.

"Do me a favor, Parelli," Utah said sternly. "Let me know if there are any other loose ends you decide to tie up."

"Something on your mind, Mister *DEA agent*?" Parelli goaded.

Utah snapped back, "Bryson and his lawyer is what. You should have consulted me on that."

"This may come as a shock to your delicate sensibilities, friend, but I don't require authorization when a guy needs to go down fast."

Utah glared, saying nothing.

"I take exterminating rats very seriously. You let them live too long and they multiply. Plus, they squeak."

"Your guy was sloppy," said Utah. "Bryson's death attracted attention. *Federal* attention."

Parelli shrugged. "Don't matter if the roaches flash a badge. They still die when you crush 'em."

21

The morgue was cold. Shiny, mirror-finish cold. Stainless steel everywhere you looked cold. Steel fridge doors, steel sinks, shiny steel surgical instruments, and other shiny equipment. Layers and layers of disinfectant, antiseptic cleaners, and bleach on the walls gave the whole building a 'just cleaned' chemical smell.

On the autopsy table, Gentry Jacobson's pale naked body lay with his chest split wide open and half his insides on a steel tray a foot from his head. Caroline watched as the medical examiner, a severe-looking man in his fifties, peeled off his gloves and tossed them into the biohazard bin.

"This was an accidental drug overdose," he said, "leading to severe heart failure. I would say death was almost immediate."

Caroline suppressed her impatience. "Accidental?"

"It certainly seems that way."

"Are you sure?"

"Am I sure?"

"Well, it's just that 'certainly seems that way' doesn't exactly imply surety."

"Ok, let's put it this way. There are no signs of struggle, he was known to use, and his blood had enough cocaine in it to OD a horse." The examiner handed Caroline the lab report. "So, seeing as how room for doubt decreases with the admission of evidence, I would say that, yes, I'm implying surety here."

Caroline handed the report back to him, unconsciously biting at the corner of her lip. "You missed something."

The examiner paused, eyes narrowed. "Come here for a second," he said. He donned a pair of gloves and grabbed a pair of forceps. With these he lifted Gentry's nose and exposed the inside of the hacker's nostrils using a flashlight pen. "See this? And this here? That's all dead tissue. The septum lining is pretty much *all* dead tissue. Only big-time cocaine users have this much damage. Now, forensics being a science of induction, we start with the specific then expand into the general in order to form a theory—looking for patterns the entire time. As indicated in my report, we have a hypertensive bleed in the basal ganglia of the brain. That's pretty much the smoking gun in a cocaine overdose. If we were to work backwards, we'd see the bleed first, we'd move on to the lining of the septum to confirm. The conclusion would be the same—cocaine overdose. There's more. Would you like to hear it?"

"You have to have missed something," said Caroline.

"I welcome any and all scrutiny of my work," he said, snapping of his gloves and tossing them onto the legs of the corpse. "If you'll excuse me..."

The examiner swept out of the room in a huff, crossing paths with Mack as he exited.

"I'm glad you're here," Caroline began. "This kid was murdered—"

Mack held up his hand. "Stop. Just stop."

"We're in the middle of a *huge* conspiracy. We need to—"

"What's this *we* stuff?"

"Mack, I—"

"You lied straight to my face," Mack yelled. "Just when I start to think we are getting close and have each other's backs you pull this stunt."

"I knew Taylor was hiding something, and I was right."

"At what cost? How'd you get this kid's name?"

Caroline stared blankly, not wanting to divulge her actions.

"Tell me now, or we're done as partners."

"I took over Taylor's Gmail account and found an email to Bryson."

"Are you for real you, *we*, can go to jail for that."

"People's lives are at stake, Mack. Or haven't you noticed?"

"You're acting like this is all about saving innocent people, but there's something you're not telling me. Is it your father? Or I'm just missing it? I don't know."

Caroline crossed her arms and looked away. She had nothing to say.

"We all have our demons, Caroline. But they're no excuse to do whatever it is we feel like doing." He gently laid a hand on her shoulder.

She jerked away. "You just don't understand. I can't help it."

"I'll let you in on a little secret, since you won't tell me yours. My biggest fear is betrayal by women I care for."

Caroline fell silent, conflicted. "I hurt you," she said softly. "I'm sorry. I promise I will never deceive you again."

Mack looked into her eyes. The look was different, complicated. "I guess I overreacted a little. It's just—"

He struggled to find the words. This was something new. Mack, so cool, so detached—he'd never had a girlfriend for more than a few weeks in all the time she had known him. Caroline thought briefly of his mother, and how he'd more than once described how his mother had left his father.

But his mother had left Mack, too.

"I would have never left you out," Caroline began, trying a new tactic. "Only I knew what I was doing was wrong, and you're too important to me to jeopardize your career. I made a judgment call, and it was stupid."

"You really mean that?"

"Partners are like family. You're stuck with me."

Whether it was the tilt of her head, the smile she gave him, or her use of the word "family," Mack perked up, almost instantly.

"I followed up on your assessment," he said dryly.

Caroline motioned to the dead body. "Thank you. But it doesn't do him or us much good now."

"Just because he's dead doesn't mean he doesn't have a story to tell. I've got the locals holding down the hotel room where he died. If he *was* killed," Mack added, "there might still be something there for us to find."

"I don't deserve you," she said, and hugged him excitedly.

Wrapped in his arms, their friendly hug suddenly felt a little more than friendly. She inhaled him. He smelled like something herbal and spicy.

"Let's get out of here," she muttered.

22

An out-of-shape man in his thirties with an unkempt beard and wearing a Yankees baseball cap walked away from the urinal at a large, rough-looking gas station bathroom. He rinsed his hands at the sink, ignoring the soap. Glancing in the mirror, he picked some long-grain snuff off his yellow teeth, exposing the massive dip tucked between his lower lip and gumline.

As the man turned to exit, Bic lunged from one of the stalls and grabbed him from behind, covering his mouth with a rag. The man struggled for just a moment and then went limp.

Bic pulled the man into the handicapped stall and settled him into a waiting wheelchair. Bic then grabbed sunglasses and a travel pillow from his duffel bag and placed these items on the man. He threw a blanket over his legs.

Bic pushed the man out of the stall. As he did so, an elderly, white-haired man entered the restroom. The man glanced warily at Bic, and then the man in the wheelchair. He nodded and made his way to the stall, whistling something semi-atonal.

Bic hummed along with the tune unconsciously as he wheeled his target out of the bathroom.

23

Mack and Caroline walked up to the hotel door and broke the crime scene seal. Mack pulled out a pen flashlight and started checking behind furniture while Caroline went down on all fours to get a look under the bed. She rocked back up, took a band off her wrist, and tied her hair in a ponytail.

Mack paused his search and plopped down in the desk chair, then suddenly found himself reliving the worst day of his life. He was seven and he had wandered into his parents' bedroom one afternoon, despite his mother telling him not to. His first recollection was of his mother's ponytail, bouncing frantically. Then he remembered his mother naked on top of his dad's best friend from college, a man Mack thought of as an uncle.

Caroline, heedless of Mack's distress, continued to examine. "They had to have left something."

Mack looked on, motionless, just like he had when he was seven. Frozen, just staring, unable to walk away. *If I would have just walked away, maybe what had happened next wouldn't have happened,* he thought wistfully.

"You going to help or just sit there and look pretty?" said Caroline. She held out her hand expectantly. "It's dark. Give me the light?"

Mack stood, shaking off the memory-burned look of disgusted shame in his mother's eyes, and tossed Caroline the penlight. "Reports said the amount of blow on this table was nearly 100 grams."

"Yeah?" she said, scrutinizing the mattress lining. "You told me that already."

"Thought it bore repeating."

She looked up at him incredulously. "And why's that?"

71

"The OD could have been legit."

"Too convenient."

Mack looked at the TV. "Hey, did we find a remote for this thing?"

Again, her look of incredulity. "Catching up on your *Gilligan's Island* reruns?"

Mack ignored the comment and turned on the TV manually. The screen stayed black, except for INPUT2 showing in the upper right-hand corner. He inspected the back of the TV.

"What are you doing?" she asked.

"There's a lock on the cable cord into Input 1. Our hacker could have plugged an HDMI cable into the Input 2 slot for some reason. See that?" He pointed to the message on the screen

"Huh, can we do anything with that?"

"Maybe," Mack went to his computer bag and pulled out his laptop. "If there were any IP addresses that sent packets of streaming data out on the hotel's Wi-Fi, I might be able to recover it."

For twenty minutes, Mack pounded away on his laptop, going through all the files from the last twenty-four hours. "Found one with video!" he said at last.

Looking over his shoulder, they both watched as a video played on the laptop. It was the hacker, setting the GoPro camera up in the corner of the room. As he set it up, the camera swiveled over the entire room, and then settled on the desk. After ten seconds, the video was over.

"That's it?" Caroline asked in disappointment.

"Wait. There's also a data file hidden inside with this video."

"Open it," she said.

"Yes ma'am. Uh… It looks heavily encrypted. Let the lab geeks figure this one out. Considering this type of encryption though, this could be juicy." He looked up at her. "And you saw it, right?"

"Saw what?"

He replayed the video. Caroline stared for a second and shook her head.

"I'm not seeing it."

"Look again. He replayed the video, savoring the coming 'gotcha' moment."

"Mack, come on, it's getting late."

"Look," he said, pointing at the pile of coke in the corner of the screen. "You saw the stuff in the evidence bag. Does that there look like a hundred grams?"

Caroline's eyes opened wide as she said, "Uh, no."

"It's twice as big, now" Mack said. "At least."

"So ... it was planted after the fact?"

He held up his hand for a high-five that never came.

"We're taking this to Bender."

"Hang on. I don't know if it counts as definitive proof of anything, but it's suspicious. The big deal is that encrypted file."

24

A man sat low inside his car, watching Mack and Caroline leave the hotel, both clearly happy about something. As he observed them getting into their rental car and driving off, he took out his phone and accessed his speed dial contacts.

"Yes?" said Congressman Tidwell.

"We have a problem."

A pause. "Is that so?"

"FBI," was all the man needed to say by way of response.

Another pause, then, "Fix it."

The congressman disconnected the call, and Phil Utah sat low in his car, taking slow, measured breaths.

Mack drove towards the airport as the buildings of San Francisco fell into the distance behind them. Caroline sat in the passenger seat, a pencil stuck through the base of her ponytail and pad of paper tossed on the dashboard, working on Mack's computer.

"Probably should leave it for the pros," Mack said.

"I'm being careful," she replied. "Just taking a peek to see if there was anything else."

He smiled. "I guess I have no choice but to trust you." It was a shared joke. At the academy, she had finished ahead of him in the cybercrime modules.

"You weren't kidding about the encryption," she said after a minute. "This kid knew what he was doing."

He heard her clicking the keyboard ferociously, and then, "No, *no, no!*

The severity with which she exclaimed this forced him to pull over.

"This isn't happening!" she said. "It was here! It was right here! Did you see it?"

"See what?"

"It must have been five pages of data. It just scrolled by real fast."

"Did you catch any of it?"

"Hang on." She typed again, and the data scrolled again. "Hang on..." She hit the spacebar and the list froze. "I found the list! It's names and numbers–"

Suddenly, the screen froze, and right before her eyes, everything began to break down, the data vanished line by line.

"What?" she said. "No."

"What the hell's happening?"

"Are you *kidding* me?" she screamed in frustration. "It's a virus."

Mack's phone pinged.

"We got another problem," he said, showing her the text from Bender ordering them to get their asses into his office immediately.

25

Caroline and Mack had been waiting outside of Bender's office for about twenty minutes. At 10:15 PM, Bender, dressed in shorts and a Tommy Bahama shirt, stormed around the corner, not even acknowledging them as he threw open his office door and entered.

"Get in here," he yelled from his office.

Caroline and Mack looked at each other.

"After you," said Caroline.

Mack took a deep breath. "Out of the stewpot and into the fire."

"Guess who my boss's boss got a call from?" Bender didn't wait for a reply. "The Chief of Staff! Who just so happens to go hunting regularly with Bubba Taylor."

"Oh boy," Caroline mumbled.

"Oh boy is right. What the hell were you thinking?"

"Sir, Taylor knows who's involved in the Bryson investigation. The man got a call moments before Bryson was murdered, and then there's a dead hacker–Jacobson–"

Bender cut her off. "Oh, I was getting to him. You put out a lookout on the hacker kid. Why?"

Caroline was resolute. "Merely part of a thirty-day assessment, sir."

"Why?" he demanded.

"Taylor has a connection with him."

"How do you know this? Did Taylor *volunteer* this information?"

All she could say was the truth, but that would just get her fired–maybe even arrested.

Bender slammed his fist on his desk. "God help you if you did anything illegal."

"Sir," Mack interrupted. "I made the connection from the prior surveillance we had done on Senator Bryson, and I found an email that led us to him."

"Did you, Agent always-seems-to-have-the-right-answer Maddox?" Bender turned back to Caroline. "Is that what happened, Agent Foxx?"

"Sir," said Caroline, "we think the hacker was killed because he created the list of the targeted people Bryson was going to divulge to his attorney."

"I saw the medical examiner's report," said Bender. "He was *very* insistent that this was an OD. Where's your proof?"

"We had it on Mack's laptop, sir, but I bricked the machine."

"Bricked...?" His eyes went from one to the other. "What the hell does that mean?"

"A virus," said Mack.

"Sir," said Caroline, "the same person who killed Senator Bryson also killed Jacobson. We have to stop them before innocent people are killed."

"Then get some real proof. And fast."

"Yes, sir."

He turned to Mack. "Don't let your partner brick your evidence next time."

Mack nodded.

"You two just do your jobs and support Moretto and TJ. And if you piss off another person in the President's cabinet, your asses are gone."

Ten minutes later, Caroline and Mack walked silently through the parking garage to their car.

"Can that man have a bigger stick up his ass?" Even though she was pissed, Caroline kept her voice low. Sounds had a tendency to carry in the cavernous parking structure.

"You got him in pretty deep water," Mack said gently. "Did you see how he was dressed? He probably was at some couple's game night drinking red wine and playing charades or something, and he gets a call from the Chief of Staff chewing his ass out."

"Please. I did my job and the boys' club got their shorts in a bunch." She clasped her arms around her midsections. "I almost got us fired, didn't I?"

"I'm with you on this one," Mack said. "We both saw that video."

"Yeah, and there were names on that list... and numbers. I can remember at least one of the names. It was W-something, White or Wicks... for mercy's sake. Let me think."

"It doesn't matter what you think, memories aren't evidence."

Caroline looked up. "After I betrayed your trust, you didn't blink an eye at risking your career for me. That's special in my book."

Mack smiled, eating up the compliment. "You know I got your back." Then he slapped Caroline on the butt in an atta-boy type of way–but as soon as he did it, he regretted it. His cheeks went red. "I'm sorry. It's habit. It's a baseball-buddy kind of thing."

Caroline looked at him dumbfounded for a moment.

Mack was sure she would chew him a new one, but Caroline just walked away, saying. "You better start working on your swing there, hotshot."

"What?" Mack replied, baffled.

Then she turned and smiled. "Oh, there's a lot you don't know about me, Maxwell."

26

The limo sped along an empty two-lane road in Bigfork, Montana.

Larry Tukenson, founder and CEO of Incubus, one of the largest communications software companies in the world, was feeling magnanimous. He'd just come from a gala at the Grand Resorts Ballroom, where he'd lavished forty of his top execs with a personalized stay–complete with fine food, a spa package, and one staff person on duty per couple. Larry Tukenson gave a speech to thunderous applause and adulation. And why not? He was the benevolent god bestowing gifts among the loyal masses.

As an added bonus, his gorgeous wife was at his side to aid in the glorification of Larry Tukenson.

They sat in the backseat of the limo, and as the vehicle sped along, she pressed herself against him, sliding a hand up his thigh. He held up a finger, focused on his phone, listening intently to the financial report, smiling. She flicked her tongue against the lobe of his other ear.

He hung up his phone. "We did it. Number ten!"

"Honey," Sharon whispered, "tonight you're mine–you promised."

"We just moved to number ten after earnings–I want to stay there. After *Forbes* makes their list at the end of the month, I promise, I will not obsess about the short-term stock price anymore."

"Sure, until next year," she said, touching his arm affectionately.

Five minutes later, the limo approached a four-way intersection located six miles from the Tukensons' house. The secluded intersection was quiet, and the pavement gleamed faintly in the dim light of the full moon as the car rolled to a gentle stop.

Without warning, a gasoline tanker with its lights off screamed through the intersection and collided head-on with the limo.

The front end of the limo crumpled like a tin can and every window in the vehicle shattered outward. The limo driver was crushed to death instantly. Larry and Sharon's bodies flew forward, smashing violently into the back of the front seat. Fountains of sparks sprayed from shrieking bent steel as it scraped against the pavement.

The massive truck pushed the limo another fifty feet before stopping, jackknifed across the road. Its front end smashed, smoke poured from the truck's engine block. The limo looked as if it had been spat out of a trash compactor.

Larry, semi-conscious, reached out to his wife.

"I can't move my legs," she moaned.

Larry tried to speak, but he was barely holding on to consciousness.

Bic took off his motorcycle helmet, looking at the limo from the driver's seat of the truck. Larry Tukenson and his wife were trapped. It would take the Jaws of Life to get them out.

He unbuckled his seatbelt, and that of the unconscious bearded man he had wheelchaired out of the bathroom, who now sat beside him in the passenger seat. He pulled the trucker's limp body over the gearshift and into the driver's seat.

The driver's side door had struck shut in the impact, so Bic rammed it open with brute strength. He pulled open the ashtray and scattered cigarette butts across the cab. Standing on the landing step, he gripped the truck driver's head under his chin and in one fluid motion, smashed the trucker's skull into the windshield, exactly where the driver's trajectory would have been in the accident. The trucker's skull crunched, and left a massive, spider-webbed impact pattern.

As the trucker lay bleeding, Bic closed the door and jumped to the pavement. He walked over to the tanker trailer's control valve and opened it. Gasoline sprayed forcefully onto the road.

Bic walked toward the limo, pulling a small package wrapped in white wax paper from his coat pocket. Just the package in his hand made him feel unstable; he ignored Sharon's painful moans from inside the car.

Sharon struggled to move as she flopped her head sideways and saw Bic. "*Help... please help us...*"

Bic slowly slid his sunglasses down then carefully pulled them off, folding them carefully with one hand and sliding them into a pocket. He stared at Sharon, and she recoiled before his radiant red gaze.

"Oh my God!" she cried out, trembling in horror.

Bic unwrapped the wax paper, exposing a thick raw single pork chop. Sharon's cries dimmed to nothing as the rage filled his body. There was his father's face. His father's blood-curdling voice.

It's pork chop-eatin' time!

He tossed the piece of meat onto Sharon's lap. The action shocked the woman to silence, her eyes fluttered, and she barely seemed to breathe as she gaped at the meat before her.

Bic walked away, outpacing the pool of gas that crept under the limo.

Near the wreck, off to the side of the road in a ditch hidden under some pine branches, Bic retrieved a black Ninja motorcycle.

He drove the bike down the road about thirty yards before stopping. He then pulled the trucker's solid steel Zippo and some butane out of his pocket. Sparking the zippo to life, he squirted excess lighter fluid on it till it was a small ball of flame, uncomfortable to hold despite the protective leather of his gloves. Taking careful aim, he hucked the lighter at the driver's side door of the truck. The lighter arced through the air, flames snapping angrily, eating up the oxygen and lighter fluid, then landed squarely in the spreading gasoline.

With a huge roar, the deadly liquid burst into flames, spreading eagerly in all directions.

The tanker exploded with stunning force, throwing the flaming limo into the air. As it ascended, it too exploded, rending open like a sardine can just before it fell back to earth. The hungry flames licked the sky.

Bic calmly patted out the flames that had spread onto his gloves with the lighter fluid then kicked the Ninja into gear and pulled away. Within seconds, he was safely concealed in the inky darkness of the valley.

27

Hot water from the steamy shower beat gently against Caroline's skin. She tried to relax as the warmth and moisture massaged her, but her bungling earlier today made that impossible. She couldn't stop thinking about how she'd fouled things up by erasing the list file. If they had the list, the case would likely be solved. Instead, more people would probably die–because of her.

Why couldn't she just have listened to Mack and waited? *What's the matter with me?* She shaved her long, tan legs. *I got carried away. What were those names again? White? Vine? And those numbers, a bank account? Social security? Phone number?*

Garbage, crap, and syringes blanketed the street. A torn tent stood, showing neither pride nor shame, in front of a boarded building without a name.

At four in the morning, Caroline walked down Skid Row with determination–and that alone made her stand out. This was where the damned lived out their sentences. No one had any purpose here. No one was determined. Unless you called survival determination.

No. No one was determined to survive. Survival was vestigial here, like an appendix. Perhaps it had a purpose once, but no more.

The thoughts made her quicken her step. *Easy does it,* she thought.

She wasn't going to fail tonight.

A car pulled up to the next street corner and a girl–not a day over seventeen–stepped out of the car after cupping her hand around something the driver handed her.

Caroline picked up pace. As the man drove off, she got a glance at him. He looked over forty. Her first instinct was to reach for her gun and shoot the scumbag, but she had purposely left her gun and badge back in the car.

With a gentle smile, Caroline walked over to the young girl. There was semen in the girl's hair. Caroline stifled any sign of shock and she asked softly, "What's your name?"

"April," she replied.

"How'd you like a nice shower in a safe place? Or something to eat?"

Someone grabbed Caroline from behind in an aggressive choke hold. "*You messin' with my property?*"

"Please don't," said April. But the grip tightened.

"Hold up?" said the man. "Ain't you got something for me?" One hand loosened from the choke hold and extended, palm open.

The girl fumbled in her pocket and produced a wad of cash. This she handed to the man.

"Now get to hustlin'," said the man. "You got more work to do tonight."

The girl started off like a kicked dog.

This was Caroline's moment. She violently snapped her head back, smashing the back of her skull into the man's nose.

"I'm gonna cut you!" he yelled as he jerked back in surprise and pain.

She followed with an elbow to the gut as she broke free from the grip. This was the first sight she caught of the pimp. He was thin too, with a face that could have belonged to any man from thirty to sixty. It too had been rendered featureless by the streets, save for the look of menace in the eyes and the fierce, permanent scowl formed by the rest of the features.

He tore her blouse as he frantically tried to restrain her. "No ho touches me and lives," the man hissed, throwing a wild right cross.

Caroline ducked and swept the pimp's legs out from under him. He went down, his head smacking against the curb. As he staggered to get to his feet, Caroline kicked him in the face. His head snapped back in a bloody mess, and he fell senseless to the sidewalk.

Caroline saw April go around the corner of the block and ran after her. Adrenaline numbed her skin and turned her blood to electricity.

The girl wasn't hard to catch. Caroline got her in a restraining hug. Her arms could have wrapped around her twice.

"He'll make me pay for that," said the girl.

"No, he won't," Caroline said confidently. She let the girl go as she stopped struggling.

April looked miserable, and hugged her own midsection, shivering. She stared at the ground. "What am I supposed to do now?"

"You're coming with me." Caroline held out her hand encouragingly.

Walking back to the car, for the first time in a while, she felt good about herself. She couldn't save them all. She wasn't even sure if she could save April. But she could try, and it was a start. The start she had been searching for.

28

A couple of hours later, Caroline rushed out of the elevator. Seemingly from nowhere, Mack intercepted her with two cups of coffee. He handed her a cup, not breaking stride.

"Your shirt... what the hell happened?" he said.

Caroline glanced at the tear in her shirt. This would have embarrassed her terribly yesterday. But today she walked into the meeting room considering it a badge of honor.

A.D. Bender, TJ, and Moretto were already discussing the case when they entered. The whiteboard against the wall had been converted into a suspect board. There were three pictures across the top of the board: Senator Bryson, Bubba Taylor, and Gentry Jacobson. Written beneath the pictures were two column headings next to each other: '**MOTIVE? HIT LIST?**' To the right of the word 'LIST,' the recorded conversation between Bryson and Taylor was written out.

Bryson: It's big... real big. And bad.

Taylor: Just lay it on me.

Bryson: Murder. Assassination. A lot of innocent people are going to die. Women too. They're being clever about it, though. No one will figure it out until it's too late.

Taylor: What are you talking about?

Bryson: They're bringing in a specialist. Do you have any idea what that means? A specialist?

Taylor: A specialist?

Bryson: A profess–a professional killer. This is big, Bubba. I've seen the list! Rock stars, all of them. And all killed to fund–

Taylor: Now take it easy, Gary. I'm sure no one's going to die.

Bryson: I–dear God, is this line secure? I've said too much, haven't I?

Taylor: Stop with the ridiculous conspiracy crap. Do I know these people?

Bryson: Of course you know them. Everybody does.

Bender looked at his watch. "What's with you two?"

"Not her fault, sir," said Moretto. "She's still trying to shake off that nasty virus she caught yesterday."

Caroline glowered. If that buffoon knew she had let a computer virus ruin the files, then everyone at the Bureau did as well.

Bender glanced at Moretto, his expression signaling the agent to knock it off. Moretto shrugged innocently, then smirked at Caroline, looking at her feet, and said, "Nice crime scene."

Caroline looked down to find her right tennis shoe with a blood spatter across the top, she smirked back at Moretto, "Just gotta know how to keep a smart ass in line."

"Knock it off, Moretto," said Bender. "Agent Foxx, would you care to address the fact that you look like you just crawled out of a tiger cage?"

"I got into a slight accident, sir. It's nothing. I'm fine. I just didn't have time to change."

Bender shook his head. His patience had obviously worn thin.

Mack had dropped a cheap cell phone on the table. "Burner phone, sir."

"Burner phone what?"

"There was an inbound call to Taylor yesterday that was from a burner phone. We got a trace on the IMEI number and were able to find out where it was scanned at time of purchase. There's a small electronics shop just south of San Francisco. The same area Jacobson hails from. Now, of course we don't know what was said, but in the last year, this is the first time Taylor received a call from an untraceable number."

"Good work, Mack," TJ said as he walked over to the whiteboard. "Taylor seems to be the key."

TJ wrote 'burner phone user' on the whiteboard under 'suspects.' Then he drew a connecting line between Taylor and 'burner phone user.'

"You were moonlighting last night," Moretto said to Caroline off to the side.

Caroline nodded, "Something like that."

"I looked into your deal–pretty gutsy leaving a gig high in the six figures to do this."

"Gutsy, maybe. Some would say stupid. But thanks nonetheless."

Moretto laughed. "Yeah, stupid for sure, but gutsy."

Mack pointed to Taylor on the whiteboard. "My guess is he's not involved. Not directly, anyway. Not his style. But whoever used this burner phone killed Bryson, and probably Jacobson, and also paid a courtesy call on Taylor to keep his mouth shut on any hunches he might have."

"Considering how reluctant he was to talk," added Caroline, "our killer probably has dirt on Taylor–or threatened to keep his mouth shut permanently like they did with Bryson."

"I want to know who bought that phone within twenty-four hours and have lockdown surveillance on Taylor around the clock," Bender demanded.

"TJ and I will handle Bubba Taylor," Moretto said.

"Good."

Mack looked at Caroline, then at Bender. "I guess that means we're going back to San Fran?"

"Don't screw this up," the A.D. replied.

29

A black scorpion scuttled out from under a rock, lifting its tail in indignation. A huge fist slammed down on it, splattering it into the sand.

Peering through the top-of-the-line Leica binoculars positioned between two prickly pears, Bic watched Steven Vorg make his way down Camelback Mountain in the cool Sunday morning air. Bic took special note of the other man's slender, well-muscled frame. He didn't want to put himself in a situation where he had to chase Vorg down. On a piece of graph paper attached to a clipboard, he mapped out the different landmarks as Vorg ran past them, seeking an ideal spot to ambush him.

Bic's mobile phone vibrated. He pulled it out of his front pants pocket and scowled at the tiny digital screen. The confirmation he had been waiting for came in—payment for completing the Tukenson job had been transferred into his account.

Almost there, he thought forcefully as he remembered standing over Chandra's freshly-dug grave holding little Gracie's hand as she stood right beside him, tears running down her cheeks. Everyone else had left the funeral.

"We'll get through this, baby girl," Bic had said as he bent down, rubbing her shoulders, his massive hand practically covering her entire back.

Gracie looked up at Bic, the tears staining her cheeks now belying the furious determination burning in her big brown eyes, "I'm going to find a cure."

"Sweet girl, we can't bring her back," he replied softly.

"I know. When I get big, I'm going to stop cancer from hurting other people."

Bic marveled at this five-year-old little girl's resolve. Inspired, he assured her, "I'ma gonna get us outta the ghetto. Put you in the type of schools where kids go on to do things like cure cancer."

Gracie reached out and shook Bic's hand, and a deal was made that neither party would ever give up on.

His phone vibrated with a news alert, snapping his attention back to the present.

He rechecked a few news sites to see if the scoop on the Tukensons had changed. No indication, yet, that their deaths had been anything other than an accident.

It's been over twenty-four hours, he told himself. *And there hasn't been a single mention of foul play.*

He went back to his binoculars and watched patiently as Vorg started down the mountain.

30

It was a misty morning in downtown San Francisco's Union Square. A cool breeze swooped down through the glitzy shops and hotels, ruffling the hair of passersby, but doing little to dispel the fog. Tidwell looked around thoughtfully. For mid-morning on a Sunday, the downtown district seemed awfully crowded.

He stood reading his newspaper outside Café Paris, a trendy new designer coffee shop he frequented since it had opened the previous month. He hid behind his newspaper, seeing but unseen.

"Sir, got any extra change?" asked a toothless man in a stained flannel shirt.

Tidwell gave the bum a baleful glance before burying his face in the newspaper again.

"Please sir, I ain't eaten in days." The bum's breath smelled like hot garbage dipped in camel turds.

Tidwell glanced around to see if anyone was watching him and snapped, "Listen, you piece of dirt, the only thing you'll get from me is a swift kick in the face! Beat it." He cracked his paper back open as the bum scurried off.

A yellow cab pulled up alongside the curb near the coffee shop's entrance. Tidwell tucked the newspaper under his arm and entered the passenger's side front seat of the cab.

"Well?"

"Well what?" came the voice from the back seat. The smell of Cuban cigar smoke was unbearable.

"Can we get on with it?"

The cab started down the street, and Tidwell twisted around to look at Anthony Parelli.

Parelli removed the cigar and gestured with it. "With all the commotion, I wanted to make sure we were still on schedule."

Tidwell nodded toward the driver. "Friend of yours I assume?"

"Vito's dad and I grew up together. He's family. Now, to business."

"That rat Bryson," said Tidwell. "Not only was he a snitch, he couldn't even do one thing right. That hacker kid was his hire. Then he goes and tries to blackmail me."

"Alright," said Parelli. "So what are you whining about? They're both dead."

"Utah said a couple of FBI agents were poking around the hotel. Are they onto us?"

Parelli snorted. "Maybe. So what?"

Tidwell looked back. "You're serious?"

Parelli blew a thick cloud of black smoke that nearly choked the congressman.

"Jesus," rasped Tidwell.

"You're worrying over nothing. They're a couple of rookies who don't have nothin' on us. However, this does complicate things. One of my contacts said that fat moron Taylor was being wiretapped by the FBI. They almost certainly have his last conversation with Bryson on tape."

Tidwell's heartbeat quickened. "What exactly did they get?"

"He didn't mention any names, but he *did* go on about a whole bunch of well-known people getting whacked."

"What?" Tidwell asked, once again twisting in his seat.

"Relax, Mr. Congressman."

Tidwell cringed at the appellation.

Parelli continued. "The Tukenson job was an ingenious hit and not a single mention of foul play," Parelli's hands sprung to life like a conductor's. "This guy's the Picasso of assassins."

"Glad you're impressed. That's twenty-seven of the two hundred and fifty billion we need into the government piggy bank. But I'm worried about the FBI. They're on high alert waiting for something to happen. We only have twenty-one days until the budget committee meets. If the projected income isn't there, it's over." Tidwell stopped in mid-thought. "Do you think we should notify the Ghost of what's happened?"

Parelli looked away and put his cigar in his mouth, his eyes wandering as he puffed. After a long moment, his eyes snapped back to Tidwell's. "I don't think so. He should just keep to the schedule."

"Do we need to take care of Taylor?"

Parelli shook his head. "We don't want to give the FBI too many dots to connect. If Taylor's removed, they'll really start jumping up our asses. And anyways, I sent Taylor a little packet, one with enough dirt to put him behind bars for two lifetimes."

Tidwell turned slightly. "Thank God."

Parelli tapped the headrest of Vito's seat, and a few seconds later the cab eased to a stop. Tidwell grabbed the door handle to exit, then paused to voice an important thought: "Are you sure we shouldn't tell the Ghost about what the FBI knows? He might need to handle things differently."

Parelli puffed on his Cuban, then said, "Here's what we'll do. The FBI is looking for some high-profile murders to test out some theory or other. Fine." He put the cigar back into his mouth and smiled around it. "We'll give 'em somethin'."

31

Bic sat at a motel room desk, booting his laptop. The room—old, outdated, with wobbly furniture and walls browned with the passing of decades—didn't faze him as much as sleeping on the dreaded cheap mattress did. At his age, his back would be tight in the morning. This hotel did not require ID from its guests, and it accepted cash, so it was perfect.

Once his laptop booted, Bic accessed the offshore account where his current employer had deposited his money, then moved the money to three other accounts he had set up under different names. He received an email ping just before he shut down and was delighted to see that it was from Gracie.

> You can now add a Ph.D. in Molecular Biology to my M.D. Thank you for believing in me all these years. I couldn't have done it without you. Love You Always, Gracie.

Bic smiled, and swallowed a small lump in his throat, as he replied:

> Great news! I showed your thesis to those investors I told you about—they were so impressed with your research they wrote a check for $2.5 million and made commitments of another $9 million over the next month. Your startup company is now funded!! I did my part—now it's your turn to find the cure!

In his heart, Bic believed that despite all the bad he had done, the good that Gracie would create would make up for it.

Then a second email came into his inbox. It was from his employer.

Mr. Blackstone, the first stage of the project went very well. I know you're anxious to complete the second stage. Unfortunately, there's a delay in our materials, but our supplier assures me that it will be only a twenty-four-hour delay. After that, you may proceed with the project as planned. I anticipate the first installment for the project was received without any problems.

Project Manager

Bic deleted the new e-mail without responding, unconcerned about the delay. He opened a small leather case on the desk and pulled out two vials of deadly toxins. After snapping on plastic gloves, he plunged the needle into one of the vials, then pulled back the plunger, filling the barrel of the syringe with 6 CC's of the first toxin. Bic then repeated with the second vial.

After capping the needle, he glanced to the corner of the room at the tightly covered white five-gallon plastic bucket labeled "CAUTION: BIOHAZARD".

32

Heather Wright exited her car, with the help of her assistant, in the front lot of Chicago's McCormick Place Convention Center. One of the top second amendment activists in America, Heather was excited about the national attention she was going to receive today. This would be the day she would get people motivated to act, to contact their congressmen, and force Congress to rewrite the existing gun laws.

Heather, at forty-eight, was an honest-looking woman, with a full figure and bottle blonde hair. She had a petite nose and close-set brown eyes that could express both boldness and sincerity at her bidding. The parking lot buzzed with activity. "It's ten AM, and we already have hundreds of protesters," Heather said to her assistant.

"We're getting stronger by the minute," her assistant replied.

Today, at noon, was the beginning of a week-long gun show. Inside McCormick Place, weapons of all kinds would be displayed. Gun enthusiasts would be able to see anything from simple handguns to some of the military's most sophisticated hardware.

Heather noticed the brisk breeze coming off Lake Michigan and worried briefly about her hair. She usually never cared excessively about her looks, but today was important. She had her hair specially done and was wearing her favorite classic red pantsuit from Talbots. One of her dearest friends, anchorwoman Loretta Rains, would be interviewing her later that evening on the 6:00 news. Tonight was the big night. On a national stage, she would reinforce her most passionate message: "Guns kill people. Tougher gun laws saves lives."

Heather waved to the crowd. Several hundred people waved back, many more cheered once they recognized her, and some showed her their protest banners–pictures of handguns with a big red X painted over the weapon and the like. A couple of the more radical protesters had enlarged pictures of police photos taken at accident and crime scenes, in which children had accidentally blown holes in their own heads or had been shot up in gang crossfire.

Heather smiled, energized by the crowd. She reached back into her vehicle and grabbed a megaphone. She was known for her inspiring speeches, and it was vital she be heard by everyone–especially today.

Heather's voice boomed: "Today's the day we take another step in making our neighborhoods and our families safer..."

"...our families safer..."

Eight hundred yards away, across the large parking lot between McCormick Place and Soldier Field, beads of sweat formed on the upper lip of a Mexican man with long slicked-back oily black hair, a dark face full of scruff, and arms sleeved in tattoos.

Positioned at the very top of the west wall of the stadium, Gabriel leered hungrily at his target through his scope. He wasn't worried about taking out the target. He had faith that Diablo, his high-powered modified Dragunov SVD sniper rifle, would not fail him. He loved the thrill of the kill so much that the waiting became a kind of torture, an anticipation that almost hurt.

He blinked his right eye as he looked through the scope lens, centering the crosshairs on the middle of her back. "Oh baby, Diablo and I want to send you to a better place," he said excitedly in his native tongue. He took his finger away from the trigger as the urge to shoot became unbearable. He wouldn't get paid a dime unless he killed her when he was supposed to–when the news cameras were there to see.

He licked his lips sensually as he continued to watch. The target's red suit separated her effectively from the mass of people around her. Gabriel visualized the high caliber bullet plunging into the woman's back, tearing through her chest explosively, leaving a soda-can-sized hole as it exited. He trembled in anticipation.

33

Mack and Caroline entered BC Electronics, a hip specialty shop stuffed with as many electronics as could possibly fit in the space without looking messy. A couple of teenagers with skateboards listened to music at an interactive music station.

A young man dressed casually but stylishly approached them. "Welcome to BC!" he said brightly. "How can I help you?"

"We were hoping to speak to the owner of the store," Caroline said.

"You got him," said the man, extending his hand. "Mason."

Before the man answered, Mack already knew he was the owner. He had on a watch that fetched upwards of $10,000 retail. He shook the offered hand. "Nice store you have here. And an even nicer watch. Panerai, if I'm not mistaken."

"A man who knows his watches," said Mason. "What can I help you find today?"

Caroline grabbed a burner phone off the shelf by the checkout area and said, "Last week a phone purchased from your store was used in a high-profile case, and we want to know who purchased it."

Mason thought for a moment. "Hmmm, that might be hard to say..."

"Our bad, we're FBI," Mack showed his FBI credentials.

Mason shrugged. "Not sure how I can help you."

Caroline glanced at the security cameras.

"Those are just a deterrent." Mason said.

"You don't store footage?" she Crossed her arms and scowled.

Mason replied glibly: "Nope."

Caroline glared at him, sure he was lying. Mason just grinned back.

Mack, eager to defuse the tension, grabbed a bag of sunflower seeds from the impulse items next to the checkout register and said, "These are the best seeds. They don't have this brand anywhere else I've been in the country."

"I love those, too," Mason agreed.

"These always remind me I'm home," Mack said sentimentally. Then added with a bit more seriousness, "look, we don't want to put you on the spot, but people have died, and more will soon. We can really use any help you can give."

Mason thought for a moment.

Mack continued, "No liability on your part–you just sold the phones. We're not here to hassle you."

In the small back office, Mack and Caroline looked over Mason's shoulder as they watched a small TV monitor showing a man with long bleach blond hair purchasing a phone from the store.

"This was purchased three days ago," Mason explained.

"You know this guy?" Mack asked.

"He runs a little surf shop at Pacifica State Beach. He's into some shady stuff, I hear."

"Great surf–I know the spot," Mack said as he patted Mason on the back. "I owe you big time."

34

After leaving the store, Mack and Caroline parked outside of a chain-type surf store, sitting in silence.

"What are we doing here?" Caroline asked.

Mack ignored her question. "What's up with you? How far were you going to take it if I hadn't been there?"

Caroline shook her head. "Mack, I know I come off as headstrong, but its hard. I can't just good old boy and make friends the way you do. So I push. I'm going to fight hard, knowing people are going to die if I don't. We had the list. I lost it. That one's on me; so there will be blood on my hands now if we don't stop them. I–I can't let that happen."

"It was your work that *found* the list, found Jacobson–without you we would still be waiting for someone to get killed for our next clue. We all make mistakes. No one's perfect," Mack said. "It's how we handle our mistakes that shows our true character."

"You really believe that?"

"With all my heart."

Caroline managed a soft smile.

Mack grinned mischievously and glanced sideling at his partner, "you ready to have some fun?"

Caroline looked wary, and a little hopeful. "Maybe. Depends on what you're calling fun."

"I've got an idea," he said with a smile. "Ready to do a little improv?"

Forty-five minutes later, Mack and Caroline were walking down the sandy beach toward a small surf hut fifty yards from the ocean shore. Caroline was dressed in a revealing bikini. The even bigger reveal was a tattoo of the name "Samantha" in cursive on her right shoulder blade. And Mack, shirtless in board shorts, despite his best efforts, could not stop looking at her. She had the type of body that stops traffic on laundry day. Mack cherished the closeness they had as partners, but was very guarded not to let any women back into his heart. He saw what that did to his father, and he was determined to avoid ruining his life in that way.

Caroline caught him staring. "I can't believe I'm walking on the beach dressed like this–this better not be the fun part."

Mack laughed, then he grabbed her hand, like a boyfriend would. "Working undercover's always fun."

"You try to make out with me, you'll be kissing a right cross," she said half-jokingly as they walked up to the hut.

35

Working inside the Surf Shack was the same man who had bought the burner phone in the video.

"Hey buddy," said Mack, "it's my girlfriend's first time— can you hook us up with a beginner board?"

The man smiled. "About to pop your surf cherry. Love it." He walked them over to one of the bigger boards and said, "This one's like an aircraft carrier–it'll keep anybody up."

Suddenly a phone rang from under the small counter.

"One second," the man said as he went behind the counter and pulled out a burner phone.

He answered the call, "Yo, I'm busy, call back," then abruptly hung up and commented, "All day long with these people–it never ends."

"You mind if I teach my girl how to pop up on the board here?" asked Mack.

The man ogled Caroline, and grinned. "Take all day if you like, brah."

After he popped up off a board several times while trying to teach Caroline, Mack asked, "Are you even listening to me?"

Caroline regarded the man in the surf hut, barely paying attention to Mack. "I'm not really getting on a surfboard," she said finally.

"You are, actually," Mack said as he grabbed her playfully, getting her to lie on her stomach on the board. He carefully positioned her then suddenly became aware of his hands positioned on her hip and long tan leg. She rolled slightly to her side, looking up at him, and her hand brushed the back of his as she moved. Their eyes locked.

In the distance a car honked and the spell was broken.

She shoved his hand off her hip and looked sheepishly away. "It's not going to happen. I hate the sand—it gets everywhere."

Mack positioned her feet then hands in the right place. "Okay. You're out there. Just try to ignore the sharks. You've just caught the crest. And... pop up... *now!*"

Caroline jumped to her feet almost reflexively.

"Pretty good. See, you're not too bad at following instructions."

"You have no idea," Caroline mumbled to herself.

"Okay, again."

Caroline rolled her eyes and whispered, "Come on, buddy, get another call so we can get out of here."

She tried again, getting more into it. After several more tries, she realized Mack was on his phone. She then looked over and saw the man in the surf hut talking on his burner phone. She turned to Mack, who had mirrored his cell with the surfer dude's burner.

"Well?"

Mack shook his head. "Not our guy."

"What do you mean?"

Mack walked over and showed her his phone. "He's using his to sell weed. He's nothing more than a beach bum pothead."

Caroline was overwhelmed with disappointment. "Well, what now?"

"All's not lost." Mack looked out at the ocean as a perfect four-foot wave broke.

"Really? People's lives are at stake, and you want to effing surf!" Caroline yelled, then turned and began to walk off the beach.

Mack shouted back at her angrily. "Maybe you should try living a little for once instead of always having a stick up your ass!"

Caroline stopped dead in her tracks and turned. "You're a bad boyfriend, you know that?"

36

L ying on her surfboard, Caroline could hear the roar of the
wave fast approaching and with it, her spirit soared.

Mack, standing waist-deep in the water and holding onto
the board said, "I'll get you right in the pocket. Just paddle like hell
and then pop up."

"Okay, I got this. What's the worst that can happen?"

"In a four-foot wave? Worst case, you get slammed down into the
sand bar headfirst and break your neck."

"I'm going to choke you," Caroline yelled, paddling with all she
had as he pushed her into the biggest wave of the set.

As the wave broke, Caroline popped up and rode it for a glorious
nine seconds before she lost her balance and was engulfed by the
crashing water.

She quickly breached the surface and shot Mack a poisonous look.
She knew she had been easily manipulated, but she couldn't hold it
for long as she cracked a huge smile.

Mack and Caroline sat on their surfboards, floating just past the surf,
with the sun setting behind them. They had surfed together nonstop
all afternoon, as if they were two worry-free teenagers out having the
time of their lives.

"Thanks," she said, leaning back and staring at the sky.

"For what?"

"In this fake world, you're able to just be you." she explained. "I
admire that so much. So, thanks."

"You're pretty fun yourself when you let loose—plus you're a natural at surfing."

Caroline smiled as she looked away.

"What?" Mack asked.

"I may have had a brief skateboarding stage in my youth," she confessed.

"You on a board? Sick!" Mack laughed.

"Never judge a book by its cover, Maxwell. You won't believe this, but... never mind."

"Try me," Mack said, pulling her close to him. "You can trust me with anything."

"What happened with your dad?" she blurted out.

"What?"

She looked at him. His eyes betrayed his secret. "You never told me about it."

Mack licked his lips and looked down. He trailed a hand through the water, thinking. "My mom left us. Dad was devastated, but we dealt with it together for years. Then out of high school, I was drafted and left home to go play baseball. I knew he still wasn't over her, but I left anyway. I was only gone a month, but I guess he couldn't take the loneliness. He tried to kill himself. So, I quit baseball, gave all the money back, and came back home to take care of him. That's it."

"You gave up your dream," she said.

Mack shrugged. "He's my father. I never should have left in the first place, but I did, and now I have to accept what happened. He's much better now. The meds he's on are working great, but that doesn't change what happens to me at night, or when I'm alone with my thoughts, and all I can see in my head is the image of him sitting there like a rock, so ruined and so sad... What about you?"

"What *about* me?"

"Was being an FBI agent your childhood dream? Or did you put all your stock into professional surfing?"

Caroline smiled at the question. "No and no. Ever since I was seven years old, I wanted to be a lawyer. I was daddy's girl, and we talked about law constantly. My whole life, he groomed me to one day have my name next to his at his law firm. I finally get there and, well, quit after a year. Pretty pathetic, huh?"

"Why'd you quit?"

Caroline turned a little, revealing to Mack the tattoo on her back.

"I wanted to help people. You've never looked in the mirror and realized what a phony you are. It's not fun. I let someone get off that shouldn't have gotten off. He hurt a child. You want to talk about not being able to live with yourself."

A man yelled from the beach.

"It's Mason." Mack said.

They immediately paddled in.

"I think I found who you're looking for," Mason said, showing them a cell phone video of a man in a tailored suit purchasing a burner phone. "He came in earlier in the week. He wasn't a regular."

"That would have been nice to know," Caroline said.

"The guy was wearing a Patek Philippe Sky Moon Tourbillion," Mason said.

"That watch costs more than most people's houses," Mack said.

"You ain't kidding," said Mason. "When I saw the watch, I didn't really pay attention to what he bought."

Caroline grabbed the phone and re-watched the video. "You can't see his face. Is there any other video or angles we can use with facial recognition software?"

"No, I double- and triple-checked. He never showed his face from under that top hat," Mason said.

"I'd like to recheck, if it's okay?" Caroline asked.

Mason thought for a second. "One condition."

"Anything," she replied.

Mason smiled. "You have to stay in that bikini."

Scowling, Caroline covered herself up with her beach towel.

37

At 5:00 PM, news vans arrived at McCormick Place. The crews emerged from their logo-plastered vehicles, hastily setting up their equipment in time for the 6:00 PM live broadcast. For three of the four networks, this was a big story; all of them had recently been overplaying every accident they could find that involved guns.

At the front of the crusade was Channel Two's 6:00 Action News reporter, Loretta Rains. A good friend of Wright, she was known for her liberal slant, especially on gun control. She had even been quoted as saying, "Gun manufacturers and the NRA should take responsibility for the violence in America's inner-city neighborhoods."

Rains was a beautiful African-American woman with straight black hair. She wore a red blazer, white blouse, and matching skirt. She played up her high cheekbones and flawless complexion—both definite pluses before the camera.

"Loretta, you look great," Heather said as she emerged from the crowd of protesters.

"You don't look too bad yourself. Nice suit. When people see us on camera, they're going to start talking." Loretta smiled.

"It would be my pleasure to be thought of in the same league as the number-one news reporter in America."

Loretta smirked. "You sure know how to make a girl feel good."

"Let's go get ready for the interview." Heather made a fist. "It's time to be the change we want to make."

113

Gabriel adjusted the scope of the tripod-mounted rifle—and reminisced about death.

His first kill-for-hire had been in his hometown of Durango, Mexico, where a Mexican politician had paid him $5,000 American to take out a rival (Gabriel had refused to be paid in *pesos*). The job went off with cool efficiency, but oddly enough, soon after he had been paid, that first politician had died in a freak auto accident.

Gabriel smiled. He had never been connected to that death. That kill had been fun, too—and no politician talked to Gabriel like he was a peasant.

Since then, Gabriel had worked both sides of the border, building a reputation for getting the job done in his indiscriminate, massacring way. He always brought Diablo with him, ever since kill number three. Those who knew of it called it "Gabriel's Trumpet," because it had called so many unfortunate souls home.

He took a deep breath, watching carefully. The second mark had arrived. Pulling off consecutive hits could be a challenge, but not here. Not with two blood-red targets side by side. He would easily get the second shot off before the second mark could even react.

He recalled the terror of his past victims, relishing all the gruesome details of the kill. Handing out death gave Gabriel an unmatchable high, as if he were an equal to his Biblical namesake, the Angel of Death, who had wiped out thousands at the behest of the Lord.

The main target dipped behind a large man.

"Little Red Riding Hood," Gabriel hissed, "come out where I can see you. I promise I'll help you get to Grandma's house. C'mon, li'l *puta*."

He sucked in short, controlled breaths of air. *All marks in red have to go*, he thought. *In his version of Biblical times, when he plays God, the red blood of the lamb is the mark of death.*

To steady himself, Gabriel began to methodically whisper to himself, "Old McGabriel had a gun, E-I-E-I-O. And in his gun, he had some bullets, E-I-E-I-O. With a bang-bang there and a bang-bang here, here a bang, there a bang, everywhere a bang-bang..."

His watch beeped: 6:00 PM. Kill time.

The targets' backs were toward him as they faced the crowd of protestors. A cameraman pointed at Loretta to signal the beginning of the live feed, and Gabriel took his final read through his scope.

"Freeze and put your hands on your head, *now!*"

Gabriel didn't move.

"I will shoot you in the back of the head if you don't put your hands up in three seconds. One..."

Gabriel threw his hands into the air, then turned around. A security guard stood five feet from him, a .38 Special pointed at Gabriel's chest.

Gabriel smiled. He took a step toward the guard. "I was just looking for the *candy store*," he said.

"On the ground, now!"

He took another aggressive step forward, "I would *kill* for some *chocolate.*"

"I said on the ground, lowlife, or I'll shoot!" The guard's hands shook slightly.

"*BOO!*" Gabriel yelled.

The guard shot him in the chest. He collapsed.

Gabriel stirred slightly. "Help..."

The guard inched toward him, the gun aimed. "Easy does it."

"Help," Gabriel repeated.

The guard took one hand off the gun and reached for his walkie.

That was enough time.

Gabriel leapt up like a cat and headbutted the man in the face. The gun went skidding across the floor. Gabriel pulled a blade from his back and slit the guard's throat before the poor guy knew what had happened.

He patted his chest. "Eez Kevlar vest," he said in an exaggerated Mexican accent as the guard bled out.

38

"People are dying, every day" said Heather. "Being frozen in a debate, refusing to act, is no longer acceptable when that inaction, that speechlessness, carries a body count. We aren't here to argue about what we should or shouldn't have done at the last mass shooting, we are here to *stop* the one that will happen tomorrow, and the one the day after that, and to save every future life we can."

The crowd cheered. Loretta was pleased with how the interview was going; animated with conviction, the two women sat side-by-side in a pair of director's chairs, surrounded by a large group of supporters. They were sending a powerful message through the camera.

Heather continued, "People talk about the right to bear arms, and yes that is the second amendment–an amendment thirteen years after the initial drafting of the constitution, by the way. But here is the deeper truth. Look to the Declaration of independence, look to the pre-amendment constitution... and ask what happened to the inalienable right to life and liberty of the kids from Columbine? What about the dead first graders in Newton?" The crowd became even louder as Heather scowled into the camera.

"I couldn't agree with you more," Loretta said, feeling the passion of Heather's message. Her voice became slightly sarcastic. "But a lot of people say that this interferes with their second amendment rights. Is that a valid reason for keeping guns in the house? Or around children?"

"Again, Loretta, if you look at the facts," Heather said, "they speak for themselves. If you want to have a gun, be willing to admit you are in a militia. Let's get a registry. Let's get thumbprint scanners on triggers." She put her hand out to enumerate her statements. "Why argue against the lives saved, the security? Because schools aren't as important as murd–"

A flat crack echoed across the parking lot as Heather Wright's chest opened up and a red mist of blood, rib fragments and gore sprayed out onto the news camera and crowd. It was the new shot heard round the world. Heather's lifeless body slumped in her seat and then collapsed to the concrete.

A bloodcurdling scream from the crowd broke the disbelieving silence and everyone frantically scrambled for cover.

Heather's gruesome death momentarily paralyzed Loretta. She sat rooted to the spot, gaping at the growing pool of her friend's blood crawling toward her feet. Then her instincts kicked in–and she rose from her chair to run.

Before she could take her first stride, her right shoulder exploded into tattered flesh and shattered bone. The force knocked her face-first to the ground, and she marveled for a mad second that she wasn't dead.

Crippled by terror and immense pain, Loretta struggled to move, and pleaded for rescue.

No one came to help her. As her consciousness faded, she saw the abandoned news camera was still pointed right at her with the little red light on–her death was going out live on TV.

Gabriel watched through Diablo's scope as his second mark fell. Upset with himself for missing her heart on the first shot, he decided to let her suffer a little before putting her out of her misery. The .338 Lapua Magnum bullet hadn't killed her, but it did keep her from running.

But her suffering bored him after ten seconds. Patience wasn't one of Gabriel's virtues.

"Loretta Rains, will you be my valentine?" he slurred softly, as he again took aim. "I promise I'll put this lead arrow straight through your heart."

On live national television, Gabriel did exactly as he had promised. Loretta's screams for help were instantly silenced as the high-powered bullet tore through her heart.

Gabriel then grabbed the rocket launcher he had laid on the ground. The crowd had scattered, so as he took aim, he muttered, "*Mis pollitos*–where are you hiding, *mis pollitos?*"

Seeing that people had taken cover behind the large news vans, he locked in and fired. The missile exploded right underneath the Channel Two van, sending it and several people into the air, on fire and in pieces. The force of the explosion blew away the nearby people and vehicles like cardboard boxes in a windstorm.

Satisfied his work was done, Gabriel carefully dismantled Diablo and returned it to its carrying case, then slung it over his shoulder. As he walked away, he smirked wickedly to himself, knowing he'd earned himself a big piece of dark chocolate.

39

In the small office of BC Electronics, Caroline was reaching her limit. Hoping to get a better idea of this mystery figure, she had been forced to watch long passes on the suspect's watch, while Mack and Mason gawked at it idiotically.

"Got it, enough with the watch!" Caroline barked "There's nothing here. Nothing we can use facial recognition software on."

"We find someone wearing this watch, we find our guy," Mack said. "You don't just see one of these walking around. It's beyond rare."

"When I have twenty stores, I'm buying that watch," Mason added.

"You two need to get a clue about wealthy men," said Caroline. "If he has that watch, he has ten others like it."

"It's better than nothing," Mack challenged.

Caroline thought for a moment. "Is there video of the parking lot?"

"Actually, yes. These punks keep tagging my wall," Mason said. "Hang on."

Suddenly, both Mack's and Caroline's phones pinged. Mack caught it first: "No way. Heather Wright and Loretta Rains were assassinated live during an interview!"

"That's terrible. I love Loretta."

"We got a flight to catch to Chicago," Mack said, then turned to Mason. "Text me if you find anything, like that guy's plate number."

"Do you think...?" Caroline asked, horrified. "Oh my..."

"What?"

"Mack... oh my God..."

"What is it?"

"Heather Wright, Mack. *Wright.* That was one of the names on that list. *She's dead because of me.*"

40

The silver moon hung on the backdrop of the twin peaks of Camelback Mountain. Bic, lying in the brush with his trusty pair of binocs, watched Steven Vorg working in his office. With the twenty-four delay, he couldn't risk the chance of a man this important being called away suddenly for business. He wanted to keep close tabs on Vorg until tomorrow.

Bic was interrupted by a text message from Hawk, his only lifelong friend and the PI whom he had hired to find his father.

"*Good lead.*"

Bic dialed him.

"You found him?"

"Brother, I said I had a good lead–that's it," Hawk replied.

"You find him, you–"

"I know, brother–I got you on speed dial." Hawk assured. "How's the little girl?"

"Just finished her final Ph.D.," said Bic. "She's gonna do it. I know she is."

"A true blessing, that girl is, to guys like you and me ..." Hawk's voice got serious. "Hey, this isn't your usual deal, is it? Seems like you're crossing some lines you haven't in the past."

Bic understood Hawk's meaning. "I agreed to it. It had to be clean, and no kids."

"Can't blame a brother for making sure his people are safe," said Hawk. "But seriously, be careful. There's a lot of strange goings on. Some of my people tell me a lot of Russians have come to port. And not the tourist kind, know what I mean? And there's rumor of some kind of shake up happening–in high places."

Bic listened without comment. Hawk had a streak of paranoia in him. It's what made him good at his job. "Don't worry about that. Call me when you get more."

"I will. And Bic, maybe get yourself a burner."

Bic hung up. But his friend's remarks made him think. *This was the biggest fee he had ever drawn, and the most precise intel he had ever gotten.* How powerful were his employers? He was making enough seed money to fund Gracie's biotech startup–

Did they know about Gracie? Did they care?

41

The cold April night's wind blew off Lake Michigan into Soldier Field, sending a chill through Mack's bones. The sky was filled with thick, dirty-looking clouds. It could pour at any moment.

Mack walked over to the spot from which the assassin had executed Heather Wright and Loretta Rains. TJ was there, squatting, scrutinizing every detail.

"Look at how far a shot it is to the McCormick Place parking lot," Mack said, gazing outward.

"My guess is a thousand yards," TJ replied.

Mack shook his head. "It's insane. I was number one shot at the Academy, and I couldn't hit a garbage can lid at this distance but two out of ten tries."

"This joker hit two hearts in three shots, then fired an RPG 100 yards past it's self-destruct range and bulls-eyed a van. Who is this guy?"

Moretto walked up beside Mack and looked at him sidelong. "This wasn't some pissed off anti-liberal. This was a professional."

TJ nodded. "What do you think, big man? Do we have anything here?"

Moretto leaned up against the cement wall that rimmed the top ledge of the stadium. He ran the hand holding his cigarette along the coarse, weathered surface of the ledge, then pointed. "Here. Right here is where he propped his sniper rifle on a stand."

"How do you know that?" Caroline asked as she walked over.

"Look. There are fresh marks here from its legs. They're exactly eight inches apart." Moretto scuffed the cement with his thumb.

"It's strange he left the rocket launcher behind." TJ looked at the pictures the Chicago P.D. had provided of the shoulder-launched weapon found at the crime scene.

"Too much to leave the scene with, quick and quiet." Moretto took a drag of his cigarette. "Any prints found on the rocket launcher?"

TJ flipped quickly though the report. "Nope."

Caroline piped up, "He probably left the launcher behind because it was a one-shot. When illegally acquired, it's hard to get them with more than a single rocket."

Moretto shot Caroline a quizzical look. "TJ, did ballistics give us anything yet?"

"I'll check my emails." TJ pulled out his smart phone.

"How does it feel to be playing with the big boys?" Moretto asked Caroline.

"I'll let you know when I find them," she replied.

"Listen to this." TJ read aloud from his smart phone: "The rounds recovered were 7N14, a type of bullet developed in Russia in 1999 to replace the 7N1—whatever that is. The 7N14 has a lead-jacketed projectile with an air pocket, steel core, and a lead knocker in the base for maximum terminal effect. This bullet was developed specifically for the Dragunov sniper rifle, or SVD. The SVD was designed by the Russian military and has a maximum range of 1300 meters."

"Wow, that's heavy. Maybe KGB?" Moretto took another drag.

"Could be—considering this guy's skill, high-level military training is likely," TJ responded.

Mack noticed a couple of sunflower seeds on the floor, and bent down to pick them up. He turned a couple over in his palm, then put his palm to his nose and sniffed. He stood up, his fist full of shells. "I'll bet he's not KGB."

Mack opened his palm for everyone to see. He took one and snapped the shell in half—it made a crisp, cracking sound.

"Hear that? This shell would have been as soft as butter if it was here from the last sporting event. These were eaten by the killer." Mack held the shells up to his nose and took a deep sniff.

"What are you, a hound dog?" Moretto chuckled. "Gonna pick up his scent?"

My guess is that he's Hispanic, not Russian."

Moretto lifted an eyebrow at TJ.

"Here," said Mack, holding the seed under Moretto's nose. "What's that smell like?"

"Meatballs," TJ said with a laugh.

Moretto laughed as well, saying, "I know a great Italian place on Division Street."

"I'm guessing you eat there often," Caroline quipped.

"It's got some type of heat to it," Moretto concluded.

"Exactly–hot pepper or Tabasco," Mack said.

"Okay," said Moretto. "So what?"

"When I played baseball, we had this guy Angel, from the Dominican, on our team. He would pour Tabasco into his bag of seeds, shake it, then let it dry into the shell overnight."

TJ bent down to examine one of the thirty or so seed shells scattered in a ten-foot radius. "I like Tabasco, too, there, Mack. *And* sriracha. Your profiling needs work."

"Still, these might lead us to something." Moretto pulled out a plastic bag and a pair of tweezers and handed them to Caroline. "Here. It's time to play detective."

She accepted the job grudgingly.

TJ nodded. "Right. We should be able to get the killer's DNA from the saliva in the seeds."

"It's starting to rain." Caroline said, rushing to collect the remaining shells. "Got them all."

"Good job–you saved the case," Moretto said. "Folks, you heard the man. Be on the lookout for a killer tree squirrel with a taste for Mexican."

A low crack of thunder rolled out over lake Michigan, and the clouds unleashed a downpour.

42

Mack and Caroline ran through the obstacle course of the parking lot's dark puddles.

Mack opened the door for Caroline and then sprinted to the other side as the wind-driven rain spattered against him. He dived in and closed the door.

"I'm soaked," she laughed.

Mack could see that. Her wet blouse accentuated her breasts. He hastily looked away and started the car. The radio came on, blaring out an advertisement for male enhancement. Distracted and a little embarrassed, he backed out of the parking spot.

"Mack, put on your wipers."

"That would help, wouldn't it?" Mack fumbled around the steering column, then stopped the car. "I promise that as soon as I find them, I'll do it."

The rain slapped heavily against the windshield. Mack looked in vain for the wipers. He grew increasingly frustrated until Caroline said, "Let me see."

She then proceeded to lean over Mack, her body pressing up against him as she reached over to the left side of the steering wheel. "Here they are, right here."

As she rose off Mack's body, she paused, caught by his stare. The pause, silent, tense, expectant, was almost palpable.

A car horn blared behind them. The startling noise killed the moment, and Caroline quickly returned to her seat.

As Mack drove, Caroline thumbed through the case files. They took turns sneaking awkward glances at each other.

Mack sneaked a peek, but then saw the photo of the rocket launcher, which triggered an idea. "Remember that case study we did several months ago on the weapons tracking program?"

Caroline pulled the photo out of the file to take a closer look. "That's right–I'm almost positive this was one of the launchers in the program."

Mack called TJ's number. "TJ, it's Mack. We found something."

"What's up?" TJ replied.

"We think that rocket launcher was part of a U.S. Army weapons tracking program."

"Our assassin would have scratched out the serial number," TJ rebutted.

"That's just it–the program was implemented to hide a set of serial numbers. A second set is concealed in the spotting rifle cartridge."

"Sounds like something, then. Good work."

"Great. Caroline and I will follow up on this first thing tomorrow."

43

Mason had spent all evening in his BC Electronics office watching video footage, and though it was past midnight, he was enjoying it. Investigating this mysterious man who had bought the phone from his store made him feel like a spy. That the man had been wearing a watch that cost about $900,000 only made it more interesting.

He had found the man's car and looked up the plates–the car was registered to Ted Jones. Mason couldn't wait to tell this to Mack, but he knew getting more information on this Jones character would only help.

He wondered after more searching if he had found the right Jones–looking up this Jones' home address on Zillow suggested the house's value was only $230,000. Why would someone wearing one of the most expensive watches known to man live in a modest, three-bedroom house? The more he dug into this Ted Jones, the questions–and not answers–began to pile up.

Finally, he found something. He picked up the phone to call Mack, not noticing the figure walking past the store video camera.

Mason got Mack's voicemail. "Hey Mack. I found the guy you're looking for, and you're not going to believe this, but ..." Mason suddenly spied the man in the live feed. "How the hell...?" Mason said to himself, hanging up the phone. He grabbed his nickel-plated 9mm out of his desk drawer and walked out into the main area of the store.

"Store's closed," Mason said, holding the pistol behind his back.

"Phil Utah, DEA," said the man, flashing his badge with a black-gloved hand. "Got a call in to follow up with you on a lead you might have."

Mason instantly relaxed, and said jokingly, "*Utah*, give me two!"

131

Utah cracked a smile. "Never heard that one before."

"DEA? Who sent you?" Mason asked, suddenly suspicious.

"Mack Maddox. Ever hear of him?"

"I was just calling Mack. You're not going to believe what I found out about this guy buying that burner phone. Come here." He motioned for Utah to follow him into the back office.

In the office, Mason sat in his chair with his back to Utah and pulled up the information.

"What did Mack say?" Utah asked.

Mason pounded away at his computer. "I didn't get to speak to him yet." He said. "Okay, here it is–I think it's a smoking gun, I found a picture of Ted Jones at a campaign fundraiser with Congressman John Tid–"

"Sorry, son," said Phil Utah with a sigh, dismantling the still-smoldering silencer from the gun barrel. "Sometimes, wrong place, wrong time."

44

Steven Vorg pumped his fists with each powerful stride as he surged up the mountain. A two-humped peak, it rose imposingly above the multimillion-dollar homes that cluttered Paradise Valley, Arizona.

Sweat clung to his forehead. The jog was taking a lot out of him, despite the cool morning air. Taking deep breaths, he mentally recapped the previous day's meeting with a startup's CEO who was asking him to invest a quarter of a billion dollars in their company. Vorg took immense pride in being America's most sought-after venture capitalist. His twenty-six-year track record of growing some of the most successful startup companies in the world meant investors would follow him wherever he put his capital. The startup knew that, too.

He was high enough up the mountainside that the bottom half of the sun had cleared the horizon. He grinned as the warm rays bounced off the shiny retractable dome roof of his most prized possession: the stadium where his professional baseball team played. Seeing it always reminded him of that day twenty-six years ago when he had walked into a startup communications company with only seven employees and had made his very first venture capital investment. Today, that company had over 90,000 employees and was one of the largest communication conglomerates in the world. It had earned him billions.

Bic waited for Vorg behind a large boulder, stealing furtive glances from his position to spot the target. As Vorg's turn-around point at the top of his jog, it was the best time to ambush him when he stopped there to catch his breath before making his descent down the mountain.

Peering again through his binoculars, Bic spotted the cheerfully focused jogger. He crawled backward, concealing himself in a crouch behind the boulder. Several seconds passed before he heard Vorg's heavy breathing on the other side of the rock.

Bic made his way silently around the rock until he stood just behind Vorg. The venture capitalist was breathing so heavily, he didn't sense Bic.

"Do you know why I'm here?" Bic asked him.

Vorg turned, his eyes wide, to see Bic and the silenced Beretta pointed at his chest. Bic stood patiently, waiting for an answer. In his left hand he held the five-gallon white bucket bearing the hazmat warning. On top of the lid lay a roll of gray duct tape.

Bic wouldn't let Vorg see his eyes—yet. That was for when it was time for the man to die.

As Bic stared at him silently, he grinned slightly. This gave Vorg a modicum of courage.

"What do you want from me?" Vorg said pugnaciously. "Money?"

Big nodded. "I need you to wire $300,000 to an off-shore account."

"That's a lot of money."

Bic put down the bucket. "That's the amount I want. That's what I need. It's nothing for a guy like you."

Vorg thought for a moment. "I can manage that amount, but I can't do it here."

"Yes, you can." He pulled out a cell phone from his shirt pocket. "You're going to do it right here. But first, I need you to put this tape around your feet." Bic picked up the roll of duct tape and extended it to the sweaty entrepreneur.

"Why?"

"Insurance," said Bic. "I don't want to have to worry about you trying to run and calling 911, or something crazy like that."

Vorg grabbed the roll of tape.

"Make sure you tape your shoes together tight."

Vorg sat in the sand and taped his feet together.

"Good. Now pull up your socks and tape your ankles together."

"Aren't my shoes good enough?"

"No."

Vorg clenched his teeth in frustration, but he complied. He rose unsteadily.

"Alright, now turn and put your hands against the rock."

With a muttered curse, Vorg hopped a couple of feet to the boulder, falling onto the stone as he put his hands up against it. "I want to make sure you understood me–I can get you the money."

Bic grabbed the bucket and walked up behind him. With the rock on one side and Bic on the other, Vorg was pinned. A thump came from inside the white bucket as Bic placed it on the ground.

"What the hell's in the bucket?"

Bic jammed the barrel of the gun in his back. "Look forward at the rock."

"I thought you wanted money. What the hell's in the bucket?"

"That's right. All I want is money," Bic said, as he peeled the plastic lid off the bucket and dumped two large diamondback rattlesnakes at Vorg's feet. With Bic holding the bucket on one side, and Vorg and the boulder on the other, the snakes had nowhere to go and were instantly agitated.

45

Mack pulled out his pistol and aimed it at his reflection, ready to fire. He smiled as he checked himself out in the full-length mirror, naked except for his boxer briefs. Serious as he swung the gun from right to left, flexing his biceps and abs and admiring their well-developed tone. *We're going to see some serious action soon—you need to be ready for anything. Faster, stronger, smarter*, he thought.

It was 6:30 AM in his Chicago hotel room. Mack usually slept until at least his second wake-up call, but he had a sixth sense of excitement about today. For the first time in a while, he didn't regret his decision to become an agent, to reject a career in finance, making the big bucks, the same way he would have in baseball.

Mack sat in the desk chair and grabbed his phone. He knew he couldn't call Mason yet—it was way too early in California—so he texted him: *'Hey Mason, sorry I missed your call last night. Call me when you get up. Mack.'*

Mack picked up his complimentary copy of the *Wall Street Journal* that the concierge had left by the door that morning. A story regarding the tragic death of Larry Tukenson segued into a column on double taxation of the wealthy. According to the author, it was downright unconstitutional for any American to have to pay estate taxes to the government. Mack, a capitalist at heart, agreed.

Then he saw the amount of the tax and whistled aloud. "You've gotta be kidding me—the government gets over *twenty-seven billion* from his estate? That really *should* be illegal," he said, tossing the paper down in disgust.

46

The snakes rattled as they coiled.

Vorg remained stiff, his breathing coming in hitches.

Bic held his ground with the bucket.

The rattling intensified.

Vorg turned his head ever so slightly and looked at the two snakes, both within striking distance. "What kind of sick game is this?"

With the slow grace of a dancer, Bic stood up from his crouched position and begun to unwrap the pork chop wrapped in wax paper.

Bic took off his glasses. "Look at me."

As Vorg did so, Bic mouthed the words, "It's pork chop-eatin' time," and tossed the thing at Vorg's feet.

The sudden movement set the snakes into a striking frenzy. Vorg screamed and thrashed as the rattlers repeatedly launched their thick heads towards his ankles and legs, thrusting their fangs into his flesh.

Vorg tried to hop away but lost his balance and fell to the sand. He curled into a ball, shielding his face with his arms. One of the snakes became disinterested and slithered off. The other, still shaking its rattle, remained coiled just two feet from Vorg's head.

In desperation, Vorg hopped up on his hands and knees. The snake sprung forward and struck him in the neck. The snake then coiled again for another strike. Not wanting any more bites on Vorg's upper body, Bic moved toward the snake. It reacted with a vicious strike at Bic, who deftly swung the bucket at it. With a loud hollow thump, the stunned snake flew several feet, where it quickly slithered away.

Vorg looked at Bic with pleading eyes. "Help me, please!"

Bic ignored him.

"I can give you billions!"

Vorg again rose to his hands and knees and attempted to crawl, but the bite on his neck had already swollen outwardly to the size of an egg. Inwardly, his windpipe was closing fast. Each breath he took sounded like a greater struggle than the last. After a few feet, he dropped to the sand and rolled over onto his back.

His throat closed up, and his eyes enlarged to the size of half-dollars. Unable to breathe, the panic of his imminent death overwhelmed him, and he flopped in the sand once, twice. His face went from blue to bluer. Then Steven Vorg was dead. It had taken fifteen minutes.

Bic went over to the body and very carefully peeled the tape off his shoes and ankles. He was pleased—there didn't seem to be any marks on the man's ankles that might reveal foul play.

Bic took the white bucket and used it to dig a hole for the pork chop. He put the tape in the bucket, peeled off the hazmat sticker, and resealed the lid.

Bic checked Vorg for a pulse. The man was dead. Bic had planned to inject him with a lethal cocktail of hemo- and neurotoxins—the bites were meant to mask the cause of his real death. But his windpipe closing up from a reaction meant Vorg must have been severely allergic. This was a break that made it impossible for this to be anything but an accidental death in the autopsy room.

As Bic made his way down the mountain, he pulled a disposable cell phone out of his pocket, and called the first number on his list.

"*Phoenix Sun*," a woman answered.

"Hello. I live on Camelback Mountain. There's a man on the jogging trail here, and I think he's dead. I think it's Steven Vorg."

The woman was in the middle of a follow-up question as he hung up.

He repeated the same call to two other papers, knowing each would contact three or four freelance photographers to try to get the best shot for tomorrow's front page caption: "Billionaire Steven Vorg attacked and killed by vicious rattlesnakes." Something like that. Ten or twenty people running all over the mountain trying to get a picture of the dead billionaire would distort the crime scene. To be sure, he shuffled over his own prints briefly before leaving the mountain.

47

John Tidwell sat in the large, airy study of his renovated Victorian mansion, sipping tea. He barely noticed the opulence that surrounded him; he was inured to it. Homes in this high-profile San Francisco suburb took more manpower and materials to build than a whole block of three-bedroom homes, just as the type of wealth found in this neighborhood took two or three generations of compound interest to accumulate.

Tidwell leaned back in his leather chair as he clicked the "send" button on an email. The laptop sat on an ornate mahogany desk. Two original Picasso pencil sketches hung on the wall behind him. A collection of English literature filled two built-in bookcases on either side of the room.

His fingernails tapped repeatedly on the glossy finish of the hardwood desk. He hoped Jones would reply to him quickly–he had promised to be online at seven. He looked at his watch to make sure.

Every time he got an email from Jones, he remembered when he first met with Anthony Parelli to set up the deal. Tidwell had asked the gangster how he was going to get in contact with him, whereupon Parelli had handed him the business card of a fund-raising consultant named Ted Jones. "Contact him," Parelli said. "He'll take care of you."

Never one to trust anonymous contacts, Tidwell had Utah run a check on this Ted Jones. The results surprised Tidwell: Jones didn't exist. Parelli had created him for the sole purpose of communicating with his clients over the internet. Jones came complete with a Social Security card, driver's license, and birth certificate, all fake–but he also had his own house, a bank account he used to pay bills, a cell phone, and a cable connection.

What really impressed Tidwell was that Jones reported an average income to the government of about $55,000 a year and paid his taxes promptly.

Tidwell figured anyone who had gone through the trouble of creating an identity just to communicate was a person capable of facilitating a deal with the Russian mafia in order to bribe the Russian government.

His eyes drifted over to the only picture on his desk. It was of him and his grandfather at his graduation from Stanford Law School. He remembered how proud his grandfather had been that he had graduated from his *alma mater*.

He recalled the best lesson he had learned from the old man.

That lesson came when his grandfather had been caught extorting money from large corporations, using his political influence to arrange for large donations in exchange for commensurate state contracts. He had been doing it for years. The evidence was overwhelming, and it looked like Tidwell's grandfather was going down for sure. The old man was all over the headlines. Everyone knew he was guilty, and there was no way to wiggle out of this political escapade, as he had done several times before.

Then his grandfather put his dollars and connections to work, buying, bribing, and extorting anyone he could. Several months later, the investigation turned its focus away from him and to an erstwhile partner-in-crime. An old-style mafia figurehead named Giovanni Franconni would go down in his place.

On his graduation day, his grandfather had pulled him aside.

"Never mind the pricks in the world, boy," he said. "Money will fix 'em for you. Enough money will get you enough power so that you can get away with almost anything. Don't be distracted by nice cars, clothes, homes, or yachts—those are merely side perks. Rewards for a job well done. Power, boy. That's what you work for."

Tidwell applied the lesson throughout his career.

The sudden ding of an email pulled him from his reverie. He opened his email to read the message from Jones:

I appreciate your compliments on the job Gabriel did to support our recent fund-raising efforts. I understand why you think Gabriel might have been a better choice to run the big campaign. But passionate as he is about the final outcome, he's not always good with the details. He's capable of running one or two good fundraisers, but boredom often results in poor job performance during subsequent campaigns.

If we need his help down the stretch to raise more money, we can always use him. And should he choose to engage in any freelance fundraising, it should distract our competition from our key fundraising efforts.

Ted Jones

In other words, thought Tidwell, never mind the pricks.
He closed his laptop and sat at his desk, thinking.

48

"No way! Did you hear that?"

Mack and Caroline were on their way to the Chicago PD when Mack had suddenly erupted.

"I missed. What was it?"

"They just said Steven Vorg was killed by a rattlesnake this morning." Mack slapped the steering wheel. "You've *got* to be kidding me."

"You know him?"

He looked at her. "You don't know much about the financial world, do you?"

"My dad's financial advisor takes care of all my investments," she admitted.

"He's one of the legends of investing–a venture capitalist worth billions. There might be a handful of men richer than him in the entire world."

She cocked her head. "What was the name of the other guy you made a big deal about?"

"Larry Tukenson?"

"Yeah, him."

"He's another one," said Mack. "Between the two of them, they had more money than most small countries." Mack paused and bit his lower lip. "This is a sign or something. These things always happen in threes."

"Here we go with the superstitions."

"You don't believe in the rule of threes?"

"Not even a little."

"I'll prove it to you. I'll bet you a fancy dinner someone who's extremely wealthy dies in the next couple of months from some weird accident."

"Define 'extremely wealthy and weird'."

"A hundred million or more. Weird? Not your everyday death. Something... improbable."

"You sure you can afford it?"

"We have a bet?"

Twenty minutes later, Mack followed Caroline up the steps to the Chicago Police Department's main precinct, carrying a duffel bag. He couldn't help but notice her hips swinging gently as she walked up the steps.

Caroline turned around at the top step to catch Mack gaping at her.

Mack felt flustered. "I ... I, are those new pants?"

"Yeah," she said with a veiled smirk. "New pants, same ass."

After a fifty-minute wait in an overcrowded room full of less-than-desirable characters, a dark-haired, swarthy-looking detective who introduced himself as Simon Reed led them down the hall. He directed them to a small interrogation room, eight-by-twelve, with all walls bare but one, which was dominated by a one-way mirror. The rocket launcher rested on a square metal table in the middle of the room.

"Good luck," Reed said.

"Why are you putting us in an interrogation room?" Mack asked.

"It's what's available," Reed said. "Look, buddy, you want a different room, you'll have to wait another two or three hours."

After a brief, silent stare from Mack, the detective shut the door.

Mack placed his duffel bag next to the launcher and pulled out a manual and a wide array of small tools.

"A man with so many tools–impressive," Caroline said.

Mack grabbed a screwdriver and began to unscrew a couple of random screws off the launch tube.

"I see," said Caroline. "The screwdriver's your forte. The rest are for show."

"You ain't seen nothin' until you've seen me wield a hammer," Mack stopped what he was doing and picked up the hammer and started to hotdog with it.

"Oh, that's hot. Now you're just not playing fair" Caroline said playfully.

And they continued like that for several minutes while Reed

looked on.

"What idiots," Reed mumbled to himself, sipping his coffee watching behind the two-way mirror.

After struggling for twenty minutes, Mack and Caroline appeared nowhere closer with disassembling the weapon. The detective made a call, watching Mack scrabbling for a proper tool.

The man he knew only as "Jones" picked up.

"Yeah?"

"I wouldn't worry about these two clowns compromising the security of the Chicago fundraiser."

A pause. "They get anything?"

"Nah, I wiped it clean myself and verified the serial number had been scratched off."

"Good. Don't take your eye off them."

49

After about twenty minutes, Mack detached the spotting rifle from the launch tube.

"There you are," he said triumphantly.

"Can you see the serial number?" Caroline asked.

"Should have it in seconds," Mack said as he glanced at the manual, then grabbed a different tool.

Suddenly the door swung open. Caroline jumped back with a start.

"Time's up—need to get this weapon back to inventory," the detective said firmly.

Caroline stepped in his way and said, "Excuse me?"

"We have a strict time limit with evidence. Your time is up," he informed her.

"You had better get your boss. We have federal clearance," Caroline demanded.

The detective got right in her face. "You don't want me to call him, honey."

Caroline pointed at the two-way mirror. "Did we entertain you much?"

"You two are typical douchebag FBI agents," said Reed.

"People's lives are at stake here." Caroline said.

"You can request another hour tomorrow. Maybe."

Caroline stepped even closer to him. Nose to nose. "I'm not leaving without that serial number."

The detective unclipped his radio from his belt, "Code red—we got a real spitfire in interrogation room C11."

"You're no better than the jackal who killed those women." She held her ground.

"I've got better things to do than babysit a pair of FBI pencil pushers." He shrugged his shoulders, feigning calm. "But hey, I just follow orders."

Mack stood up. "Let's go, it's not here."

"I'm not going anywhere. We need to double and triple check," she said.

"It's not there. I'm positive." Mack ushered her into the hall.

A group of uniformed officers were approaching from one direction.

"Time to go," Mack said to Caroline.

Mack started to walk in the opposite direction, but Caroline held her ground.

"Run along now, kids," the detective taunted.

"Screw you," Caroline said, then followed Mack in the opposite direction of two approaching officers.

The agents said nothing as they walked back to their car. Mack refused to speak, despite querulous glances from Caroline.

"Who are you right now?" Caroline said as they approached their car.

Mack entered the vehicle without even acknowledging her comment. Caroline followed as she slammed the passenger door shut.

"You need to relax," Mack said calmly.

"I thought you had my back. Instead you run like a scared little girl and leave me standing there."

"Are you finished?"

"Oh, I'm just getting started."

"Here." Mack opened his coat and pulled something from the inside pocket. "See that?"

"What about it?"

"Know what it is?"

"It looks like a pen light."

Mack smiled. "That's right. It *looks* like your ordinary pen light." He held it up for her inspection. "There's a camera inside. And see that?" He turned the end of the pen toward her. "There's a lightning connection there. I can upload the pics to any device. I stuck this baby down into the rocket launcher's trigger mechanism body while you were playing Wonder Woman with Barney Fife."

"Sorry for the 'little girl' comment."

Mack handed the pen to Caroline. "That's what I love," he said. "I mean appreciate–respect!–about you. You're not afraid to call someone out if need be."

"You're amazing, Maxwell. Anyone ever tell you that?"

"Never get tired of hearing it." He started the car and put it into gear. "Now, don't ever make fun of my tools again."

50

Mack raced to the fax machine in the LA FBI office. A dozen pages sat waiting. He snatched them up, glancing at his phone for the hundredth time in the last hour—he had sent Mason three texts and called him twice, and still hadn't heard back.

"How's the hunt, Columbo?" Moretto muttered as he walked by Mack on his way back to his cubicle.

"Your shoe's untied," said Caroline, pointing.

Moretto continued on without acknowledging her.

Caroline sidled over. "He can dish it out, but can't take it. Any luck?"

He nodded absently. "You look nice today," he said quietly.

"Glad you noticed," she said before pointing at the profile

"You're not going to believe this," he said, handing it to her, "but this man was the last person known to have possession of the rocket launcher used in Chicago. I would bet my life this is our guy."

TJ appeared out of nowhere, startling Mack with his usual stone face.

"We got a hit on our suspect, one Gabriel Hernandez," Mack said as Caroline handed the profile to TJ.

TJ took it, but continued to stare stonily at Mack.

"What's wrong?" Mack asked.

"Your guy Mason was found shot in the head by one of his employees this morning."

"Dear God, is everybody in this case going to wind up dead?" Caroline hastily grabbed her purse from her cubicle and walked off.

Mack looked down at his phone in disbelief at the unseen texts to Mason, realizing the terrible truth: This young, innocent man had been murdered because of him.

51

Bic was disappointed that he had been unsuccessful in executing his plan yesterday. In order to accomplish all ten hits in twenty-two days, Bic had to make the first round look like freak accidents. If he didn't, the remaining hits would turn into suicide missions, with the FBI setting traps to catch him at each target's home. Or worse, the remaining targets on the list would go into hiding.

Bic crouched down by the riverbank and watched the Yellowstone River flow toward the sea. Cupping his hands, he lowered them into the water. He noticed trout swimming away as his hands disturbed the calm surface.

He wore a khaki jump jacket, bush shirt, and pants tucked into his old military-issue jungle boots, prepped for hiking. His massive backpack held enough supplies to sustain him in the mountains for days. He also carried a tranquilizer rifle. The high-end weapon had the accuracy of a sniper rifle from less than a hundred feet.

Bic moved downstream, the cool April breeze stirring the pine trees within the valley. This stretch of the Yellowstone lay between two mountains trimmed in verdant forest, though large outcroppings of rock were exposed in several places. The area was privately owned. After searching all morning, Bic found what he thought to be a pile of fresh scat. He examined the droppings to confirm they were what he was seeking–spoor of a grizzly bear.

Bic pulled out his rifle and loaded it with a red-tipped tranquilizer dart. The bear tracks he located left the clear path of the riverbank, so he made his way into the thick forest. He glanced at his watch. If he didn't check off this part of the list by day's end, he would be forced to execute Plan B.

Bic's mobile phone vibrated in his pants' side pocket. He pulled it out and scowled at the tiny digital screen. A text from Hawk, another dead end.

A rage began inside him. He pulled the only photograph he had of his father, faded with age, out of his pocket. The buzzing hatred in him intensified.

Once again, he relived that day just after his seventh birthday, the day he had last seen his father.

He sat on a wooden crate in the kitchen late that Sunday afternoon. His mama, making dinner, was singing "Blessed Assurance." She could have recited a shopping list to him and made it sound beautiful.

She stopped singing when his dad stormed through the front door of their small housing-project apartment. In about six steps, Bic's daddy had walked through the living room and stood face-to-face with his mama in the kitchen. He was coming down from a cocaine high and needed money bad. He had already sold everything they had to fuel his drug habit. There was nothing left in the apartment except the crates and boxes they used as furniture. Bic's father told his mama that she was going to start turning tricks for his drug dealer to pay off his debt.

Bic's mama refused, and his daddy started screaming, backhanding her across the face. She fell to the floor and rose immediately, screaming at him to get out. Foaming at the mouth, he grabbed a hot pan off the stove. Bic remembered the sickening thud as that old cast-iron skillet connected with his mother's skull. Fear turned into a blind rage in Bic, and he leaped onto his father's back—punching, biting, and scratching. Bic fought ferociously. It was no use. From his father's back, he watched the man beat his mama to death, smashing her beauty into a bleeding mass of ruined bone and flesh. His dad then yanked Bic off his back and slammed him onto the floor. With the red of the devil glowing in his doped-out eyes, Bic's daddy grabbed him by the throat so hard Bic thought his neck was going to snap. His daddy then snatched a raw pork chop from the counter and jammed it into Bic's mouth.

"It's pork chop-eatin' time!" his daddy growled as he choked. Everything went dark.

52

Late afternoon, Mack stood outside the main conference room. TJ and Moretto waited for him. His text chain to Caroline had no responses. Mason's murder and Caroline's unresponsiveness fueled Mack's feelings of anxiety and guilt.

He looked up and saw TJ waving for him to join them. He impatiently glanced at his phone, a deep-rooted sick feeling growing in his stomach.

He called her again. No answer.

"Angry Birds will get on without you," Moretto called. "Let's go. We got work to do."

As Mack made his way to the room, a female agent passed by, leaving an unmistakable scent of patchouli in her wake.

Patchouli, that awful scent his mom used to wear. He took a deep breath, then exhaled. *She didn't leave us because of me–I was just a kid who saw her doing something terrible. She left for what she did, not for what I saw.*

Mack entered the room.

"Nice of you to join us, Cinderella," said Moretto.

Mack smirked darkly at Moretto. "It was a princess move making us come back to LA instead of helping put the heat on that crooked detective until he told us what he knows."

"Relax, kid. You don't know what you're talking about," Moretto said.

"A friend of mine is a detective on the Chicago PD. Turns out, this Reed character pulled some strings to be in charge of our case. And yet he tells us when we're there that he was *ordered* to babysit us. And this dirtbag has a history of dirty dealings.

"Mack," TJ said sympathetically, "I understand your frustration, but we're not going into the Chicago PD and shaking down a twenty-five-year vet."

Mack pointed to Gabriel's name written on the white board. "That detective is a direct link to whoever hired this scumbag."

Moretto raised his eyebrows and shrugged. "He wouldn't have said a word."

"He doesn't have to. I bet if we pull his cell phone records, we'll find he made a call to either Gabriel or whoever hired Gabriel yesterday."

"Sounds like you have this whole case figured out." Bender walked energetically into the room, smiling. "How about we just pull the phone records of everyone within a twenty-mile radius of the building?"

Bender sat at the head of the oval table, wearing a dark navy suit with a fashionable tie.

"I appreciate you taking the time to join us, sir," said Mack.

"I like how you two have contributed to this investigation." Bender looked at everyone in the room, then gazed through the glass wall out into the open office space, where all the cubicles could be seen. "Where's Agent Foxx?"

"She's in the field," said Mack. "Trying to dig up additional information on the suspect."

Bender nodded. "Alright. Now, tell me why you think I should let you cowboys go down to Tijuana to apprehend a suspect?"

Mack blinked, surprised—and a little impressed—with the A.D.'s directness. He pointed to the white board and said, "He's our one lead, sir."

"This perp may have information—" Moretto began.

"Don't fill this kid's head with ideas, Moretto. If he does have any information, we'll extradite him. Personally, I think Gabriel Hernandez is nothing more than a hired gun who knows only as much as he needs to know."

"Sir," Mack interjected. "He may know things he doesn't realize he knows. Even two more names of potential targets could reveal a pattern."

"And the dirty scumbag's gotta pay for this!" Moretto added.

"It's vigilante justice now, agent?" Bender asked Moretto. "The FBI isn't going around assassinating anyone, for the record. As for you, Agent Maddox, I realize he *may* have information, which is why I'm prepared to go forward with extradition. Hernandez has major ties to the drug cartels. We're going in on that. I've already been notified that the DEA is going to handle it. San Diego department head Phil Utah has confirmed that Hernandez is back in Tijuana, so he will be sending in a SWAT team."

"Can this Phil Utah guarantee he'll be taken safely for questioning?" said Mack.

"You're overstepping, Agent Maddox," warned Bender. "It's not your place to question. Utah's an old friend, and he's good at his job. You'll leave him to it."

A disconsolate silence filled the room.

"Good. Then we're done here, gentlemen," said Bender, rising. "By tomorrow, this particular individual will be dealt with."

"Sir?" said Moretto, raising his hand.

"Agent Moretto?"

"Permission to refer to the suspect as 'the rodent'?"

Bender left without an answer.

53

The room had no air conditioner. It was close, muggy and hot inside. Sweat clung heavy to Gabriel's skin, and to the half naked flesh of his two female companions. He smiled through the heat, liking his threesomes hot and nasty. He felt powerful here. His unlimited supply of hard drugs made him feel like some master vampire with his own harem. Instead of a thirst for blood driving his underlings to obey, they had a craving for his dope.

The queen-size bed dominated the small bedroom. The only other piece of furniture in the room was a small, scarred wooden desk located where other people might keep a nightstand. On top of the desk were some pieces of surveillance equipment and a lamp. The room's décor of plaster walls, each a maze of different-sized cracks and holes, was a motif of rot and corruption. The room's most unique feature was a platform mounted above the doorway, with a section of the ceiling cut out so a man could stand upright on it into the attic above.

The dark-haired Latina and blonde white girl waited anxiously as Gabriel fixed a hit of heroin.

"Old McGabriel had a needle, E-I-E-I-O. And in that needle, he had some horse, E-I-E-I-O," he sang lustily as he filled the syringe.

The blonde woman grew more excited.

"Easy chica, it's comin'." He flicked his tongue out at her as he placed the syringe on the bed and reached into another massive pile of cocaine on the table. He scooped a mound of the fine white powder with two fingers and drew a thick, messy line on his chest.

"Yeah, baby," the blonde said, as she bent down and wildly snorted the coke, while simultaneously licking his chest with her long tongue to clean the rest.

"Show me why I need to party with you next time," Gabriel said as he picked back up the glass syringe.

"With pleasure," the blonde replied.

Gabriel motioned to the Latina to join in as he made a couple new lines.

High as kites, the girls snorted and licked Gabriel's chest and stomach.

"I like hard working chicas," he said as he moved the glass of the syringe above the flame of the candle.

At that moment, a red light came on near his head, piercing the gloom. Gabriel pushed the women off him unceremoniously and turned his attention to the electronics on the desk. The red light was a perimeter sensor, indicating something was moving within five feet of his house. Gabriel grinned wickedly, his mood changed from the erotic to a possibility of even greater pleasure: killing those coming after him.

54

Gabriel quickly put on pants and grabbed two silenced 9mm Beretta pistols. He ran out of his bedroom and dove to the living room floor. He crawled along the splintered hardwood and squatted below a window, careful not to give anyone a shot at him. The living room was the only room in the house where the windows weren't boarded up.

He snatched up the small pocket mirror lying on the floor near the window and lifted it carefully above the sill. Using several different angles, he was able to see down the side of his house all the way to the backyard. He didn't see anyone coming from either direction, though a second scan did reveal a beat-up white Ford van that he had never seen before. In this neighborhood, vans were mainly used for two things: transporting large amounts of drugs, or bringing in a crew to snuff someone out. His guess was the second.

Feet scuffled on the front porch, and he heard a few metallic clinks. His eyes narrowed. The raggedy old boards in the front porch cracked and squeaked, like he had fixed them to do, and he estimated that at least four, maybe five, men stood on the other side of the front door.

Another shuffle came from the front porch, and then some whispered dialogue. *These* pendejos *are real amateurs,* he thought. Anyone with any sense would have worked out hand signals in advance.

Before they could knock his door down, Gabriel rose and unloaded both pistols into it. Bullets snapped through the thin wood as if it were paper. He didn't know how many he had hit, but he was sure it was at least some.

He spun to the side, expecting return fire. Nothing. No groans or screams, even. Huh. He retreated into the bedroom, baffled, amazed he hadn't made contact. The two women were huddled naked in the corner, attempting to shoot up as much of his dope as they could, oblivious to the gunshots.

Then it hit him: this *had* to be some type of government raid. The people conducting the raid would be well-equipped, wearing body armor everywhere.

Well, he had the answer to that, too.

Gabriel opened the desk drawer and grabbed several clips loaded with armor-piercing bullets. Then he grabbed the white hooker by her hair and pulled her to her feet. "You still have to earn that dope. Go check and see who's at the front door."

The hooker was too high to be afraid and didn't question the command. She stumbled her way, naked, to the front door. Gabriel stood in the dark hallway, making himself a shadow against the wall.

She unlocked the door and opened it.

"Hold your fire!" someone yelled in English. "It's one of the girls."

Gabriel smiled, then took aim and shot the woman in the back of the head. Her brains sprayed across the front porch as she fell face-first out the door.

Complete silence followed the thud as the woman's lifeless body hit the floor. Gabriel fed off the eerie stillness of the moment and the horror of his action.

The silence was broken by frantic calls to act and then by the sound of a small bowling ball rolling toward him across the hardwood floor. He took three quick steps back before diving deeper into the hallway. The grenade exploded loudly, briefly flooding the house with searing light.

Gabriel rose to his feet and ran into the bedroom. The Latina whore sat in the corner, rubbing her eyes and crying out.

He had no doubt some type of American strike force had come for him—probably the DEA. If this were a gang or drug hit, he would have just been blown up ... none of this whimpy flashbang stuff.

He stood up on his bed and shattered the naked bulb dangling from the ceiling with the butt of one gun. With the windows in the room boarded up and the hallway leading to the room unlit, the only lights left in the room were the burning candle on the desk and the ready lights on the surveillance equipment. Gabriel reached under his bed and pulled out a strobe light box. He plugged it in and placed it in the corner of the room along the same wall as the doorway.

He turned the strobe light on and blew out the candle. Then he put his foot in a hole in the wall and climbed up onto the platform above the doorway.

He waited, squatting on the one-by-three-foot plywood platform directly above the entrance. As he waited, he stared at the Latina crying and pleading in the corner of the room opposite him. He raised his gun and took aim at her forehead; the strobe effect flickered in and out of life. He almost squeezed the trigger, but he lowered his weapon, realizing she made the perfect bait.

Gabriel could hear shuffling feet in the hallway, and saw the laser scope-lights of the men in the hall beaming across the room. He counted five total.

"We have you locked down, scumbag!" a harsh voice yelled. "You have two choices: come out with your hands on your head, or we're coming in and taking you down!" The demand was immediately repeated in Spanish.

Gabriel reached up into the attic, where he had more weapons stashed than Santa Anna had fielded at the Alamo. He made sure two grenades were within easy reach. If they did fatally wound him, he was going to make sure he took everyone out with him.

"Let's this dog down," a different voice muttered.

Another flash grenade rolled into the bedroom; Gabriel stood, lifting his upper body through the hole in the ceiling and into the attic while covering his ears. The device exploded.

With his ears ringing, he squatted back down. Two men entered, leading with their automatic weapons as they swept the room. Undetected above and behind them, Gabriel took aim at the tops of their helmets. He then squeezed off two rounds.

The two men fell to the floor. "Men down!" someone bawled.

The men in the hallway blanketed the room with automatic weapons fire, a constant spray of slugs snapping into the walls, bed, and desk within the light-dark-light-dark of the strobe. A haze of dust, generated by hundreds of bullets plunging into plaster, filled the room.

The bullets stopped. Dead silence. Gabriel smiled as he waited for someone to come into the room to retrieve their dead comrades.

One man charged deep into the room to cover a second, who went to the team members who had been shot. The man on the other side of the room turned and saw Gabriel standing on the platform above the doorway entrance–above his teammates. With both pistols aimed at the agent's goggles, Gabriel squeezed off a shot from each before the man could fire. Before the second man realized the teammate covering him had been shot, Gabriel put two slugs in the back of his head.

Amateurs, he thought.

55

William Bennington waded alongside his wife, Lynn, in a calm stretch of the Yellowstone River. The tall man moved hardly at all as he cast his fly rod. A perfectionist, he knew the fish feared movement above the water much more than they did movement below the water's surface.

He had never felt better, which was a relief. He peeked over at his wife, Lynn, in wading boots to her armpits. After his second heart attack, it was she who had convinced him to retire and buy this 2,000-acre ranch in the Rocky Mountains. He had been only fifty-nine at the time, and had been planning to work for another ten years. If it hadn't been for her, instead of fishing nearly every afternoon for the past three years, he would have been stuck in constant meetings with his execs, feverishly strategizing on how to stay ahead of the competition—until he dropped dead.

A very tall black man was walking downstream toward them. He was wearing a backpack and carried a large canvas sack slung around his shoulder.

"Who the hell is that, and what he doing here?" said William, starting toward the riverbank.

"Don't cause a fuss."

"Fuss nothing. This is private property. I've a right to defend it."

The very notion of having to defend his property made his blood boil. He sloshed back to the riverbank, and his wife followed. Once ashore, he opened his tackle box and pulled out the knife he used to fillet fish.

"What are you doing?" she asked.

"I have a right to defend my property," he repeated. He put the knife, still in its plastic case, in his back pants pocket.

"Hello," the man yelled, waving.

William lifted his chin and said loudly, "This is private property."

"I know, and I apologize," said the stranger, ten yards away and still closing. "I was canoeing down the river and spotted this little guy on the shore."

He unzipped the bag enough to show them the face of a grizzly cub.

"Dear God," said Lynn. "What's wrong with him?"

"I'm not sure yet. He was like this when I found him—listless and unresponsive. The abandoned cubs I've worked on before are often malnourished, or end up eating something bad. They get lethargic and usually wind up dead. He should be okay. His vitals are strong. With food, he should be alright."

"Who are you?" said William Bennington.

"Name's Green. I'm a biologist."

Lynn Bennington stepped forward to pet the cub's head. As she did so, she pulled on the forehead, forcing the left eye to open. She recoiled slightly.

"He's been tranquilized," she said. "You can't miss it once you've seen it a thousand times. I'm a biologist myself."

The man called Green stared at her. He unshouldered the sack and placed it carefully on the ground. He did the same with his backpack.

"Who are you?" she said firmly.

"Bic Green, ma'am."

She cocked her head. "What's the scientific name for a grizzly bear?"

Bic didn't respond.

"Answer the lady" said William Bennington. "What's the scientific name for grizzly bear? William reached back and pulled out his knife.

Bic Green stood silent.

"Listen," said William, "if I were you, I'd haul ass on outta here."

Bic removed his sunglasses.

"*Oh my word*," said William, staring into the misty, lifeless red eyes. His hand faltered and fell to his side.

"I didn't come for the bear," Bic said too calmly.

William knew what Bic meant to do. He lunged forward with all the speed he could gather and thrust the eight-inch blade toward Bic's abdomen. Bic moved faster than William, redirecting the blade away from his body with his left hand. As William's body extended outward, Bic's right fist exploded into his side. The punch landed right on his kidney. The pain was excruciating and he fell to the ground.

The man grabbed Lynn, who was too shocked to resist. He reached into a side pocket of his cargo pants and pulled out a Ziploc bag with a rag inside. He removed the rag and buried her mouth and nose in the cloth.

"*Ursus arctos horribilis*," he whispered into her ear.

He moved toward William and placed the damp rag over his nose and mouth.

56

ight, dark. Light, dark.

Gabriel Hernandez stood on the platform, five bodies scattered below him. Four agents, one hooker. But a creak of wood told him there was at least one more agent to take out.

The wood below his feet came to life as a spray of bullets popped into the platform. Ah, there was Number Five. Having lined the platform and surrounding attic floor with Kevlar vests, Gabriel avoided being hit. He quickly retreated upward, going through the ceiling opening into the attic. He lay on a bed of bulletproof vests as he waited for the last man to enter the bedroom.

He saw a flicker of movement, but it turned out to be the hooker in the corner of the room. She was covered in blood, but she was alive, and now stood up, crying. *Dumbass* puta.

The man in the hallway opened fire again. Lines of bullets torpedoed through the ceiling and into the roof. Splinters of wood fell from the rafters. Several slugs popped into the Kevlar blanket beneath Gabriel. Each struck like a ferocious two-hundred-pound man's punch.

The bullets stopped. Gabriel heard the unmistakable click of a weapon magazine releasing beneath him. Before Gabriel even thought, "he's reloading," he acted. With catlike agility, he jumped feet first through the hole in the ceiling, dropping into the bedroom, facing the hallway, and fired shots into the hall.

He crouched, his gun at the ready. In the intermittent, strobing light, he was unsure if his shots had hit the agent.

The room lit, and he caught a glimpse of the agent dropping his automatic rifle and reaching for his sidearm. Gabriel dropped to his belly, rolled to the right, and took aim.

The strobe light flashed. Catching a glimpse of the agent in the hallway, Gabriel emptied what was left in both Berettas. He fired twelve shots total in a tight box pattern.

Gabriel watched the agent fall eerily in the stuttering light to the floor.

Unsure if the agent was playing dead, Gabriel reloaded his weapon with his final clip. He lunged toward the agent and put two bullets in his head.

He bent down to identify the man, whose ID was emblazoned on his jacket. *DEA!* Gabriel thought. He would never be able to step foot in this house again after killing five of their agents.

Well, no great loss. He went back into the bedroom, grabbed his bed's metal frame, and flipped it up against the wall. He then bent down and pulled up several floorboards up to expose a safe. He opened the safe and removed his "travel gear:" a duffel bag containing about a $150,000 American in cash, several bricks of uncut cocaine, Diablo, and two handguns.

Gabriel walked to the front door and dropped his bag. He went to the kitchen, opened a cabinet under the sink, and smiled. With an evil little chuckle, he grabbed two Molotov cocktails he had stored there for emergencies. "Time to redecorate."

Each tightly-capped glass whisky bottle was filled with a murky liquid, and had a tampon tied to its side. He grabbed a lighter off the counter and lit the tampons. The cottony material quickly ignited.

Seeing the trembling woman's eyes stare at him confusedly, he began to sing in a slow methodical voice, "Old McGabriel had a cocktail, E-I-E-I-O. And in that cocktail, he had some gas 'n' oil, E-I-E-I-O... With a shake-shake here and a shake-shake there..."

Standing in his bedroom doorway, Gabriel whipped the first bottle up against the wall. It shattered, and the room burst into flames with a huge roar. As fire screamed toward him from the bedroom entrance, he made his way down the hall.

He stopped and bent over the hemorrhaging woman lying on the floor.

"*Te veré en el infierno,*" he said to her, and as he walked out the front door, he threw the bottle hard against the wall beside her.

57

Lynn Bennington opened her eyes. Everything was blurry, and she felt a numbing pain radiating all over her head. She raised it sluggishly and realized she was lying on the ground at the base of a large tree.

She had been drugged, but sobered suddenly to see–and smell–the pile of bloody fish guts draped over her stomach. Feverishly, she pushed the rank remains off her body. A chaotic panic swept over her. In its wake, she noticed her husband lying to her left, just out of arm's reach.

She looked around but saw no sign of their attacker. "*William,*" she whispered. "William, answer me, please!" He didn't respond, but he was breathing at least. He, too, was covered in fish parts.

She tried to go to him but couldn't. Her wading boots had been removed, and her right ankle was wrapped in a thick leather shackle attached to an iron stake by a single chain link. She thrashed with all her might but couldn't shake the stake loose.

Lynn tried again, but was too woozy to continue. She found it odd that the leather cuff's insides were lined with a soft fleecy material.

She heard rapidly approaching footsteps and looked up. Their attacker was sprinting down the edge of the river toward her.

"Please don't hurt us anymore," she whimpered as he approached. "We're good people." Tears rolled down her cheeks.

The man ignored her pleas as he passed by her. He stopped at his backpack and rummaged through it with haste, looking several times over his shoulder.

He pulled a thick rope and a syringe out of his pack. Lynn gasped as she saw the pre-made noose at the end of the rope. "Dear God! Don't hang us, please!"

Ignoring her, Bic walked over to his duffle bag, unzipped the pouch, and pulled the tranquilized cub out. He placed the noose first over the cub's head, then its front legs, and then pulled it snug. After checking to make sure the rope was secure, he injected something into the cub. After a moment, it started to move.

Bic walked up to William.

"Leave my husband alone, you animal!" Lynn snarled.

As if in answer, the cub whined, low and wet. The sound was horrifying.

Bic took something else out of his pocket and waved it below her husband's nose. William regained consciousness.

"Honey, are you okay?" Lynn cried.

He could barely mumble.

Lynn watched her husband's pale face for some time, before Bic's movement regained her attention. She watched as Bic, rope in hand, climbed the large tree. She still had no idea what he was doing, but quickly the rope tightened as Bic ascended the tree, which dragged the cub nearer to her. The cub struggled helplessly in the other direction. As it struggled, its cries grew louder.

"Are you *crazy*?" Lynn shrieked. She'd recognized this behavior in the cub, having seen it many times in the field.

It was calling for its mother.

58

Bic secured himself on a large branch about fifteen feet above the ground. The cub's calls grew increasingly more distressed.

Lynn's voice caught in her throat. She found she was unable to scream.

The cub was dragged directly between William and Lynn. It now thrashed in its bonds.

"*William*," she said with barely any voice at all, her breath coming in hitches. Her husband lolled his head toward her, his eyes like glass.

A stream of water splashed onto William's face from above. The man in the tree had just emptied his canteen onto William. The water roused him. He sat up and looked to Lynn. He squinted, in obvious pain, and asked her, "What the hell's happening?"

"*We're... we're...*" The words skipped and slid. Her horror was absolute.

Her husband, suddenly conscious of the bear, shook and thrashed from side to side as he attempted to free himself from the leather shackle. Fish guts flew off his body.

There was a sound. Something rumbling and low and hollow. A red glare of terror flashed in her brain, blotting out all reason. She had no scream left in her as she spotted the mother grizzly charging toward them in full stride.

The thing was at least a half-ton, with a short, stocky neck and massive shoulders.

Something landed in Lynn's lap. It looked like a pork chop.

The grizzly barreled into both William and the tree. Unfazed, it rose up and struck William and Lynn wildly with its front paws.

The death had been a messy one.

When it was done, Bic pulled the cub up into the tree, immediately drawing the attention of the mother.

The big grizzly stood on her hind legs and swatted at Bic. Her swinging paws rattled the tree branches far below him. Bic quickly loosened the noose and lowered the cub to the ground, letting go of the rope. The cub struggled at first, but quickly worked its way free. Without a glance back, both the mother bear and her cub ambled off into the woods.

He waited for some time before climbing down out of the tree, his rifle loaded and ready. He scanned the area briefly and began to clean it up.

He removed the shackles from the corpses and the stakes from the ground. He then filled the holes with loose dirt and poured water over both to tamp it down. Walking down to the river's shoreline, he pulled a collapsed one-person raft out of his backpack. He yanked the pack's ripcord and the thing inflated in seconds.

Moments later, he was far downstream.

59

Caroline braced herself when she saw him through the coffee shop window

"Where have you been for the past twenty-four hours?" Mack growled at her.

"I needed to take care of something," she said, avoiding his gaze.

He sat down at the round table across from her. "And that's it? You can't just up and abandon the case when you like. We're partners here."

"I'm sorry. It's just, after hearing about Mason... he would be alive, you know, if we hadn't... I don't know. It's just hard to process." She pushed the cup of coffee she had bought him across the table.

"I get it," he said. "But we have to man up here. This is the big league, Caroline. This isn't some cozy little law firm job."

Mack looked at her grimly and buried something behind a swig of coffee. "You left me hanging in the middle of a hot mess," he said.

"I'm sorry. That wasn't my intention."

"Where were you?"

"Helping a friend," she said coolly. "Like I said, I just needed to get my mind off things for a sec." She felt warm inside knowing that she'd gotten April moved from the not-so-nice homeless shelter to the best prostitution recovery center in California.

"What did Ashton need?"

"I didn't tell you? We broke up."

"A rebound?"

Caroline didn't meet his eyes.

Mack's eyes narrowed. "So there's a new guy."

She looked at him now. "Yeah."

"And who is this mystery man?"

"It's none of your business. But if you must, an old friend helped me with a new friend," she said.

"What kind of kinky hippie stuff do you have yourself into?"

Caroline looked all over the diner, scanning for anything that would help her escape the conversation. Then her eye landed on something, and it made her breath catch in her throat.

She walked over to an empty table and grabbed an abandoned newspaper. "You're not going to *believe* this," she said. She showed him the headline. "Looks like I owe you a nice dinner," she said. She took a long, slow sip of her latte as he read.

Billionaire Couple Killed by Bear

He tapped the headline with his finger. "I can't friggin' believe this."

"You want to make it double or nothing?" she said without affect.

Mack looked up quizzically. "Did you know the government is going to receive over fifty percent of their money in death taxes?"

"They should."

Caroline immediately regretted her comment, as she watched Mack's face turn a shade redder. "Any money that was taxed once shouldn't be taxed again. It's un-American. We had a revolution about too much taxes once."

She held her hands up in surrender. "Relax. Everyone's entitled to an opinion. I think it makes sense for wealth to be redistributed to the less fortunate."

"Redistributed? Why, so they can–"

Caroline held her hands up again. "Are you going to take the bet, or what?"

"Maybe we should just give it to the government. They're so efficient with the other trillions of dollars we give them. I'm sure they'll put it to good use."

"I guess you don't want to up the bet. Where do you want me to take you? Applebee's?"

"Ha, ha. No thanks. I'm ready to let it ride, but the stakes just changed. If I win, I get to cook a candlelit dinner for us."

"You get to cook for me? Okay then. I guess it's my funeral."

Mack thought for a moment. "I'm sticking with the threes," he said, "so I'll bet you another billionaire *doesn't* die by the end of the month."

No kidding, another billionaire isn't going to die. But it seemed to keep him from asking her about her little escapade of the previous night.

"It's a bet," she said.

He stood behind his chair. "So, are you interested at all in what's going on with our case?"

Caroline leaned back. "What's going on?"

"Bender called for a briefing."

"Are you kidding? Mack, I'm sorry."

"Yeah. Makes sense now why I called your cell phone twenty times in two minutes. It wasn't because I missed you."

"Well... no." She paused, "so, what's going on with the case?"

"They located our perp–the only living link to this investigation–in Mexico. Turns out, the DEA went in, and pretty hard, too. They sent in a strike team."

"What?"

"Bender said he was, quote, confident the DEA would handle it." Mack shook his head. "Anyway, according to Bender, with Hernandez dealt with, the case is closed."

"That's insane. This isn't a one-man operation. Senator Bryson sure didn't make it sound like that." She paused. "Wait, you said with Hernandez dealt with? So, the case is definitely closed?"

"There's more to this," he said. "The whole SWAT team was killed and burnt to a crisp in the suspect's house."

Caroline blanched. "And the suspect?"

"Still at large."

"We'd better get back to HQ," she said, gathering up her things. "Am I in trouble with Bender?"

"I told him you were doing research off-site," he said.

"Thank you."

"I'll always have your back," he said, turning away from her. "It's what partners do."

She followed him out to the car without another word.

60

Bic sat reading a newspaper at an outdoor café in downtown Austin. Across the busy intersection was the entrance to the main campus of Texas Computer Corporation, the largest computer hardware manufacturer in the world. It was huge and solid, built of thick Texas granite and concrete, and looked more like the portcullis of a medieval castle than the gateway to one of the world's largest corporations.

Bic looked at his watch. If his intel was correct, the sixty-nine-year-old CEO and founder of TCC, Henry Barron, would be leaving the campus at 6:00 PM sharp–like he had done every single day for the past twenty years. Bic mused over how widowers grow set in their ways as they age.

A black Cadillac stretch limo pulled out of the campus drive and turned right, exactly at 6:00 PM. Bic watched carefully to confirm the vehicle's course. His intel was perfect–as it had been for every hit so far.

His employers had gathered astonishing amounts of information on the targets. Bic frowned at that thought. People like that were not to be defied. He was sure they were linked to the government somehow. The intel packets just had that kind of wordy-yet-bland feel about them.

The first three hits had gone exactly as planned, but these hits wouldn't stay accidents for much longer. Somebody, the FBI or a clever cop, would connect the dots. Recent newspaper articles written were playing to the imaginations of the readers, invoking all sorts of theories. Some were uncomfortably close to the truth.

Bic shuddered as he pictured himself gunned down like a wild animal. But that's just how it would end. He would never allow himself to be taken alive.

That's right. Die, then go straight to hell and make Clarence Green suffer remorselessly for–

A fear such as he had never confronted nearly overwhelmed him.

What if I die and find out that monster somehow found forgiveness? I'll be in Hell while that bastard is sitting upstairs in the country club having the last laugh.

61

Congressman Tidwell was sitting at his desk in his office when the phone rang. He looked at his watch, thinking, *It's almost five on a Friday. Pam knows better than to let a call through this late.* He let the phone ring. Working diligently, he continued to map out a strategy to ensure the budget committee took into consideration the extraordinary death taxes that would be paid into next year's budget. He had it planned out in detail, right down to the congressmen with whom he would plant the idea to bring it up in committee.

Eight rings later, frustrated that he couldn't concentrate, he shouted, "Pam, what's with letting a call though this late?"

"I'm sorry, sir. Mr. Jones was so persuasive I couldn't say no."

Tidwell picked up the phone. "This is John Tidwell."

"John, this is Ted Jones, calling about our fundraising efforts."

"Now's not a good time to talk. Why don't I contact you when it's more convenient?"

"John, I can appreciate your concern, but I wondered if you had heard about our number two fundraiser, the one who ran the campaign in Chicago. This morning a rival organization attempted to cancel his contract."

Shocked, two thoughts collided in Tidwell's mind: first, who had attempted to take out Gabriel? Second, had Parelli already given an order from someone to take *him* out?

Tidwell said slowly, "No, I wasn't aware of any issues with that fundraiser. I'll look into it and get right back to you." He hung up the phone, then grabbed his dark navy pinstripe suit coat. Time for some damage control. He hurried out of his office, barely saying goodnight to his secretary.

Before leaving the building, he ducked into an unused office ... he wanted some privacy with the call he needed to make.

He stepped into the office and closed the door behind him. Sweat clung to his forehead as he considered the implications of Parelli's news, and how it might affect his plan.

He dialed the number of Parelli's alias. "Ted Jones," the voice answered.

"Ted, this is … It's Jim." Parelli wasn't the only one who could use an alias.

Parelli chuckled, "Great, Jim," before growing more serious. "I need to know what happened with the number two fundraiser."

"I have no idea."

"My guy in Chicago said he didn't think our business rivals knew who our fundraiser was."

"I'll have to look into it."

"I already have. The people who tried to cancel the fundraiser were working for our Salt Lake City correspondent."

That meant Phil Utah. "That doesn't seem likely, does it?"

"Does it?" Parelli growled, "I hope for your sake you're not playing with me."

"I'd never put the campaign in jeopardy."

There was a brief silence. "Okay, what next?" Parelli finally asked.

"The next two big fundraisers are in Texas. Our people have already emailed the profiles and schedules of the main contributors we're targeting to our number one fundraiser. Once he contacts those two, that'll be numbers four and five on our list."

"Halfway home. That's good."

"That will leave us about ten days to approach our last five donors."

"Good. In the meantime, I'll keep our number two fundraiser busy. He's a little upset about someone trying to take him off the campaign trail."

"Okay, I agree, let's keep him busy." Tidwell hung up the phone without saying goodbye.

62

The red Razr cell phone buzzed, and K-six rolled his eyes as he answered. "Yo," he said emotionlessly.

"Is this the *slob* K-six?"

The large, muscular black man, sporting cornrows and gang tattoos over each arm, calmly exhaled the drag he had just taken from his one-hitter. He looked around at the three other OGs sitting in the red leather seats of his custom-refinished 1980 Coupe de Ville, wondering if one of his homies was playing a joke on him.

"Yo, turn down that music, TP," K-six said to the driver. TP or Tiny Pete—all 250 packed pounds of him—complied.

"Is this a dirty *crab*?" K-six asked into the phone.

The unknown caller laughed. "Call me what you want, playa, me and my folks is gettin' ready to move into your hood. We'll need to carve out a little of that drug money for ourselves."

K-six instinctually grabbed the 9mm tucked in his belt and pulled it out as he said, "Street's hot with *crabs*." The other three men in the car quickly reached for their own weapons. This part of Austin belonged to K-six and his boys. Nobody else was taking it without a fight.

Driving in one of two lanes going northbound, TP slowed the pace of the vehicle strategically, making sure vehicles from behind didn't speed up next to their car and vehicles ahead didn't slow down to get a shooter's angle. He would have to be especially careful at stop signs and lights. When the car was stopped, they were the most vulnerable.

Everyone looked out their windows, intensely scrutinizing the other vehicles on the street, looking for signs of Folks in the area. They watched fast food restaurant parking lots and the endless strip malls lining both sides of the road.

As K-six looked into a gas station parking lot, a young black man pumping gas caught his attention. He was wearing a bright blue T-shirt, and a sure sign of Folks was someone dressed in blue, green, or black. Considering the call he had just received, if the kid had been wearing clothing with strong representation, like a North Carolina Tarheels jersey or a Detroit Tiger hat, K-six would have already opened fire. But seeing that the shirt was plain and the young man was alone, K-six decided he wasn't affiliated.

"Where you at?" barked K-six into the phone again. "I'd like to pay you a visit."

The caller had hung up.

"Rose, you believe this crab?" he asked, looking at the man sitting in the back seat next to him.

K-six's number two was called "Rose" because if any rival crossed his path, they would be getting roses the next day at their funeral.

"Call the gutter rat back," Rose said, his eyes hidden under a pulled-down red bandana.

K-six hit the callback option on his phone. He remained calm. His cool is what kept him alive all these years. Act before you think it through and you wind up dead.

The phone picked up, and after a confused pause, the voice said, "Tell your driver it's pork chop eatin' time!"

Before K-six could reply, a single bullet burst through the windshield, entered TP's forehead, and exited through the rear of his skull, spraying fragments of bone, blood, and brains all over K-six and Rose in the back seat.

The car lurched right, jumped the curb, and then crashed into a telephone pole. Nobody was wearing their seatbelts, so on impact, everyone flew forward. K-six dropped his gun.

With his head ringing and ribs aching sharply with every breath, K-six rapidly recovered his gun, expecting to be sprayed by bullets any second.

K-six nodded to Rose, and Rose replied, "Let's take some of them crabs down with us."

K-six kicked the door open and waited for gunfire ...

Rose pointed toward the windshield, "That crab put a slug in TJ from the front–gotta hit the poser from there!"

Then K-six's phone rang. He looked to Rose.

"See what that crab's got to say," Rose hissed.

K-six answered his phone. "Folks is comin' to take your hood, slob. My crew'll be here in the next couple days." The caller disconnected before K-six could say a word.

63

Gabriel bent over the motel bathroom sink, inhaling the heady fumes of the bleaching mix he had just applied to his hair. It made his eyes burn, but he continued massaging it through his hair.

The motel was off Highway Five in Chula Vista, California, a town just south of San Diego—a crappy little place that was used to the type of clientele that rented by the hour.

The small bathroom's outdated wallpaper was peeled, and the tacky corroded light and bathroom fixtures didn't work reliably. Many would find the room disgusting, but for Gabriel, this was an upgrade from the dump he had just burned down.

Every twenty seconds or so, Gabriel popped his head up and looked to see if his jet-black hair had changed color yet. At first it didn't seem to be working, but after twenty minutes had passed, he began to see results. He then took a quick shower to wash the product out. Exiting the shower, he immediately looked in the mirror and smirked, pleased with how it had turned out. Changing his hair color to a light brown, plus taking the length of his hair down to about an inch-and-a-half, had completely altered his look.

He walked into the bedroom and grabbed a bag full of new clothes and other items he had bought the day before at a big-box discount store.

He pulled out a new outfit from his bag—a nice pair of khaki pants, a collared long sleeve blue button-down shirt, a brown sweater vest with a baby-blue argyle pattern, matching socks, and boat shoes. He hated this gringo look, but he needed to blend in.

Gabriel dressed, then grabbed a smaller bag from inside the larger one and returned to the bathroom. Inside was a box containing non-prescription contacts.

Gabriel put the contacts in his right eye, followed by his left. He blinked a couple of times, to get accustomed to the lenses. He looked in the mirror approvingly; his dark brown eyes now appeared to be a deep-water ocean blue.

His finishing touch was a pair of non-prescription wire-framed glasses. He looked himself over in the mirror. *Bueno. Muy bueno.* He no longer looked like Gabriel Hernandez, public enemy *numero uno,* instead he looked like one of these gringo dorks.

He returned to the bedroom and retrieved an 8 x 11 manila envelope from the bed's side table. He had received it yesterday when crossing the border. He sat on the bed and opened it. Inside were the details about a job from his Chicago hire. He didn't know who that employer actually was, and he didn't really care. But he knew they were very wealthy and powerful, because of two things: they had arranged his passage across the border without any interference from the law, and he had been paid $200,000 for the Chicago job. In Mexico, he got paid five or ten thousand for the same work. *Ain't complainin', ain't complainin',* he told himself.

Gabriel studied the photo of his target: a man with a strong build, tan skin, and a brown, bushy mustache. To Gabriel, he looked like someone he'd enjoy killing. Then he read the letter that came with the photo, and his nostrils flared. His target was Phil Utah–the one who had sent the SWAT team to kill him. He shredded the letter violently and dropped it into the garbage can. The picture, though, he kept.

Grabbing his duffel bag, Gabriel left the hotel room. The game was on.

64

K-six sat in an oversized chair in the darkened living room of a run-down apartment in one of the rougher areas of Austin. He tilted his head back, watching the ceiling fan circulate the cloud of smoke he and the fourteen other homeboys in the room had created. Everyone in the room was smoking. That's what they usually did after a funeral: pack into a room with their closest friends, listen to classic rap with the volume turned down low out of respect for the dead, and get high.

K-six heard a ringtone and looked down at the rectangular glass coffee table where the phone was perched. He had been hearing imaginary rings from his phone, hoping the fool who took out Tiny Pete would have the nerve to call him.

K-six reached for it as all the reminiscing conversations about TP went silent. Everybody in the room knew the story about the crab calling.

He answered.

"How was the funeral?"

K-six immediately recognized the voice. His grip on the phone tightened. A blazing fury washed through him, sending him into a blind rage. All he could see was red.

"You dirty crab, where are you?"

"You slobs are soft. I'm bringin' the hardcore g's into your hood today."

K-six's anger ripped tears to his eyes, his fury so overwhelming he could barely get his words out. "Where are you?"

"Downtown, at the corner of North and Wells." The caller hung up.

K-six stood. "It's crab-killin' time."

191

65

ic sat on the concrete sidewalk a block and a half west of the Texas Computer Corporation's main entrance. He wrapped himself in a dirty old gray woolen blanket leaving only his head and his right hand exposed. He held a ragged cardboard sign which read *Vietnam Vet* in big crudely-written letters, with *God bless you* in smaller letters below.

Next to Bic was a cardboard box filled with ragged clothes, aluminum cans, McDonald's bags and a couple of half-eaten rotten bananas. Wearing his dark sunglasses, he sat still as a statue and mumbled "God bless you" every time some change jingled into the old coffee can in front of him.

Directly behind him was Tina's Flower Shop, one of the many businesses lining both sides of the four-lane road. Vehicles were jockeying for position in the downtown rat race along the road, trying to beat the rush hour traffic.

A Cadillac Escalade caught his attention. With the windows tinted dark, he couldn't tell if a gang member was driving or not. Probably. Three other vehicles closely followed the Escalade in what looked like a pimp convoy. As they passed, he watched to see if K-six went to the suggested intersection. He kept his head down and waited.

The four vehicles pulled into the parking lot of a Walgreens. The gangsters were at the intersection between him and the main entrance of the Texas Computer Corporation. He grew slightly concerned over the number of men exiting the cars. They were all dressed like members of a basketball team: Red-and-white Bulls jerseys, sweatshirts and baggy pants, wearing red bandanas or Starter hats, the bills tilted to the right.

Bic's watch alarm vibrated. Ten minutes to six. They were right on time.

He watched closely, trying to keep tabs on all the gang members at once. At first, they stayed in a tight group, but then they started to spread out. Five of the gangbangers crossed the street; two went east, and three came west toward him.

Bic knew that if there was a confrontation and gunshots were fired, TCC campus security wouldn't let anyone exit the facility. They especially wouldn't let Henry Barron's limo leave.

The three men made their way toward Bic. He could hear them asking people, "You a crab?" as they randomly grabbed and shook people walking on the sidewalk. Finally, they noticed Bic. "Look at this big ugly hood rat," one of the men said. His teeth glittered with gold fronts.

"May God bless you," Bic said, as he slowly rocked his head back and forth. He stared forward at the knee level of the three men standing in front of him.

"I bet this dude ain't even blind," another one said.

"If he ain't blind, I'm gonna kick his ass," the one with the gold fronts returned.

"That's a big black piece of meat there. He might put a big ol' whoopin' on your skinny ass, Fronts."

"May God be with you," Bic said in a soft, weak voice as he gripped his 9mm under the blanket.

"What's a blind po' fool need nice glasses for," the man with the gold fronts said, reaching down and removing Bic's glasses.

Bic looked up at the three men.

"Oh man, look at them jacked-up eyes. He's blind as a bat."

Without warning, the man with the gold fronts slapped Bic across the face hard. "Don't look at me with those buggin' ghost eyes."

"Fronts, you done pissed him off–steam's coming from his big bald black head."

The man slapped Bic again. "Didn't you hear me?" He then turned to the other men, laughing, "Fool looks at me one more time, I'm putting a bullet in his watermelon-sized head."

Bic kept his head turned from the slap. Looking down the street, he saw a black stretch Cadillac cruising through the intersection of North and Wells, coming toward him.

Bic then looked up at the man with the gold fronts and said, "You remind me of someone."

"Who that, you blind fool?"

"Clarence Green," Bic said in a low tone, the rage of a thousand trapped tortured souls burning through his veins.

"Who's Clarence Green? Black Santa Claus?" Fronts blustered.

"My father," Bic said as he stood, tossing the blanket from his body. They had time to notice he was wearing a North Carolina Tarheels jersey and held a 9mm pistol in each hand, extended toward them. A special magazine holder was strapped around his waist, holding clips for the nines–and several larger clips for an M-16.

"Oh no," said Fronts, as Bic pulled the trigger on his right-hand pistol and a slug cracked into the thug's forehead.

The left-hand gun put a bullet into the chest of a second gangbanger, dropping him instantly. A third man tried to pull his weapon from the waistband of his pants, but Bic patiently aimed and put a slug through the man's chest. The gangster's eyes rolled up, and he collapsed on top of one of his buddies.

Bic unloaded his remaining bullets into traffic. Bullets shattered windows and punched holes through metal auto-bodies. Tires screeched, and the sounds of crunching metal filled the street as vehicles collided into each other from every direction.

Traffic ground to a halt. Pedestrians on both sides of the road screamed and fled for cover, trampling each other in their rush to escape.

Bic released both spent clips and reloaded his pistols. He then slid the weapons into their holsters under each armpit and dropped flat to the ground.

66

Phil Utah sat glumly in his white Ford Taurus on the fourth floor of a parking garage in downtown San Diego, head down, pressed against the wheel. He wondered how he was ever going to make it out of this mess alive. He had sent five good men, five friends, to their deaths.

Not consulting with Tidwell had been a big mistake; he knew that now. He figured he would just clean up a loose end by taking out Gabriel. Cleaning up people who were sloppy at their jobs was what he had been brought into this project to deal with. After all, when someone became a liability, he took them out of the picture, just like he had done with the hacker kid. The hell of it was, *he* was the one who had been sloppy this time. Harold Bender informed him of his investigators finding Hernandez. Phil saw that he had to make this the DEA's problem. He had to make sure Hernandez wasn't taken by the FBI, not knowing what the crazy psycho knew.

But Phil had messed up. And was there now a price on his head? Probably.

He had left a message for Tidwell on Saturday, but the normally punctual congressman had yet to call him back. Utah wasn't sure what his next move would be. It all depended on whether he was now considered a loose end that Tidwell and Parelli wanted to clean up. If Tidwell didn't contact him by the end of the day, he would have to assume he was.

"Dammit!" He gripped the steering wheel with such intensity that his knuckles turned white. Teeth clenched, Utah glanced at himself in the rearview mirror, muttering, "I should've sent in twenty men to kill that sick Mexican psychopath."

Three knocks on the driver's side window startled Utah. His heart raced at the sight of a tall, well-dressed man motioning for him to roll down his window. Utah couldn't get a good look at his face, but noticed the outline of a handgun under his suit coat. He was no match for an enemy in a fast draw.

Instead of opening his window, he cracked the door open slightly, holding the handle with a tight grip, just in case he needed to thrust the door into the man's body to buy him some time to draw his weapon.

"Phil Utah?" the young man asked.

"Who's asking?"

The man began to reach for his weapon. Utah lowered his left shoulder and pushed on the door open with all his might. The door flew open, but the other man side-stepped it easily, looking bemused.

"Who were you expecting?" he asked, then flashed a wallet full of credentials. "Mack Maddox, FBI."

Utah felt a flood of relief. "What the hell are you doing sneaking up on me like that, kid?" he barked, trying to regain his composure.

"I didn't sneak up on you. Who did you think I was?"

"I just had five good men killed, so a stranger packing heat makes me a little jumpy." Utah pulled out a handkerchief and wiped the perspiration off his forehead. "You just never know when it's going to be your day."

"Sorry about your men."

"Yeah. It's a tragic shame."

"I'm assigned to the case involving the victims Gabriel killed in Chicago. I wanted to see if I could help in any way. Do you think we could talk for a couple minutes?"

"Not right now, kid, okay? I've got a lot of things on my plate. I'll tell you what though, give me your card. Once I deal with … I'll help you out."

"Fair enough," Mack said, and handed Utah one of his business cards.

67

The floor-to-ceiling window of Tina's Flower Shop shattered under a barrage of bullets. The gangbangers had finally gotten their act together.

Bic reached deep into his beat-up cardboard box and pulled out a fully automatic M-16 rifle. He stood and sprayed several rounds into the vehicles that the gang members were using for cover. Windows burst and bullets pocked the car bodies with lines of large black dots. Looking forward, Bic located Barron's limousine about three car lengths in front of him. He charged toward the limo, wildly spraying bullets in all directions.

Barron's limo driver tried to flee, but he made it only two steps out of the vehicle in the gangbangers' direction before he was mowed down in the crossfire.

Bent down behind the limo, Bic reloaded his M-16. Bullets from the gangbangers continued to clank into the big car's chassis. Bic figured they were firing shotguns and handguns, and one of them was shooting a small automatic weapon, probably an Uzi. Their bullets wouldn't make it all the way through the limo.

He stood suddenly, firing several bullets over the limo's roof and into the vehicles in front of the gangbangers. The weapon kept the men pinned down, and their vehicles already looked like they had been through Armageddon.

Bic bent down and pointed his M-16 inside the rear door window of the limo, which had already been blown out. Henry Barron lay curled in a fetal position on the floor, his back to Bic. A dozen or so incoming slugs hit the side of the vehicle opposite Bic, and Barron frantically covered his head with his arms.

With the rifle resting on the bottom of the doorframe, Bic fired a tight pattern of bullets through the interior of the limo and out the other window into the vehicles protecting the gang members. While holding the M-16 steady with one hand, he continued to pepper the gangbangers' position with an occasional short burst. With his other hand, he pulled a raw pork chop wrapped in wax paper out of a side cargo pocket of his BDU pants.

He unwrapped the wax paper and tossed the cut of meat into the limo. "It's pork chop-eatin' time," he said solemnly.

Bic then grabbed his weapon with both hands and shot several more rounds at the vehicles in front of the gangbangers; as he did, he dipped the barrel of the gun downward. Five slugs zipped through the interior and blew out Henry Barron's spine.

Bic turned and squatted with his back up against the car. He released the empty clip and reached for another.

Shots clanked into the limo only feet away from Bic. The two gangbangers who had originally gone east were now behind him to his left at a forty-five-degree angle, shooting from the entrance of one of the storefronts up the street.

Bic fired at the two men, and they retreated expeditiously into the sunken entranceway as the bullets whined off the marble cladding around them. Bic took the opportunity to dart deeper into the street, making his way east toward the intersection while he alternated fire between the men across the street and the two in the store entrance.

Bic took a position behind two vehicles that had collided and formed a V in the middle of the street. In this position, the men to his right and left were both at forty-five-degree angles to him, but Bic had cover from a vehicle on each side. He was aware he had put himself into a flanked position, but his intentions were to eliminate one of the two groups immediately. As he reloaded, he noted he had four magazines left, and presumed the men behind the vehicles were also running low. They had been returning fire with substantially less vigor lately.

Bic crawled out from behind the car and fired toward the men behind the vehicles. This time, with his different angle, he aimed at the pavement underneath the vehicles. The bullets skipped off the pavement, clanking into the underbellies of the vehicles—and from the sound of the screams, he had hit a couple of gangbangers, too.

His watch alarm vibrated. 6:10. Time to leave the scene before the cavalry showed up. He popped up and ran toward the entranceway where the two gangbangers had been taking cover, spraying it with M-16 fire. The bullets slammed into the stone like miniature sledgehammers, relentlessly pounding the hard rock into pebbles.

Bic rushed into entranceway and turned the corner firing, his bullets chewing the gang members to bloody rag. Then he nonchalantly retreated west down the sidewalk, toward his original position. Having reloaded his weapon as he walked, he turned every ten paces and shot a round of suppression fire back toward the main concentration of gang members.

He returned to his cardboard box, then bent down and pulled out a duffel bag. He tossed the bag over one shoulder and continued down the sidewalk before abruptly turning right down a long, wide alley.

He stopped halfway down an alley. Behind a dark blue dumpster was his Ninja street bike. He dumped his gun and his gangsta outfit in the dumpster and mounted the vehicle.

He drove the bike out of the alley, made a right turn and then opened up, heading west. A half-mile down the road, he entered the traffic flow on I-35 and left the scene.

68

Mack walked away from the vehicle to an exit, thinking that something was very wrong with Phil Utah. He looked back and thought: *For a man who doesn't have any time to talk, you'd think he would've started his car by now.*

While in the elevator to the ground floor, he decided that his first step would be to find any connections between Utah and Heather and Loretta in Chicago. It never sat well with him how eager the DEA had been to take over "handling" Hernandez. Had Utah been going after him for a different reason?

As he exited the elevator, Mack called Caroline to have her see if there was any connection between Utah and these killings. The call went directly to voicemail. *She ditching me again?*

Mack left the parking lot with a scowl. All around him people dressed in shorts and T-shirts were window-shopping and enjoying the 80° weather, but Mack saw only gloom. He made his way to a gourmet sandwich shop he had seen earlier.

As Mack walked, something Utah had said popped into his mind: *You never know when it's going to be your day.*

Wasn't that true? thought Mack, looking at the people passing by with more care, taking extra notice of the little subtleties of the people around him.

A man to his right, walking in the same direction as him, was holding a woman's hand. Neither the man nor the woman wore wedding bands, but he noticed a tan line on the man's left ring finger. Had he taken his wedding ring off? Was this man having an affair?

A woman walked toward him in high heels, her calf muscles flexing tight with every step, trying to maintain balance. She didn't usually wear heels; so why was she wearing them today? *She's going somewhere she doesn't usually go, or doing something she doesn't usually do,* he thought. *What is it?*

A man behind the woman looked "off" to Mack in his preppy, soft colors. He had the strut of a street thug—and his cargo pants didn't exactly nail the preppy look. The guy also had crude tattoos on the hands below his knuckles. *This man is hiding something.*

Or was he? Mack shook his head. *Could make yourself crazy thinking like that.* As the man with the strut passed, he spat a sunflower seed shell from his mouth.

Mack took a step and the bottom fell out of his stomach. He stopped, turned, and picked up the seed. He regarded it in a kind of fog, smelling the faint peppery sour smell in the air. He then saw movement out of the corner of his eye. *Gabriel Hernandez!*

Mack reached for his weapon, yelling, "Freeze! FBI!"

But the man before him was already facing him.

Mack froze.

His mind screamed *draw your weapon,* but his arm didn't respond. And in that split second of hesitation, the preppy man reached into his pockets; pistols instantaneously appeared in both of the man's hands.

The preppy grinned coldly. Mack's gun was barely clear of his arm holster. The last thing Mack knew before the man shot him was the writing across the knuckles of his right hand, clearly visible now: *Gabriel.*

Two slugs struck Mack simultaneously in the chest.

As he flew backward, gun soaring into the crowd, a final thought echoed through his head before it smacked against the concrete:

I guess today's my day.

69

Bic sat in the leather chair of the majority shareholder and CEO of Kempco Oil, one of the world's largest privately-owned oil and natural gas companies, in a plush executive office on the 33rd floor of the Kempco Building in Dallas. He looked across the vast cherrywood desk stretched out before him, out to the two banks of tall windows that stood in for two of the office's walls, and lost himself in the abundance of stars decorating the night sky. He leaned back, feeling more relaxed than he had in days.

And in that moment of contemplative relaxation, he began to question what he had become—or scarier, whether this was who he really was all along, someone who needed to kill to fill a deep, dark desire.

It wasn't the sort of thinking he often allowed himself. He had started out killing thugs and other killers, but had somehow devolved to murdering innocent people solely for money. Was the money just an excuse he used to fulfill some perverted desire to kill? Did Gracie's mission to find a cure even matter to him?

The spray of stars in the window blurred and vanished, replaced by his own faint reflection in the glass. For a moment, he saw his father in that reflection. An anger alloyed with pure hatred overwhelmed him as he thought about the day he would finally get his hands on that evil man.

He bent over and took the sealed pork chop out of his backpack. He put it on the cherry wood desk as his eyes became moist. He did what he did because of his father. Whatever else Bic Green might have become in his life, the day his father forced him to witness the brutal murder of mama, he had made Bic into a soulless killing machine. Bic was going to find his dad, one way or another. If the old man was still alive, Hawk would eventually track him down. And if he was dead, Bic knew now he would settle this score with his father one day in Hell.

This was no grand epiphany. He had known this from the very day his mother had been killed.

Clarence Green would never escape from him.

70

Jonathan Killebrew sat at his desk reading *The Wall Street Journal* as he did every morning when he arrived in the office. But today he couldn't get past the front-page headlines.

In his late sixties, Jonathan retained the strong jaw and broad shoulders he had sported back when he played football at the University of Texas. He looked ten years younger than his age and worked hard to maintain that. He kept his gray hair short and spiky and tousled forward in a nod to the current fashion. His stylish red power tie set off his crisp, white dress shirt perfectly.

He was devastated by the murder of his good friend Henry Barron. Henry had helped him work through the sudden death of his wife Melody only a few years ago. And had counseled him to keep his company and acquire more assets when oil prices crashed, rather than sell it as he intended. He'd recouped a fortune in the oil recovery all because of Henry.

Jonathan wanted to do something special for Henry's family. "Shirley," he said into the intercom.

"Yes, Mr. Killebrew?"

"I need your help. Come in here for a second."

Killebrew's secretary entered his office through one of the two oversized twelve-panel cherry doors.

"Shirley, did you see that Henry Barron was killed yesterday?"

Her eyes glistened slightly. "I did. Are you ok, sir? I know how much he meant to you."

"I'd like to do something for his family," Jonathan said stoically.

"Beyond just flowers, of course."

"Of course."

"Can you help me think of something?"

"I'll give it some thought and let you know, sir."

"Thank you, Shirley," he sighed. She nodded and left.

Jonathan stood slowly, feeling every one of his years, and walked over to a mahogany table on the other side of his office. He sat in one of the two dark leather chairs to consider how he could best eulogize his friend.

When sitting still didn't help, he went to his private bathroom. All hunter-green marble and matching wallpaper, with solid gold fixtures and a shower. The private bathroom was a small indulgence that he allowed himself.

He turned on a faucet, leaned over, and splashed his face. The cool water was an instant relief.

When he turned, he found he wasn't alone.

71

"Where the hell did you come from?" Jonathan asked the big, bald African American man standing before him. The intruder, in sunglasses, had a satchel hanging from his shoulder. He wore one of the navy-blue jumpsuits maintenance employees in the Kempco Building wore. Even aside from the bulky satchel over his shoulders and the sunglasses indoors, in the sixteen years Shirley had worked for him, she had *never* let anyone into his office unannounced–not even family.

Jonathan's eye saw his conference room door open. "How did you get in here? My secretary..."

"Was called away," the man said in a deep, detached voice.

He tried to keep his voice calm, despite the menacing figure before him. "The maintenance crew is not authorized to be here unless... called for." He paused, licked his lips, and said softly, "What are you here for?"

"I'm here for you to make a choice."

"I'm calling security." Jonathan strode toward his desk phone, pausing only a moment before the two new items on his desk: an iPhone and a small item wrapped in butcher paper.

"That is certainly one choice," the black man said. The calmness and strength of his voice gave Jonathan further pause.

He had just lifted the phone from the cradle when the man's hand touched his. It was large and delicate. Jonathan withdrew his hand as if it'd been burned.

"Hear me out," said the man.

There was something about this man, so full of dread, that compelled him to replace the phone back in the cradle. "If we're going to talk," he said, "I need to know your name."

"Bic."

"What do you want from me, Bic?"

Bic pulled a silenced pistol from his satchel and pointed it at Jonathan as he said, "You cooperate and take your own life. Or, if you choose not to, I'll take your life, and then your daughter's and her family's."

The iPhone on the desk suddenly rang. Bic motioned with the silenced pistol for Jonathan to answer the call. Jonathan's hands trembled as he hit the connect button.

Numb with terror, Jonathan watched a live FaceTime video of his daughter and three grandchildren playing in their backyard pool. *Dear God*, he thought, *this is real*. His eyes welled up as his mind overloaded with emotion. "This is some kind of sick prank?" he managed to choke.

"No joke. The man on the other end of this phone in Malibu is an assassin." Jonathan continued to watch his family play in the pool. "You have sixty seconds to do exactly as I say. If you follow my instructions, your family lives. If you don't, your family will die."

A sinister-looking man's face appeared on the iPhone screen. "Targets are secure. We will execute in sixty… " The video feed then returned to Jonathan's family.

Jonathan looked at Bic as he mentally played through the thousands of wonderful moments he had spent with his daughter and grandchildren. Then he squared his jaw and said, "What do I need to do?"

Bic pulled two round yellow tablets out of his pocket. "Take these two pills. That's all."

Without hesitation, Jonathan grabbed the pills, then reached with his other hand for the glass of water on his desk. He tossed the pills into his mouth, paused, and looked at Bic.

Bic looked at his watch and said, "You have fifty-five seconds left."

The hand holding the water started to shake. He couldn't believe he was even hesitating this much. Looking at his family on the phone, Jonathan knew he had to do this. He could only hope Bic would hold up his end of the bargain. He took a big drink and washed the pills down.

His heartbeat quickened. "Call the man," Jonathan demanded, short of breath. "Call this off."

"I will, but we're not done yet," Bic said, as he drew a pen from his jumpsuit pocket.

Bic picked up the desk phone and dialed 911. "Tell them who you are and that you're having a heart attack."

Jonathan waited several long seconds until someone picked up. By then he was sweating, and his heart was pounding so hard he was sure it was audible. "911, this is Wendy. Is this an emergency?"

"Yes. This is Jonathan Killebrew in the Kempco Building. I'm having a heart attack. Send help quick, and please–and tell my family I love them." His voice broke on the last words.

Bic disconnected the call. He then turned the top half of the pen. A small needle extended out from the bottom.

Bic put the gun in his satchel and zipped it closed. "I'm going to inject this into you. If you cooperate, I'll make the call."

Jonathan nodded, realizing he was going to be dead in a matter of moments.

Bic took Killebrew's finger and injected something under the tip of his nail.

Jonathan grew briefly terrified as he lost control of his body. His arms first, then his legs. They twitched and shook with increasing violence.

Bic reached for the wrapped pork chop on the table. Jonathan gained control of his hand long enough to weakly grab Bic by the wrist. They locked eyes, and though unable to speak, Jonathan silently pleaded for Bic to make that call.

Bic grabbed his phone, then said, "Full cooperation. Abort mission. I repeat, full cooperation."

"Ten-four," the man replied.

Jonathan smiled, or tried to. His sweet daughter and her children were safe. He couldn't move now, and no air was coming into his body. Though paralyzed, he could turn his gaze to the picture of his wife on his desk and thought, *I'm coming, sweetheart, finally. I'm coming home.*

72

Mack opened his eyes, mildly amazed that he still could. He lay on his back, disoriented– a light shone on him from above. He wasn't sure if he was dead or alive, though he felt as if an eternity had passed since he had been shot.

He glanced around: plain white walls, plain doors, and manila-colored cabinets with a countertop and sink below. He knew he wasn't dead then; heaven couldn't be this bland. He had an IV in his arm and a monitor sensor on his finger. He was in a hospital room.

He winced, touching his chest … it hurt to breathe, but more like the worst workout strain in the world kind of pain and not the "where are the holes?" kind.

A man dressed in green scrubs walked into the room. "It's not your chest you should worry about," he said, smiling, "it's your head."

"Who are you? Where am I?" Mack sat up, and realized his mistake as the world reeled sickeningly. The man was right about his head.

"I'm Dr. Ross, and you're at St. Rita's hospital. You were unconscious when you came in here."

Mack reached up and felt the stitches on the crown of his head. "Anyone know I'm in here?"

"Your partners visited yesterday–a loud Italian guy and a well-dressed black man." The doctor picked up an ophthalmoscope and shone a light into Mack's eyes.

"Yesterday?"

"You've been in and out for the last twenty-four hours. You suffered a concussion from hitting your head on the concrete. Luckily, there was no severe swelling or bleeding on the brain." He shone a penlight into Mack's eyes. "Your pupils are responding better than yesterday–that's good."

As Dr. Ross scribbled something on a clipboard, Mack took a deep breath and glanced toward the bulletproof vest draped across a chair next to the bed. *Caroline,* he thought. Her ridiculous insistence that he wear his vest anytime they did field work had saved him.

Dr. Ross placed the clipboard at the head of Mack's bed and said, "Get some rest. I'll check up on you in a couple of hours."

73

Mack woke up suddenly. According to the clock on the wall, only three hours had passed since he fell asleep. Staring at the ceiling, he wondered what Gabriel was doing back in America?

His thoughts became a jumble once he heard a woman's shoes clacking down the hall. His heart fluttered.

"Mack!" Caroline called, practically jumping into the bed, hugging him tightly. Mack didn't want the hug to end; her warm body and gentle breath next to his ear revived him better than any medicine.

Her eyes were glistening with impending tears. "I'm so sorry I wasn't with you," she said softly.

Mack wasn't sure what to do. Their lips were now only inches apart, and the painkillers were making him feel reckless. But he could smell a trace of another man's cologne still clinging to her. There was that stab of jealousy again. Feeling too exposed, he let go of her.

"I should have been there for you," she said, sounding ashamed.

"You *were*." His eyes went to his Kevlar vest hanging off the chair.

Caroline's eyes followed his, and she smiled. "Wow. How many times did we argue about that vest?"

"I've got a crazy one for you," said Caroline. She showed Mack the news feed on her phone. "Looks like you got out of cooking me that candle-lit dinner."

He sat up and winced, his head feeling like a pressurized bowling ball as he focused on the headline: *Jonathan Killebrew, 58, Found Dead in Office*. And the byline below: *CEO suffers massive heart attack*.

Caroline took a deep breath. "The day you were shot, Henry Barron was killed in a gang crossfire."

"What? That's five billionaires in a couple weeks." Mack thought

215

for a moment. "What if these aren't accidents?"

"I have to admit, it's getting a little creepy now."

"What just happened is statistically impossible. We need to get Bender to assign some agents to investigate."

"Taking this to Bender? After the stunt you pulled with Utah? That sounds like a man who's just been concussed."

"All we need to do is follow all that money."

"Follow it where, Mack?"

"Well, that's the question, isn't it? But all these guys combined have a net worth equal to the GDP of several small countries."

She had a strange look on her face. Like one who was starting to doubt reality as she knew it.

"What is it?" he said.

"I was just thinking that's enough to kill for."

"Welcome to my brain," he said.

74

Bic headed north to Nebraska, driving 65 on I-35 in a late-model black Cutlass Supreme. The AC didn't work, and only warm air flowed through the rolled down windows. The car sped past perfect rows of fields, marred only by the hot grey two-lane highway.

It was a half-hour past dusk, but a full moon had risen in a black sky bright enough to illuminate the seeded tips of the tall, wild wheat grass along the roadside. From time to time, sporadic gusts of wind brought the tall grass to life, and it swayed like an endless carpet of people dancing wildly in a nightclub.

Bic drove on, glancing at the passenger seat and at the wrapped pork chop from Killebrew's desk there. For the first time when his target had been at death's doorstep, he hadn't been overtaken by a ferocious blinding rage about his father—the rage that always stopped him from feeling any compassion for his victims.

Unlike the criminal marks of the past who had deserved the spoils of his rage, these were good people he was killing. Jonathan Killebrew had, without fanfare, sacrificed himself to save his family. When he looked into his eyes, Killebrew's love for his family trumped Bic's rage in a way that had never happened before. Instead of showing Killebrew his exotic eyes, then pulling out the pork chop in a blind rage and reciting to him the last words he would hear on Earth, Bic let this man die in peace, knowing his family was okay.

Bic suddenly applied the brakes and veered off onto the gravel shoulder. He reached into his backpack on the driver's side seat and pulled out his iPhone. He recalled the conversation he had with Hawk on his "work" phone, and the conversation regarding Gracie.

He didn't want to complete his contract. He no longer wanted to kill–but if he stopped now, what would happen to Gracie?

Chest tight, he opened his email and pulled up his list of sent items. In the past seven days, he had emailed Gracie several times. Was she in danger?

Bic decided to test the theory. He sent a simple email, asking if there were any backup contingencies in case something was to happen to him. He knew he was taking a big chance. No one in his business ever asked these kinds of questions without a reason, and almost always, it was a reason that didn't suit the employer.

Bic phrased the question simply and blandly. He didn't wait five minutes before he got an answer:

Alteration of the timeline is not possible; no contingencies exist. Failure to follow the contract would result in severe penalties, including a reshuffling of targets for a future potential contractee, to include the following targets [list follows at bottom].

Confirm immediately that there will be no changes in schedule.

And congratulations on your future philanthropic endeavors.

Bic read on down to the bottom. The reshuffling included Bic's present list plus the addition of two names: Hawk and Gracie.

And that last line? *Philanthropic.* Not only did they know what Gracie meant to him, but what he was paying for. Frustrated, he looked in the rearview mirror, and the rage he felt from the near-perfect image of his father overwhelmed him as he wondered if they knew where his father was, as well.

He needed to know that, too.

He answered his employer's email with one word: *Confirmed.*

He sent another email to Hawk, making it clear that if Hawk didn't find his father in the next week, then Bic would have to drop what he was doing and start looking for his father himself.

After sending the email, he pulled back on the road, his mind racing.

75

"You sure you're alright?" Bender said, almost genuinely concerned.

"I'm fine," said Mack, easing his way into a chair across from him with Caroline's help. "If I could just shake the feeling that I was just bludgeoned with a *sake* bottle, I'd be perfect."

"Well, I want you to take some time off. I think that's a given."

Mack's heart sank. "Is it the report?" He nodded to the folder on Bender's desk.

"I was thinking more of the fact that you happen to have a bad concussion."

"That's not why we're here, though," said Caroline.

Bender looked at her, surprised at her bluntness.

Bender put his hand on the folder. "What do you think I would like to know about your incident, Agent Maddox?"

"Sir, you're probably not going to like the truth," he said softly.

Bender maintained his grave expression as he nodded. "By all means, lie to me then."

"Well, sir, I went to the San Diego DEA office for two reasons. First, I felt a little responsible for what happened to the SWAT team, since they were following up on my lead. I wanted to see if there was anything I could do to help out. Second, I wanted to have a talk with Agent Utah. I was curious about–"

"Why did you think it was okay to question a Special Agent in Charge?"

"Well, sir, I went there with the hope of gathering some additional information to help me with my inquiries. It was part of my investigation."

"And what kind of information did you think you would find?"

"I didn't understand the DEA's—and by extensions Agent Utah's—need to send a strike team in to 'deal with' Hernandez."

"You didn't understand? Do you need to understand the workings of another agency before you let them do their jobs, Maddox? Or are you just burned that another agency was going in to bring down your man?"

"No sir," said Mack defensively. "I just assumed—"

"You shouldn't assume *anything*. I've known Utah for twenty years. I called him to run my situation by him, and he said he already had a team down at the border ready to go in, so he did me a favor—and that psychopath killed five good men because of it. Would you rather it had been you?"

Mack remained still, biting his lip.

"I'm taking the two of you off the case. TJ and Moretto will handle it from here."

"I understand."

"Mack, you have great instincts, but great instincts combined with inexperience have the potential to get people killed in this business. You need to let your experience catch up a little, so you don't make more stupid mistakes like you did on Sunday."

"Thanks for the advice, sir." Mack said, attempting to stand. Caroline's firm hand was on his back and his shoulder.

"Mack, I'm glad you're okay. Wearing your vest—that shows some foresight."

Mack nodded toward Caroline. "It's this pain in the ass you should thank. She's the one who's always badgering me about the vest."

"Sir," said Caroline, "since we're off the case, what will we be doing?"

Mack looked at her. She was ballsy today.

"The reason I ask is Mack and I have been following the news about the five billionaires who've died in the past couple of weeks."

"You have any inklings about it?"

"Well," said Mack, "it doesn't look like there was any foul play involved, but that's just the thing: it *looks* like there's no foul play involved."

"We thought it would be prudent," said Caroline, "for the FBI to reexamine some of the scenes to verify that."

"It is very likely that there is nothing to it, but we figure it would be a great learning experience," Mack added, referring to the A.D.'s advice.

Bender folded his hands, then looked away for a moment, thinking. When he looked back, he said, "Henry Barron was a huge supporter and friend of the President. I'm sure the White House would appreciate us taking a provisional look."

"Thank you, sir," said Caroline.

"The key word here is *provisional*. If you get yourself into any more trouble, I'm transferring both your asses to Alaska."

After shutting Bender's door, Caroline smiled ruefully. "He was really pissed, huh?"

"Wow," said Mack, "I thought you'd be through the roof when he took us off the case."

"Moretto gave me a heads-up just before we went to see Bender. He agreed to keep us up to speed on the case–let us help where we could."

"That's a curveball."

"I've learned in the last couple of days if you try to save everyone you wind up saving no one," she said.

76

The details of the dream receded too quickly into the fog of wakefulness, but he knew it involved that murderous Gabriel.

Mack was drenched in sweat. He grabbed his phone and powered up the screen. 10:17 AM.

He'd missed a call from his dad. He'd been so into the case these last couple of weeks that he'd forgotten his daily calls he'd promised to the old man–every day for a week straight.

"Hey Dad," he said into his phone.

There was no reply.

"Dad? You there?"

"Yes," the father replied curtly. Something was wrong.

"Everything okay?"

"I'm fine," he replied.

"Dad, have you been taking your meds?"

"I saw her," the man mumbled.

Mack paused and licked his lips. "Where? How?"

"Facebook. She looks so happy. How can she?"

"Dad, it's Facebook, everyone looks happy. It's going to be okay"

"No, it's not."

"Dad, I'm driving home. I'll be there in a couple of hours, okay?"

"No," he said with authority. "I'm fine."

"Dad, don't be ridiculous. I'm coming home."

"No, you're not. This is all your fault."

He almost dropped the phone. "You don't mean that," he said after a pause.

"You ruined my life!" the man said, and hung up.

Mack stared at his phone. Well, this wasn't shaping up to be a good day.

He texted Mrs. Lawrence. The neighbor had been a godsend in checking in on his dad. She had a knack for getting the obstinate old man to take his meds.

Mack was offered a week's leave with pay to recover, but he'd turned it down. Instead, he'd settled with Bender that he'd at least work from home for a couple of days and take it easy.

He stared at the laptop screen. He'd been granted access to countless files from different departments, including a database of every news organization that had any tiny bit of info on the billionaire deaths. Despite a few holdouts, most were eager to cooperate with the FBI. Following up on these new leads helped Mack keep his mind off what had happened with Gabriel. Mack had changed the story a little bit in his report, but it didn't matter. He knew what had happened. At the most important moment, he'd choked again, freezing up like that little boy who stood there stunned, watching his mother.

He turned his mind back to the present, determined to prove to Bender that he wasn't a total screw-up and cringed inwardly. In the era of the twenty-four-hour news cycles, where the meatiest stories get a total of 72 hours' coverage at best, each death was just taken at face value and forgotten once the next random blood-soaked lead story hit.

Mack ran through the causes of death in his mind. Killed in a grizzly bear attack: reported and forgotten. Died in a car wreck: reported and forgotten. Died of rattlesnake bite: reported and forgotten. Shot in a gang battle's crossfire, heart attack: same forgotten story, different days.

So far, the only lead he could follow up on was in Austin. One of the gang leaders from the shootout had been apprehended.

A text from Caroline: *Here. You awake?*

He texted her back: *Working.*

77

Mack heard the key he'd lent Caroline rattle in the door. And in she came, a small brown paper bag in her teeth, two coffees in either hand, her foot and her butt on the door doing the work of an arm.

"You come across anything?" he said.

She placed a cup on his workstation. "Glad to see you too. And you're welcome. I got you poppyseed. They were out of sesame. How you feeling?"

He eagerly took the wrapped bagel she handed to him. "Much better now."

"Glad I can help."

"So?" he said around a mouthful of bagel. "Find anything?"

She shook her head. "So far everything seems fine."

"Same here. No patterns, except for death by strange circumstances." He grimaced and peeled the top off the bagel. "Is this low-fat cream cheese?"

"You serious?"

"This six pack demands it." Mack lifted his shirt showing off his stomach muscles.

"I'm sure your abs of steel can handle it."

"True that."

She stared at him a moment.

"You want to see them again, don't you?"

"Please. Are we sure we shouldn't be helping TJ and Moretto behind the scenes?"

"*I'm* sure. There are fewer than thirty people in the US with over five billion in net worth."

"And what does that prove?"

"That's one sixth of their demographic dead. And five of them dying within a few weeks of each other? What if 50 million Americans died in the same time period?"

"Okay, Mr. Wall Street. You're aggregating where you shouldn't be."

"Only one way to find out," he muttered. "I'm going to call and see if I can talk to some of the scene investigators. Maybe we'll get some leads."

"Sounds great, you do that. Listen, I'm going to get going. I have a lunch date."

"Anyone I know?"

"Probably not. Get some rest maybe, okay?" She kissed him on the forehead.

"Sponge bath?"

She smiled and turned to leave, but then turned back, "I spoke to the Austin cop at the scene. He'd mentioned something that wasn't in the report–probably nothing."

"What's that?"

"There was a pork chop on the floor of Henry Barron's limo."

"A pork chop?"

"A raw pork chop. Pretty weird, huh?" Caroline shrugged. "Maybe it was his dinner. I don't know. Speaking of, I'm gonna be late. I'll see you. Get some rest and try not to go chasing down psycho killers without me, will you?"

"Right, boss. Have fun"

Mack turned his attention back to his computer screen. He opened the FBI ViCAP database, where he ran a search on pork chops. He could feel the hair on the back of his neck rise as he scanned the list that flashed on the screen. There were at least fifteen cases in which a pork chop had been left at a murder scene. More intriguing, the words "unsolved" appeared next to every case number.

He opened one of the most recent files and read the comments about the suspect:

UNSUB is believed to be a high-profile assassin informally known as "Ghost." He is a highly efficient killer who employs a diverse range of methods, strategies, and weapons to eliminate his targets. The often elaborate, strategic manner in which the assassinations are conducted, along with the skill level of the different weapons utilized, indicates a high level of military training. Despite the impressive variety of killing styles, and a proven record of performing killings for hire, an undercurrent of ritualistic behavior suggests possible psychosis or dissociative personality condition; UNSUB has been repeatedly profiled as a high-functioning serial killer for hire.

Over the last fifteen years, UNSUB has been responsible for twenty-two killings.

Mack spent the next two hours reading each of the files, amazed by the things this suspect did to take his targets out. This killer could have easily murdered these five billionaires and made their deaths look like accidents. And in every case, a raw pork chop had been found at the scene. In some cases, the meat was stuffed in the dead person's mouth. This was the ritualistic behavior cited near the end of the file.

He put himself in Bender's shoes. Finding one pork chop in the billionaire deaths was a coincidence. He needed at least one other.

He shook his head and chuckled. "Pork chops, huh? Friggin' whack job for sure."

78

Phil Utah sat at the kitchen table of a one-bedroom condo on the 15th floor of a high-rise in downtown San Diego. The condo was one of the DEA's transitional safe houses, where witnesses in drug cases and the like were usually placed before testifying.

Plain beige furniture and unadorned white walls heightened Utah's feeling of isolation–he was all alone in this mess. He was up against an adversary he didn't want to have to face. Well, he had done it to himself, hadn't he? And he had taken five good men down with him.

He set his pistol and glass of Scotch down, then picked up his cell phone and called Tidwell. It had been two days, and he hadn't heard a word from the bastard.

When he finally heard Tidwell's voice, he snapped.

"I knew after my last email you'd pick up my next call, you piece of crap!"

"Have *you* lost your *mind?*" Tidwell hissed.

"Lost *my* mind? You're the one who sent that sick psychopath after me, aren't you?" Utah grabbed the glass off the table and took a deep swig. His hand was shaking.

"Phil," Tidwell said coldly, "Gabriel is in San Diego to do another job for us."

"Enough lies! He shot an FBI agent right outside my building. I *know* he was coming for me." Utah clenched the glass, drank, and slammed his glass down hard. "Now, you listen, and listen close," he said, grabbing his gun. "If I–or anyone in my family–so much as breaks a fingernail, I'll blow this thing wide open. I have our whole Wasatch Mountain meeting on tape."

"You shouldn't bluff without the cards."

"You wanna try me, pal?"

Utah listened to the congressman's measured breathing on the line, then continued. "Now listen very carefully. I will email this conversation—the pipelines, the oil, the bribes, the Russian mob, the death taxes—every bit of it to every legal and political agency in the country, along with a nice, neat transcript with attributions and everything. You prepared for that, *Mr. Congressman?*"

"Phil, you're overreacting," said Tidwell. "But just so we're clear, I have five different contracts in place on you and everyone in your family. If I go down, you and everyone you've ever cared about will be gone."

Utah was silent as he walked over to the window and peeked out at the San Diego skyline. "So, I guess we're still partners, then," he said at last.

"Glad to have you down here in the muck, Phil," Tidwell said, then disconnected.

Utah threw his phone onto the couch in disgust.

He licked his dry lips and thought for a moment then retrieved his phone and dialed a number.

"I've been waiting for your call," said Bender.

"Is that so?"

"The kid was right. About Hernandez... and you."

Utah sighed. "That kid has great instincts."

"Mack's one of the good ones. Plus, he's pure."

"What are you trying to say?" Utah asked.

Bender was silent for a long moment. "I took him off the case."

"You trying to kick an old friend when he's down. I did you a favor and got my men killed."

"Listen, Phil, I don't want this kid or his partner to wind up dead. We both know how these deals work. If it was just chasing after the bad guy, then fine, but when things are more complicated than that—well, he's just not ready to cover his front and back."

"Listen, we need to do a little house cleaning, is all. Hernandez somehow found out I called for the raid and now he's after me."

"Phil," Bender said weakly, "I'm always willing to help out the DEA any way I can. What do you need from the Bureau?"

"I want Mack Maddox back on the case."

"Can't do it. We have two of our top agents already–"

"The kid IDed the guy from a sunflower seed. I want his help finding Hernandez before he finds me."

There was a moment of silence. "I'm sorry, Phil. Mack's already working on another case."

Utah growled. "Don't go using some smoke and mirror excuse like that."

"Phil, I'm telling you this in confidence. This morning he came in here and laid out a pretty compelling case alleging those five billionaires all over the news the last couple of weeks had all actually been murdered."

"Yeah?" said Utah. "Well, I'm a little confused."

"Confused about what?"

"About how you can so casually allow a friend to get killed by some Mexican junkie."

"Moretto and Jackson are still after Hernandez for murders in Chicago. They'll get him. Don't you worry."

"Well, you know, friend, any help would be appreciated."

"Listen, Phil, you keep safe out—"

Phil Utah disconnected the call mid-sentence. He downed the last of his drink, then prepared to tap out an email to Tidwell outlining Mack Maddox's investigations into the billionaire assassinations. It was the last card he had, one that would ensure his survival.

It was nice down here in the muck.

79

Mack found himself locked in a dingy, gray, cement-walled room, sitting at a steel table in an Austin County jail cell. He had pulled some strings, stretched some truths, to convince the warden to let him interview the inmate. He had even dropped the president's name into the conversation, insinuating he was here by his request–Mack didn't even want to think about what would happen if any of this got back to Bender.

It had been less than a week since he'd sustained his concussion, and though it felt pretty good to be back out in the field, the stale compactness of the room brought a bit of nausea into his head.

The door buzzed open, and an exceptionally powerful-looking man shuffled in, his legs and wrists shackled and connected to his waist by a thick leather belt. He was flanked by two guards and dressed in an orange jumpsuit. The guards directed him to the chair opposite Mack.

"You sure you don't want us in here?"

Mack looked at the man, whose stony eyes were fixed on him. "I think we'll be alright."

The guards were buzzed out, and it was just the two men, face to face.

"Can I call you K-six?" Mack said.

The man just stared in response.

"I'll take that as a yes." He flashed his badge. "FBI. Do you mind if I ask you some questions? I thought maybe we could talk a little about what landed you in here."

"Nothing to talk about," said K-six.

"That's too bad. One of the people killed, Henry Barron, was one of the richest men in the world."

"That supposed to impress me?" the man rumbled.

"Judging from the report, someone killed most of your friends and you wound up in jail. So, I guess you'll take all the blame and let the Crips just punk you like that. I think it's great you're not scared of the death penalty."

The gang member's stone-cold eyes narrowed. "What do you want?"

"Would it surprise you if I told you I believe Henry Barron was the real target in that incident? That you and your crew were set up to take the fall?"

K-six leaned back, looking thoughtful for a long moment, then his expression hardened.

Mack leaned forward. "I can tell it grates on you, K-six."

The man's hard eyes bore into him.

"What can you tell me?"

"I can tell you about your mama. I did her last week, and she's juicy."

Mack kept a deadpan expression on, one eyebrow barely twitching. "She lives too far away. What else?"

The man smiled and shrugged.

Mack kept his gaze fixed in the man's eyes. "Listen, screw that 'snitches get stitches' bull. We're not talking 'bout being a snitch. We're talking about justice here, K-six. You got set up."

"Alright," said K-six, "we'll play your little game. What's in it for me?"

"I can work to have your sentence commuted."

K-six smiled skeptically. "I like your soft language."

Mack smiled back. "What do you mean?"

"You can *work* to get me off. You ain't a ho, and you ain't getting me off. I know your type, all promises. I know you ain't letting a me out easy, not with what you've got me in on. You get me minimum security and a private cell. Guarantee it ain't nowhere near the Arian brotherhood, and I'll talk."

Mack slid a finger across the cold steel of the table, thinking. Finally, he nodded. "I'll get it done. Tell me what happened."

K-six leaned his huge frame back in his chair and looked over at the wall. "Not yet. My baby sis, 4.0, 35 on her ACT." He turned back to Mack. "There was a drug raid at the house. She's never even touched the stuff, but because she's related to me, she's now got a dope felony on her record."

"I'm sorry to hear that."

"No school will even look at her for a scholarship. I need it erased. Give her what my life has taken away."

Mack smiled again, this time at the thought of Caroline. "You're in luck. I just happen to know a passionate attorney who lives for these cases.. I will get her help, you have my word."

He met the inmate's stone eyes for a cold, unwavering minute, until he saw something soften in there.

"Tell me what happened, K-six."

The man took a deep breath through his nose. "This dude calls me on my cell and starts throwing a bunch of insults. A couple of minutes into the call he shoots TP in the head."

"While you're driving?"

"Not fast or nothing, but all of a sudden there's a shot, and TP's messy brains are in my lap."

"Did he take any more shots after that?"

"Nope, punk just disappeared until after the funeral. Me and my boys was sittin' around, and I get another call from the clown. He says meet him to kick pistols.

"So, we go lookin', and it turns out the dude has some kind of automatic weapons. Man, I don't know what happened. He pinned us down and killed half of us, then just walked away." K-six lowered his head.

"How many of you were there?"

"Thirteen solid soldiers."

"How did you guys fight him off?"

K-six looked away. "I told you, Junior G-Man," he said, his hissing in anger. "We didn't fight *nothin'* off. When he was done, he walked away."

"Did you get a good look at him?"

"No, I never got within a hundred feet of the dude. He was big though."

"How big?"

"Big as me, probably bigger."

"Anyone else get close to him?"

"Didn't nobody get a look at that joker, at least that didn't get shot. He closed-casketed three of my boys. He shot Fronts right in the forehead. Our cars was all shot up and the heat was comin', so we all ran on foot. I saw Fronts and went to him. He's dyin', but he kept on jabberin' about the dude havin' 'crazy eyes, the dude had crazy eyes.'"

"I have another question," Mack said, "and it's gonna sound crazy. Do you know of any reason why someone would have left a pork chop at the scene?"

"A pork chop?"

"Yes. Raw," Mack added.

K-six snorted derisively. "You mean like an actual pork chop? Nah, man." He shrugged his shoulders, then his face became focused. "Wait. Before he shot TP in the head, he said something."

"What did he say?"

"Dude said, 'Tell your friend it's pork chop-eatin' time.'"

80

It was a late Thursday night and Mack was sitting in his apartment. He stared at the yellow legal pad where he had written the phrase, "It's pork chop eatin' time" at least twenty times.

Before he brought this to Bender, he needed a motive. If these killings were hits, and not random accidents, and this man named the Ghost was involved, then it must be an elaborate scheme with some high-end players involved. It wasn't a personal motive. Not for this assassin.

He tapped his pencil gently on his cheek as he tried, for the umpteenth time, to figure out why someone would want this particular group of people dead.

Mack sighed and opened the reply to an email he had sent out earlier. It was from the head coroner at the morgue who had handled the bodies of Larry Tukenson and his wife. The email read:

Dear Mr. Maddox,

Per your request, I have attached the coroner's report for Larry and Sharon Tukenson as a PDF file. Given the circumstances, the bodies were burnt to the bone, and there wasn't much to investigate. The one interesting thing you'll note is one of the bones taken from the scene was not human. The unknown bone was eventually identified as a thoracic vertebra from a pig. At first, the question of how this bone got in their vehicle puzzled us. The report concludes that the Tukensons must have been taking a pork chop home in a doggie bag from the dinner they had attended.

Take care,

Leonard G. Pullen

KAPOW–there was number two, staring him right in the face. Mack could feel his heart pumping hard in his chest. He took a couple of deep breaths to relax.

Just then his cell phone rang. He answered shakily, "This is Mack."

"Mack, it's Phil Utah." His voice was muted, strained.

"Yeah, how you doing? You okay? You sound a little–"

"I think you were right, Mack. That guy, Gabriel, was maybe coming for me. I might want your help. I can give you some insight into this problem of ours."

"Hate to break it to you Phil, but you got some lousy timing there. I've been taken off the case."

"Yeah, Bender told me that." A pause. "Why?"

"He wasn't happy with me for going to San Diego on my own and, well, speaking to you. By the way, I'm sorry about that."

"You were just doing your job. For what it's worth, I put in a good word to Bender to try to get you back on."

"Well, I appreciate that, but I've started a new case. And it's big."

"Yeah, he'd mentioned that, the billionaire deaths. He said you had some pretty interesting theories."

Mack opened his mouth to share his breakthrough, but his instincts told him not to. "No, it's really just a training exercise. Henry Barron was a big supporter of the President. Bender thought it was a good idea to look into it."

"Anything come up?"

"No, just another tragic wrong place-wrong time situation."

"Well, if you have any ideas on the Hernandez case, I want you to contact me immediately."

"I'll do anything I can to help take that guy down."

"Good man," said Utah. "We'll be in touch."

81

Mack stood anxiously outside the closed door to Bender's office. Hopped up on his third cup of coffee, his juices were flowing fast. He'd been thinking about the breakthrough in his case all night, and had concluded the best course of action would be to set up twenty-four-hour surveillance teams to watch the remaining six billionaires on the top eleven list. He knew he would have to hard-sell Bender to get that type of support.

He cleared his mind, and feeling sharp, knocked on Bender's door.

"Hold that cab," Caroline said as she walked up to him.

At first glance, he almost didn't recognize her. Her normally straight hair was extravagantly curled; her light natural look had been converted into a flawless painting of base, eye makeup and lipstick. Her red and black dress suit was all business, but seductively tailored and, as casually worn by his partner as it was, suggested a wild kind of business, too. Mack did a double take.

"What do you think?"

"I–I don't know."

She smiled and posed like a model on the runway. "Good or bad?"

Even her teeth looked whiter, he thought, as he grasped for something to say.

"You okay?"

"You look … great. What happened?"

"Freddie treated April and I to a complete day of pampering at the Beverly Wilshire. We felt like movie stars."

"So the new guy's rich. Great," Mack said out loud by accident. He then deflected, "Who's April?"

"A young girl I've been helping get off the street. This is important to me. It's a life I can fix."

"Huh. Well, you look like a movie star. Better."

"I've been waiting my whole life for you to notice," she joked.

The door to Bender's office opened. "What is this, an office party?"

"No sir," Mack said quickly. "I wanted to see if you had a couple of minutes to talk."

"Sure, come in." Bender took a head-to-toe look at Caroline. "You look... different."

"Thanks, boss."

Bender then looked at Mack. "And you look like someone beat you with a carp."

Mack ignored Bender's comment and sat down as Bender eased into the chair behind his desk.

"What's on your mind?" the AD asked.

"I've been up all night working on this billionaires case. I believe an assassin was hired to kill all five of the victims." Mack pulled the manila folder from under his arm and placed it on Bender's desk. "Possibly more."

Bender opened the file. "Interesting."

"Behind my summary page are recaps of files on twenty-two unsolved assassinations that were performed by a profoundly skilled assassin–one who's never been caught. All these hits and not one solid clue–except the trademark item connecting all the cases."

Bender closed the file and lifted an eyebrow. "Where's your evidence?"

Mack took a breath. "I know this sounds odd, but the assassin's trademark is leaving a raw pork chop at the scene. In all twenty-two of those cases, a pork chop was found in association with the body. I think this assassin has killed our billionaires, too. In Texas, they found a raw pork chop on the floor of Henry Barron's limo, and in Montana, in the remains of the Tukenson explosion, investigators found a bone from a pork chop mixed with the victims' skeletal remains."

Bender eyes narrowed. "How about the other three?"

"At this point, no pork chops have been found at the scenes."

"Very interesting, Mack, but at this point, it's *just* very interesting."

"Five of the wealthiest people in America have been murdered. And though I haven't isolated a clear motive, I believe the other six people on the list are potential targets. As a precautionary measure, I recommend we have surveillance teams watch the remaining six families."

Bender shook his head. "Mack, I like what you've done, but at this point we're just stretched too thin. Between this Hernandez case and all the terror threats we're following up on, there's no way I can do that. The best I can do is give you and Caroline some breathing room to investigate further. Figure out who you think is next on the list, and you two go stake them out. If you come up with something concrete, you'll get all the support you need. But you have to bring me something soon, or I'm pulling you both out to support other cases."

"Fair enough." Mack stood. "Thanks for listening, sir."

"Well, that was quick and painless," said Caroline. "I didn't get a word in."

"He's prejudiced against this case for some reason."

"Now why would you say that?"

"Come on. You heard him in there. The guy can't come up with enough stock reasons to take us off this thing. I'll bet he only said yes to it in the first place because I blindsided him."

"Well, Sherlock, what do you need me to do? Talk to every pork butcher in the country?"

"Very funny. No." He stopped walking and turned to her. "There is something though. Remember the gangster I interviewed? K-six?"

"Yeah."

He smiled at her. "His little sister, this total genius, her life was ruined because of him. I volunteered you to fix it."

82

Bic sat in the driver's seat of a yellow cab in the Old Market area of downtown Omaha, pretending to read the *Omaha World Herald*. He was parked on the southeast corner of an intersection, with an unobstructed view in every direction. Bic played up his role of a slob on a lunch break, working his way through a big ham sandwich. He wore blue jeans with a red Nebraska T-shirt and a red ball cap decorated with a white N.

Quaint mom-and-pop shops and restaurants occupied the bottom storefronts of the eight-to-ten-story brick buildings on all sides of the intersection. Bic's watch read half past noon, but it was dark as dusk outside. Not a drop of rain had fallen yet, but storm clouds were gathering to the east. In his rearview mirror, he saw a tricky wind pick up a small plastic bag lying in the middle of the street and dance it in slow circles.

Bic figured the crazy weather was to his advantage. When he had cased the area yesterday, people were constantly popping in and out of the little shops and restaurants and the interior passageways that honeycombed the Old Market. Today, however, the streets were mostly bare. There were only a few people out, quickly darting back and forth, hoping not to get caught in the rain. The traffic in the usually busy intersection was much lighter, too.

Bic examined the photo of Mr. and Mrs. Sam Wilkes from the manila envelope resting on the passenger seat and slid the photo into his open newspaper. The intel on Wilkes was dead-on. Every Thursday, Sam Wilkes, took his wife of fifty-seven years out to lunch at Jimmy's in the Old Market. Bic was parked in a metered parking space right in front of Jimmy's and had confirmed the Wilkes' arrival ten minutes ago. The multi-billionaire's well-kept Lincoln Town Car was parked two spots down.

Bic rechecked the photo for verification. In his mid-seventies, Sam Wilkes was a tall, slender, fair-skinned man with a long face and thin lips. His most distinguishing feature was his comb-over: so much hair was flipped over his crown, the thin light-brown strands created a small dome on the top of his head. Penny, or Mrs. Wilkes, was an attractive older lady with healthy-looking shoulder-length white hair, gleaming blue eyes, and a good figure for her age.

The comb-over would be a dead giveaway. Confident both marks were present, Bic reached over into his duffel bag and pulled out a compact remote-control car. Only this toy had a round metallic ring the size of a doughnut set on the top of its shiny chassis. The expensive upgrade was capable of releasing enough voltage in a single massive charge to kill an elephant. The metallic ring was attached to a miniature hydraulics system designed to raise it vertically into the air about ten inches—more than enough to do the job.

Bic peeked over his newspaper and silently scanned the area in all directions. Satisfied no one was around, he cracked open his door just enough to slide the remote-control car directly under his cab. He closed his door, then resumed reading his newspaper and eating his ham sandwich.

Five minutes later, a sight in his peripheral vision startled him.

Bic slowly looked toward the window. He didn't see anyone. He quickly looked around, wondering if someone was sneaking up on him.

Then he looked down and saw a little brown-haired boy who couldn't have been older than six or seven. The boy was holding Bic's remote-control car, looking around as if trying to confirm that the thing had no owner. Stifling a curse, Bic immediately rolled down his window.

"Hey," he said, "come here with that."

The boy put the thing down and started to walk away quickly.

"Yo, come here. I'm not gonna hurt you. You like that car? You can have it."

The kid started and stopped, started and stopped. From the state of his clothes, Bic suspected he didn't come from much money. Patiently, he said, "But not that one. I need that car."

The boy bent down and slid the race car back under the taxi.

"Where are your parents?" Bic asked him as he stood up.

"They live back there," said the boy, jabbing a thumb toward the west side of town. *Nothing but concrete and depressed buildings*, Bic thought.

He quickly scanned the area for anything else suspicious. "I'll tell you what, kid. I'll make a deal with you. I'll give you some money to get your own car if you promise not to tell anyone I gave it to you–not even your mom."

The little boy squinted. "What's the catch?"

Bic smiled. Good kid, smart. Unfortunately, he might go far in the neighborhood he was from.

With some trepidation, Bic handed the boy two $100 bills. "You go to the toy store and tell the person at the register that you want the best remote-control car this money can buy."

The boy nodded. And Bic enjoyed a feeling he didn't get to enjoy very often.

"Hurry up. It's gonna start raining soon."

The feeling was of warmth like when his mother sang as they drove to church: "*Amazing grace, how sweet the sound, that saved a wretch like me! I once was lost, but now am found, was blind, but now I see.*" He remembered feeling it only once since her death–when he had first held little baby Gracie in his hands.

He took a deep breath. Memories of his mom were something he hadn't enjoyed in a long time. He missed her, or at least what he remembered of her. For the first time, he wondered if what he was doing hurt his mom. He was about to kill two Christians who had probably never deliberately hurt anyone their whole lives. The violence he'd seen, that he'd been responsible for– he'd heard some of his kills praying before he took their lives–where was God for them?

You can't know, his mama had told him. *No one can.*

If there was a God, there was no way li'l ol' Bic Green was gonna be able to figure Him out. And if there was doubt, there was hope. It was that gray area, that space of not knowing, where Bic Green had found his strength all these years.

He made up his mind and started the car. He depressed the brake pedal and put the vehicle in reverse. As he turned and looked behind him for other vehicles, his iPhone rang. Sighing, he threw the car in park, picked up the device, and opened his email.

A flash of thunder cracked through the sky as he did so. The violent snap seemed to release the rain pent up in those puffy, dark clouds, and instantly the cab was shrouded in a heavy downpour.

The email was from his employer, and it read:

Great job so far. Your work is impressive.

But there cannot be any deviations in the schedule. Failure to complete all items left on your list in the next six days would be considered a breach, and action against you will be implemented.

For the sake of your fee, and to avoid other consequences, keep to the schedule.

Good luck.

Bic pounded his fist into the dashboard so hard the change in the ashtray rattled.

Other consequences. They knew about Gracie, which meant he had no choice but to go through with the job—at least until he could guarantee her safety. Bic looked at his watch. His targets would be coming out to their vehicle at any moment now.

And where was God?

Dammit.

83

Mack sat back in his cubicle with a frustrated sigh. Looking for this guy was like searching for smoke in a strong wind.

Then a thought occurred to him. If he couldn't find the killer, maybe he could track down whoever had *hired* the killer.

He remembered noticing how much the value of some of the dead billionaires' company stocks had gone down when their deaths were announced. If someone had possessed prior knowledge of their deaths and had sold their stocks short, they would have made a mountain of cash.

At his computer, he reviewed what had happened with Incubus's stock. The stock had gapped down 27% at the opening bell on the first market day after Larry Tukenson had died. Incubus would have been the perfect short-sale target for anyone who knew Tukenson was going to die.

He then pulled up the short sale data from the week before the Saturday Tukenson was killed. Considering a great quarterly earnings report had come out that week with record insider buying and positive guidance for the remainder of the year, there was no way short sales should have increased.

Except they had. The week before Tukenson died, short sales were up 19.13% That massive, bearish activity made Mack suspicious. Tukenson had died on a Saturday, so his death could not have impacted the short interests for that week of trading.

He did some quick calculations. To bump the percentage of short interest up by 19.13% in a single week, an additional two million shares of Incubus stock would have been sold short. The week the short sales were made, Incubus stock averaged $76.50 per share. The Monday after Larry died, the share price dropped to $55.84. The two million shares shorted on average the week prior to Larry's death would have earned their purchasers $20.66 per share, or $41 million in one day.

"Now that's motive," Mack muttered.

He needed to find the person or group who had heavily shorted Incubus stock the week before Tukenson's death. The task would be difficult without the help of the NASD and obtaining clearance through the SEC could take weeks, even months. He couldn't stand the idea of another person dying while he waited for permission.

He rubbed his eyes and ran his fingers through his hair. "There's gotta be a way around this."

He stared blankly at the Incubus data on a financial site when something caught his eye. Out of eighty-nine firms covering the stock, only one had a strong sell recommendation. And when he saw the lead analyst who had made the recommendation, Mack felt like someone had punched him in the gut.

A name from his past stared at him from the screen, practically begging him to crack.

84

The little black car sped across the empty parking spot like a toy dog on wheels. Through the pouring rain, skirting the puddles dappling the pavement, the toy came to rest just under the rear door on the driver's side of the Lincoln.

Bic looked hard to the right, his eyes concealed behind his sunglasses. The toy car sat unassumingly under the Town Car. He pressed the button on the bottom of the remote, and watched the hydraulic arm raise the metallic doughnut into the air. The ring contacted the underbelly of the vehicle. A different button, and a flash of blue light came from underneath the Town Car as the device released hundreds of high-amperage volts into it. The remote car sped back obediently.

Five minutes later, a waiter with a large golf umbrella walked the Wilkes to their car.

Thirty seconds later, the car had not yet moved. It was time. Bic drove up the cab next to the Town Car and rolled the passenger side window down. Raindrops flooded in, slapping against the plastic interior of the door.

Mr. Wilkes tried to open his window but couldn't, so he cracked his door open and shouted, "Our car won't start."

"Sorry to hear that!" Bic yelled. "Tell you what. I'm just about off my shift, but I'll be happy to give you a ride."

Sam Wilkes leaned over and said something to his wife, then swung his door open, got out of his vehicle and came into the back seat of the cab. He was pretty quick for an older man.

Mr. Wilkes' shirt was drenched from being in the rain, despite being outside only briefly. His comb-over looked like a bad science project.

249

Bic pulled to the other side of the Town Car. He got out of the vehicle, using his newspaper to shield himself from the rain the best he could. He swung open the door on the Lincoln and extended his hand to help Mrs. Wilkes out of her vehicle and into the cab, shielding her from the worst of the rain with his newspaper.

Bic returned to the driver's seat. He looked at the couple through the rearview mirror. "Where to?"

"416 Gilbert Drive."

"No problem," said Bic, pulling out of the parking spot.

The rain was pouring down harder than before, and the poor visibility caused Bic to drive extra cautiously. A car accident, even a small fender bender, could derail everything.

He faked a double-take at the old couple in rearview mirror and said hesitantly, "Say, haven't I seen your picture somewhere?"

Mrs. Wilkes smiled. Bic could tell how proud she was of her husband, "He's Sam Wilkes."

Bic nodded, wide-eyed. "Hey, I thought so. I tell you, I can't wait to tell all my buddies I gave Sam Wilkes a ride in my cab." Grinning, he went back to peering at the road.

He exited the Gerald Ford Freeway onto the ramp to head south on I-29.

"I think you've just made a wrong turn," Mr. Wilkes said dryly. "We're heading south."

"Yeah, I thought so. The visibility is terrible. I'll turn around as soon as I can."

"Maybe you should take the sunglasses off," said Mr. Wilkes.

"I'm afraid they're prescription, sir, for an eye condition."

"How long have you been driving around here?" Bic could sense the irritation and suspicion in Mr. Wilkes's voice.

"A couple of months."

"Where do you live?"

Bic didn't answer him. With the weather, and with Gracie possibly being in trouble, he was in no mood to play games.

"Well?" Wilkes said in a louder voice.

"I'm sorry, Mr. Wilkes, but we're going to take a slight detour."

"What do you mean?" Mrs. Wilkes asked, her voice quivering slightly.

"I'm taking you both to Arkansas to visit an old friend."

Sam Wilkes leaned forward and thrust his face into Bic's until they were nose to nose. The old guy had balls, Bic had to give him that much. "I *demand* you take us to our home!" he shouted, the veins showing through the paper-thin skin of his neck.

"Sam, don't. He's going to hurt us," Mrs. Wilkes said fearfully.

You're right there, Bic thought regretfully, *but I'll try to be as gentle as I can.* He reached over and pulled a stun gun out of the central console. In one swift motion, he turned and jabbed the stun gun into Sam's neck.

Mrs. Wilkes screamed as she watched her husband's body spasm violently. He sank, unmoving, back into his seat. Bic wasn't sure if the old man had survived the shock or not.

Penny Wilkes clutched her husband's hand, still screaming. Bic zapped her in her upper chest. Her body shook as the voltage flowed through her. Her teeth clacked together like castanets.

Once again, the rage began in Bic Green.

85

Brooks Balter, Mack's dad's best friend from NYU, was that analyst. Brooks was once part of his family–he was like an uncle to Mack, until that day the young boy caught him nailing his mother.

From there, the wheels fell off, and she eventually left Mack and his dad to move to New York with Brooks.

The wheels fell off Mack as well, and his will to solve the case suddenly went out the window. He leaned forward, his elbows on his desk, trying to not relive all the pain he and his dad had experienced after she had left. First guilt, then blame. *If only I hadn't seen them, maybe it would have passed. How could she have done that to us? We were such a great family until she messed things up. She broke our hearts.*

And then the inevitable: *It's all my fault.*

He felt the walls of his cubicle close. Guilt seemed to clog the air around him. He texted Mrs. Lawrence, his father's neighbor, if she would head on over and make sure his dad took his medication. He hadn't seen or talked to his father since that blowup. Guilt on top of guilt. His mind was an anxious mess. He needed to get out, get some air. He made for the nearest exit.

"Mack," Caroline called happily as she approached him. "So, that girl? K-six's sister, Sydney? I got my dad's firm to agree to some *pro bono* work. He'll have the felony off her record in a month."

"I have to get out of here."

"What's wrong?" she said, reaching out to him.

"I have to get out."

"Hey, partner, talk to me?"

In that instant, anger suffused Mack's expression. "Talk to you, who's never here? Who's always letting me down, going off every afternoon with this new guy, getting pampered or getting–no… I'm not doing it. I'm not falling like my dad–"

Then, before Mack surrendered to an emotion he couldn't come back from, he walked out of the office down the nearest stairwell.

86

Gabriel hugged the wall with his back, pointing his 9mm Beretta with a 3" suppressor toward the open door, waiting to pump lead into anything foolish enough to charge through. When the FedEx truck rumbled off, he closed the door with his foot.

Safe in the dark hotel room, he grabbed his package and retreated to the small, windowless bathroom. He turned on the light and opened the package.

There had to be safer ways to receive his contracts, he thought. Any deliveryman could be intercepted and replaced by a federal agent. He thought for a moment if an iPhone or something electronic would work. But then he realized, no, the FBI and CIA could track the things with their satellites.

Gabriel pulled a single piece of paper and an eight-by-ten photo out of the envelope. The paper outlined his new instructions:

Your #1 target has changed to FBI agent Mack Maddox. THE FEE IS $50,000 US. IF BUSINESS CONCLUDED WITHIN 24 HOURS, FEE INCREASES TO $200,000 US.

Call 1-800-446-6464 anytime for target's location.

Gabriel looked at the picture and immediately recognized the face of the man he thought he had killed a couple of days ago. He never forgot a target's face, especially the eyes. What a person's eyes told him when they realized they were going to die was euphoric to him. He felt as if he were God, standing in front of them with cold steel in his hand as an inner fear erupted from the depths of their soul, pleading for his mercy, begging him to decide not to move his index finger. Some doctors have God complexes because they can save lives. And then there were men like Gabriel.

Gabriel looked at Maddox's photo. He remembered the strong eyes. The look in his eyes had been very different than most when Gabriel had shot him. At the moment he realized that he had been shot, his eyes didn't beg for mercy. They showed only hostility and a confused embarrassment.

Gabriel had been gypped. He had shot the guy twice. He'd certainly looked dead lying there on the concrete. He had put two bullets in the guy's heart, or so he'd thought. He usually used supersonic armor-piercing rounds, but on that day, he had chosen subsonic ammunition. He had been planning to sneak up behind Utah, tap the bastard twice in the back of the head from point-blank range and walk away from his falling body without drawing any attention to himself. He mentally shredded himself over the choice.

He cursed, long and fluidly, in two languages. He stared intensely at the photo, vowing that the next time they met, he would open the bastard up like a balloon full of blood.

87

"Give me another," Mack said even before the shot glass landed on the scarred hardwood bar. Nine others had preceded it.

He grimaced as the aftertaste of cheap tequila burned his throat and nasal passages. He didn't even bother to use the lime—all ten sat in a sad little pile on the napkin.

The small, lonely joint had room for only a couple of round high-top tables and a bar that seated twelve. At 1:00 PM, a handful of diehard drunks had already assumed their positions for the rest of the day. They sat staring at the mirror behind the bar while drinking at a pace fast enough to make their problems go away. These were his soul brothers.

Mack found himself blurry-eyed. The tequila was catching up.

"Give me another," Mack said again, anticipating a black out.

"You sure?" the female bartender asked.

"Yeah. I'll have another."

"I'll join you for this one," she said. She poured two shots.

Mack cupped the small glass. "Here's to oblivion," he slurred, and flipped the ounce of liquor down.

The bartender took Mack's hand, turned it palm-up, then licked and salted his wrist. She licked it again and poured down, then grabbed a lime off the sad pile and bit into it.

Mack leaned forward. "When's your shift over?"

She closed the gap between them. He could feel the moist heat as she whispered into his ear, "I'll meet you in the bathroom in ten minutes."

Mack nodded.

Ten minutes later, the bartender winked at Mack then headed

toward the back.

Mack stood—and the world spun, just for him. He reached for a bar stool to regain his balance. As he watched the bartender strut toward the back area of the bar, the excitement sobered him up enough to take a step forward without falling.

"Mack!" a female voice called out from the entrance of the bar. It was Caroline's, and it rattled him even more toward sobriety.

"Anyone ever tell you that you suck at timing? I've got a lot on my mind. Just let me be." He turned his back to her.

But before he could take a step, she grabbed his arm and spun him around. It felt like a drop from a rollercoaster.

"What is your problem?" she hissed.

"Are you kidding? Where do I start?"

Caroline didn't reply. She just stood there, waiting.

"Okay, fine," he slurred. "First," he started, then stumbled over to the right, bumping into one of the other patrons. "Sorry. First, you have abandoned me as a partner. I can't even count on you to answer my calls, let alone have my back."

"I'm sorry, Mack. It all just happened."

"Yeah right. Just like my dad's best friend just *happened* to wind up beneath my mother."

"You're drunk, Mack."

"Very observant. And you are unpredictable with your emotions, little lady."

"You want to know about Freddie?" she began. "I owe you zero explanations for my actions. They're mine. You understand? The sooner you understand that, the sooner you'll find yourself maturing. But whatever, Mack. You're drunk as hell and you'll forget all this anyway."

"You sure fell for him fast."

"Is that what's bothering you?"

"What's so special about him that you'd fall so fast?"

"We didn't just meet, first of all. We met when I was at Stanford."

"You and the rich guys."

"Screw you, Mack. He was my first love—I thought I was going to marry. The other day, he just called to catch up, I asked for his help with April and..." She shrugged. "That's just that."

Mack blinked his eyes and realized he had nothing, so he reached for something. "I got shot twice last week while you were getting

258

filled out by some old fling who already broke your heart once."

"You have no idea what I've been doing."

Mack turned and stumbled his way toward the bathroom.

Struggling to enter the bathroom, Mack couldn't stop thinking about Caroline. He mumbled to himself, "It's better this way. She'll break your heart."

Mack entered the bathroom.

"Hey stranger," said the bartender. "I thought you forgot about me."

Mack took a step toward her, trying to zero in on the ample cleavage her low-cut shirt left exposed. With the room spinning, he fought to control the buzz as he wrapped his hands around the small of her back and pulled her to him. He began kissing her neck and chest heavily. Her hands quickly undid his pants

Mack closed his eyes as something erupted inside of him. In an erratic motion, he pushed himself away from her, then turned to his left and barfed profusely at the toilet.

He struggled to hold himself up with a hand on either side of the toilet. He wasn't sure if he was going to pass out, so he looked to the bartender for help.

"Ugh," she said. "Break's over, chum." Then walked out of the bathroom.

Mack fell to his knees and rested his forearms on the dirty, puke-covered toilet rim, then barfed again.

The bathroom door swung open. And a soft hand went under his chin and gave him the support to stop his face from dipping down into the toilet water.

"You're okay," said Caroline. "Just get the rest out, and I'll take you home."

Mack tried to look at her to apologize, but the sudden movement was more than he could take, and the room faded to black.

88

"I don't wanna have to shoot your wife in front of you," said Bic, holding the gun to Penny Wilkes's ear.

After a couple of hours, they were awake and alert. He'd purposely used a low voltage on the couple. He couldn't risk either one of them even bearing a tiny scar from the thing–or worse, dying of heart failure right there.

Sam Wilkes sat nervously in the back seat of the cab, the cell phone clamped to his ear.

"Hello, Louise, this is Sam," he said as steadily as he could, squinting at the index card that Bic held for him to read. "I'm good. No, everything is fine, Louise." He squinted at the card. "I've... decided to take the wife on a little trip... we needed a break. We'll be gone for the week... yes, very sudden, I know. I'll call you if I need anything... alright... you take care now."

As instructed, Wilkes disconnected.

"Good," Bic said and lowered his weapon.

"What do you want with us?" Mr. Wilkes demanded.

"I just need your help for this week, and then we'll part ways." Bic took the phone from Sam Wilkes and handed it to Penny. "Your turn."

Mrs. Wilkes's hand trembled so much she could barely hold the phone. Bic scowled at her and said, "It's real simple. All I need you to do is call Mrs. Peppercorn and invite her out for lunch." He pulled out a second index card and held it up.

She started to cry. "I can't help you kidnap my friend!"

"You're not kidnapping anyone." Bic raised his slick black 9mm and pointed it at her husband. "But if you don't get that lady to come to lunch with us today, you'll be responsible for your husband's death.

Penny sobbed softly, trembling. Bic lowered his weapon.

"Listen, you'll be fine. You hear me? Just insist she come to lunch with you, no matter what."

"But what if she's busy?"

He tapped the index card. "Read this as written and she won't be. Understand?"

She nodded in agreement, her face streaked with tears.

Bic handed her the phone and she dialed, then put the little black phone to her ear. "May I speak to Virginia?" she asked after a moment. "Tell her Penny Wilkes is calling."

Bic looked steadily at Mrs. Wilkes, watching her every move, he tried not to be too intimidating. He wanted her to sound calm on the phone.

"Virginia! How are you? Oh, that's good to hear... no, I'm not so good. Actually I'm in town, and I wanted to come... get you for lunch... so we can talk." Mrs. Wilkes anxiously nodded through Peppercorn's reply. "My goodness, Virginia, it sounds like you have a full day." Before she could say another word, Bic raised the silenced 9mm and pointed the weapon at Mr. Wilkes.

Seeing this, Mrs. Wilkes became emotional. "It's Sam. I didn't know what to do . . . who to turn to, so I found myself in a cab... all the way out here. I'm not but ten minutes from your house, and I really need to talk to you, even if we just go for coffee..."

She paused, listening, nodding.

"Okay... I'll pick you up soon... *thank* you."

She handed the phone back to Bic, who disconnected the call.

"You did good, ma'am."

"Now what?" she said.

Bic turned to face the road. "We drive." After a moment, he caught their eyes in the rear view and said, "You're gonna sit back there and behave, right Mr. and Mrs. Wilkes?"

"We will," came the reply.

"Good," said Bic. "How 'bout a little music then?"

He flicked on the radio. *Bad Moon Risin'* came on.

Bic smiled.

89

The cab idled outside the enormous wrought iron gate of Virginia Peppercorn's estate. Penny Wilkes was alone in the back seat of the cab, because Sam was gagged and hogtied with plastic zips in the trunk.

The gates swung open. Bic drove down the brick-paved driveway, glancing at the numerous white Greek-style statues that lined the way. The house seemed better suited to the Hollywood Hills, or else the deep South—something straight out of *Gone with the Wind*.

And at the top of the driveway, dwarfed to insignificance between massive white columns, stood Virginia Peppercorn.

Before Bic had fully stopped the cab, Virginia had marched down the front steps of her home and had already opened the cab door. She was in the cab almost before he realized it. Wasting no time, she said, "Alright, Penny. Talk to me."

Bic glanced at her in the rearview mirror as he put the cab into drive. Virginia Peppercorn was in her late seventies, and despite her best attempts, she looked every bit of it. Her hair was dyed a bit too blonde; her makeup was too heavy, with thick foundation and lots of color around the eyes. She reeked of expensive-smelling perfume.

Penny began to cry, and Bic knew this could get real ugly, real quick.

"What is it? What did Sam do to you?" Virginia demanded.

"I'm so sorry."

"Sorry for what?"

Bic drove through the gate and turned left onto the street. He kept one eye on the road and one on the rearview mirror. Penny just trembled as she stared at the back of his head.

Virginia put her hand on Penny's shoulder. "It's alright, dear, you can tell me."

Penny's lips quivered as she tried to speak.

"What is it?"

"We've been kidnapped."

"Excuse me?"

"We've–we've been kidnapped. Sam and I... and now you."

Bic pulled the cab over to the side of the road. He didn't want to be driving while dealing with whatever was about to happen with his new passenger. They were still in the exclusive neighborhood. There weren't any cars on the street, and he didn't see anyone around at all.

Virginia pointed at Bic. "Kidnapped... by this man?"

Penny nodded.

"Sir, do you know who we are?" Virginia Peppercorn said haughtily. "If you don't turn around this instant, the *best* thing that's going to happen to you is you'll spend the rest of your life in prison."

Bic turned and rested his 9mm on the seat, pointed towards Virginia. "I'm only going to say this one time, ma'am. Shut your mouth."

Virginia's eyes narrowed to slits. Her aggressiveness took Bic by surprise.

"You, sir, are nothing but an animal."

"Virginia, please, he's serious," Penny pleaded.

"He's not going to do anything with that gun," she said, pointing at Bic. "If he shoots me, he wouldn't get one dollar–just the electric chair."

"Virginia, please stop."

"What are you looking for, some drug money?"

Bic just stared at Virginia through his dark sunglasses. He had never seen someone express this kind of courage when staring down the barrel of a gun. Old lady Peppercorn ought to be pissing her pants.

Virginia tried to unlock the cab door, but she couldn't, so she rattled the door handle. "How much money do you want for your drugs? Hm? Five thousand? Ten?"

Bic smiled, thoroughly amused by this crazy lady's actions.

"Well?" Virginia said with wide-open eyes.

"I want a billion dollars."

"A *billion* with a B? Good Lord, you people are all the same. You're probably no better than your deadbeat father. How many kids between the two of you have you abandoned?"

Bic turned away from her and tried to stop the fuse of the cherry bomb she had just lit inside of him.

"Daddy issues," she continued, "what a big surprise. Is he the one who taught you how to cheat and steal like this?"

Bic looked out the front window, trying to stop the red sea of rage overtaking his body.

"Please stop," Mrs. Wilkes begged Virginia.

"Here's a novel idea—why don't you get a job and pay your own bills?" Virginia said as she reached into her purse, pulled out a wad of cash, and shoved the money into Bic's peripheral vision. "Here's a couple grand—now let us out of here so you can go get high and then crawl back into your cardboard box."

Bic slowly removed his sunglasses, still looking forward, as he asked calmly, "You want to know what my father gave me?"

"No, I couldn't care less," Virginia said.

Bic turned. His fiery eyes shook Virginia's confidence as he said, with a tornado of fury swirling within him, "He gave me a pork chop."

He squeezed the trigger. The lead slug made more noise snapping into Virginia Peppercorn's chest than it did exiting the silenced weapon.

She died instantly, her painted eyes wide in shock. Bic grabbed the wad of cash from her hand and stuffed it into her slack, racist mouth.

Penny, screaming like a madwoman, tried frantically to open the door, clawing and pounding at the window like a trapped animal. Bic turned the gun toward her and shot her.

Bic then put the cab back into drive, and drove out of the neighborhood, making his way toward I-40. Several minutes into his drive, his fury faded, replaced by something else, something heavy and sore—he hadn't felt guilt often, but he had when Killebrew died, and he felt that now. What was he doing? How could he justify taking out these innocent people? His father had become an excuse to do something Bic feared that he liked to do: kill people.

This feeling was redoubled when he pulled his car over to a secluded spot and put two bullets into Mr. Wilkes, still in the trunk from being tied up and thrown in hours before. The look on the man's face—resigned. He had heard Bic kill his wife. His eyes had been red and wet, and he didn't look away when Bic shot him.

Returning to the road, he buried the guilt and the brewing self-hatred. The question was how best to dispose of these bodies and get on to his next kill. There was also the matter of disposing of the Wilkes's Town Car, which his employer had promised to take care of. Then it was off to a secluded area about forty miles east of Albuquerque to get the new vehicle and equipment his employer had arranged for him to pick up.

From there, it was on to the next kill.

90

Mack woke up in his bedroom with the taste of puke in his mouth. For an instant, he thought he might throw up again. With his head still thumping, he reached over to his phone. 9:42 PM.

He had a missed text from Caroline: *Call me when ur up.*

Somehow, he mustered up the energy to sit up. Miserable and with a head full of jackhammers, he dutifully grabbed the water glass. After the first few tough gulps, he found himself guzzling the cool water like a clean drain.

He was determined not to call Caroline, but seconds later, he had his cell phone to his ear, waiting for her to answer.

She picked up. "Mack, how are you feeling?"

"I'm okay."

"About what happened at the bar—"

"I'd rather not talk about it."

"Mack, I—"

"Caroline, what's going on between us?"

A pause. "What do you mean?"

He sighed. "I don't know how it happened, but I've started to look at you in a different way."

"I'm sorry, Mack. I don't know what to say."

"I guess I needed to let you know where I stand."

"You're important to me... but right now, it's just... "

"I understand." The knot in his stomach loosened a little. "How about we make this less awkward. Any thoughts on the case?"

She chuckled. "Right. I've been digging all afternoon and I think you're dead on." She took a deep breath. "You're not going to believe this."

"What?"

"I called the six remaining families to tell them what we thought was happening–and found out that Sam Wilkes, his wife, and their friend Virginia Peppercorn are unaccounted for."

"They're probably dead already."

"I think so, too. And there's something else," Caroline added. "It was the Wilkes I saw on the list, not Heather Wright. I'm sure of it. And the numbers next to the names, they must have been net worth amounts. They were all very large."

"So, if we're right, then who do we stake out?"

"I'm looking here at a map. Logically, if he were coming from Arkansas, he would take out Colin Shepard next. He's located just outside of Denver."

"Who's the next closest?"

"Frank Deeds, in Vegas. But his representative said not to worry about Mr. Deeds–he's living inside his casino."

"He might as well be living in Fort Knox. Looks like we're going to Denver."

"There's one more thing."

"What?"

Here she paused, "Who's Brooks Balter?"

"He's a stock analyst," said Mack.

"So, who's Brooks Balter?"

He took a deep breath and looked off to the side. "It's ridiculous."

"Okay. But I saw your notes in the file. You wrote 'home wrecker' next to his name."

Mack felt something tightening his face. "He slept with my mother when I was a kid."

"Well, that sucks. Wait, is that why... ?"

"Mom left? More or less."

"The one-night stands, the non-committal relationships. This is something you never dealt with, did you? Like, seriously dealt with it."

"Guess not. Anyway, just seeing the guy's name with everything else going on, I just lost it."

The phone went silent.

"Caroline, you there?"

"Yes."

"What is it?"

She took a deep breath. "Please don't be mad, but I kinda called him.

Mack sunk slightly. "You called Brooks Balter?"

"I didn't know, Mack. I swear. I'm sorry."

"Don't be sorry. Someone had to call the prick."

"Good, because we may have something here. One of their accounts shorted 200,000 shares of Incubus just before Larry Tukenson's death."

"Did he give you the name of the client?"

"Here's where it gets interesting. This account has been with the firm for over twenty years, and no one knows who really owns it. The account is set up as a limited liability corporation. Brooks says the account is now worth over a hundred million."

Mack scowled. "So, did he say why he gave the recommendation to short the stock?"

"That was also interesting. He said the LLC makes only a couple of trades a year, but when it does, they almost always turn a big profit. Brooks then goes in and finds out anything negative or positive he can on the company, and puts out a recommendation in the same direction as the picks for the LLC."

"So, he basically knows that whoever's behind the LLC is getting inside information, and he's not questioning it–he's even taking advantage of it. Good old Brooks."

"That's what it sounds like."

"Shady bastard. I'm going to report his ass to the NASD tomorrow."

"Um... you can't."

"Why?"

"To get him to talk, I gave him a deal."

"Screw him, he's got no proof. We'll still turn him in."

"Yeah, about that. I already emailed a signed deal to him."

Mack sighed. "What a slippery dick."

"Brooks will get his one day, but for now, we need to focus on this LLC. They could be our assassin's employer."

"Good call. I'll call my buddy Tom Walton at Langley. He's good at digging out information. If anyone can find it, he will."

"Great, so we'll have this thing wrapped up by the end of the week," Caroline said playfully.

"I've drunk to greater lies than that," he said without a shred of mirth.

91

Mack and Caroline left Denver International Airport in a rental car on their way to pick up a surveillance van at the local FBI field office. From there, they were going to Colin Shepard's house.

"Tell me about him," said Caroline.

"Fourth wealthiest man in America. Worth around $62 billion."

"Is he single?"

"I'm afraid you're outta luck. Shepard is a notorious family man. Married for over thirty-seven years. Father of five. There're all these photo ops of him at his grandkids' soccer games and dance recitals and whatever."

"Norman Rockwell material, huh?"

"Aside from the sixty-two bil, pretty much. But there's a catch, and see if this doesn't raise a few of those pretty little hairs on your neck. Why is Colin Shepard, dedicated family man, not leaving one stinking cent to any of his kids or grandkids?"

"Nothing?"

"Not a dime. When he and his wife are gone, all that cash is going into a foundation."

"Jeez," said Caroline. "I take back my question of his being single."

"Makes you think, doesn't it?"

"That we should be following this money?"

"Bingo. And I know just the guy."

"Let me guess. Tom Walton from Langley?"

"Bingo again."

A moment later, the man's voice came over the car's speakers.

"Listen up," said Mack, "I got you on speaker, so none of your usual filthy talk about Caroline. Think you can put some of those MIT skills of yours to work for me again?"

"What's the target?"

"I'm going right to the top of the food chain with this one. It's in reference to all these billionaires that have been dying lately. Perhaps you've heard of them."

"Um, yeah? What do you think, I live under a rock?"

"Well, listen, there's an LLC created under the name J.F.T. Enterprises that shorted 200,000 shares of Incubus right before the CEO died. The LLC is supposedly over twenty years old, and we can't figure out who owns it. I believe if we find the owners, we'll find who's behind these murders."

Tom Walton scoffed. "I thought you said you had a challenge for me."

"You the man," Mack said. "Oh, one more thing. Could you check and see if a DEA agent named Philip Utah has any weird money flows or is associated with any offshore accounts somehow?"

"Yeah, um, you sure you want to go there?"

"Why? Do I have to worry about you leaving any fingerprints?"

"Not a chance."

"Then what could it hurt? If he's clean, he's clean."

"But if he's not ...? Tell you what, I'll call you when I've got something."

"That's what I like to hear. I owe you big time, buddy. Talk to you soon."

"Checking Utah's sheets, huh?" Caroline commented. "If Bender finds out, he'll have your hide."

"He's got a connection to Gabriel Hernandez that he's not owning up to. I just have a bad feeling about him."

"You've got a bad feeling about everyone lately," she said.

92

While Mack and Caroline sped along the Denver roads, Bic Green was glancing at his reflection in the decorative mirrors of the Grand Cayman Casino foyer in Vegas.

He was more than a little embarrassed by his appearance. He had changed into a black Adidas sweat suit with a red three-line pinstripe, a Yankees ball cap tilted to his right, old-school Jordans with fatty red laces, grossly oversized rings with diamonds, and Gucci shades–and to top it off, a large steel chain with a big-ass padlock dangling from his thick neck.

His employer had arranged for him to check into the penthouse of the Grand Cayman under the alias of Black Magic, a little-known rapper from the East Coast who had just dropped his first album. The Grand Cayman was located on the Las Vegas Strip directly north of Frank Deed's casino, South Beach. The north end of the penthouse at the Grand Cayman, according to Bic's intel, was exactly 702 feet from the south end of the penthouse where Frank Deeds was currently living.

Bic felt like he was wearing a bad Halloween costume–in his business, you didn't want to be memorable, and you especially didn't want to draw extra attention to yourself.

At the same time, he realized he didn't have to worry about casino security snooping into his business. As long as he was disguised as Black Magic, security was used to every wannabe newcomer to the rap game coming to Vegas and throwing money around like it grew on trees. He knew they wouldn't give a second thought to him renting the penthouse; it was almost part of the cookie-cutter marketing plan of the music business.

Bic had never been to Las Vegas and was amazed by the grandiose magnitude of everything. At 1:00 in the afternoon, the place was hopping, the huge room echoing with the ringing of slot machines and sporadic howls from the craps and blackjack tables as people cheered on a hot roller or a dealer bust.

"May I help you, sir?" a young, dark-haired lady asked him with a brilliant smile.

He hesitated as he prepared to talk like he figured Black Magic would. "Yeah, yeah, I could use a little help." He smiled, showing off the gold front in his mouth.

He was nervous, waiting for the girl to burst out laughing at how ridiculous he was acting—but to his surprise, the lady looked at him with a flirtatious grin.

"Your name, sir?"

Bic cleared his throat, "Black Magic."

Her eyes enlarged a little. "We were expecting you. Welcome to the Grand Cayman. I see you're staying in the penthouse. You'll love it."

Bic nodded. "Ya know it."

Twenty minutes later, Bic stood on the balcony of the Grand Cayman's penthouse. The area on the roof of the hotel was more like a backyard, completely planted with grass, a sundeck area, and a nice-sized pool with an offset Jacuzzi. More importantly to Bic, this area was on the far north end of the building and couldn't have been more perfect for the job he needed to do tonight.

Bic walked to the railing and looked over at the top floor of the South Beach casino. Just like his penthouse, the one on the top of South Beach was built with ceiling-to-floor windows.

After determining the angle was acceptable for a kill shot, Bic rolled his golf travel case into the bedroom and lifted it to the bed. He opened the case, but where a true East Coast rapper might have been greeted by the sight of gem-encrusted platinum Honma clubs, this golf case had been retrofitted to hold his own special type of equipment. A .308 sniper rifle with Sound Tech M-CAM suppressor, a Raptor 6-power night-vision scope, an Omni-Mission telescopic sight with Horus reticule, a Leica LRF 1200 laser rangefinder, all set snugly in the case, along with a pair of Leica 8X32 binoculars and a box of HJ Ballistics 168 HPBT ammo.

Satisfied, Bic grabbed a burner phone, sat down on the bed, and dialed.

"Hello?" said Gracie.

"It's so good to hear your voice."

Her sweet laugh came back at him. "What, did you get a new number?"

"Yeah, I don't want to alarm you," he said, gathering his thoughts.

"What's wrong?" she asked quickly, "Oh no, please don't tell me the investors took their money back. I just signed a ten-year lease on that building in Chicago I told you about."

Bic laughed, "Don't worry, the money's already in your account–they can't take it back."

"Silly, I mean are *you* okay."

"I'm fine, sweetie, but we do have a slight problem."

"You know I can't handle the unknown! What is it?"

"One of our potential investors that I showed your thesis to might be trying to steal your idea," he said, his eyes closed. He hated lying to her, but the truth was not an option.

"Oh my goodness!"

"Don't worry, this is part of the pharmaceutical business. A cancer-curing drug is the crown jewel to these people, so it's no surprise someone might be coming after it."

"What should I do?"

"You need to be very secure with all of your information. I have a friend who can help us out–he's going to give you a secure new phone number and internet access. But until then, I need you to go completely off the grid for a few days–maybe even stay with a friend."

"Unc, you're scaring me," Gracie said.

"I'll have it sorted out in a week. We've worked hard for this. I just want to be extra careful."

"Okay."

"One last thing," Bic paused. "I need you to put your phone in the microwave and destroy it, then go buy a phone off the shelf–with a new number. Then call me at this number, and I'll have your number."

"You serious?"

"I'm afraid so. Don't take chances with security when it comes to something this big."

They said their goodbyes and hung up.

Bic lay on his back on the soft silk sheets with his eyes closed. *Not enough*, he thought. *But enough for now.*

93

Mack glanced at his watch: 8:10 PM. He and Caroline had spent the last two hours in the back of a surveillance van watching over Colin Shepard's ranch. The van was parked to the far-right side of the long driveway that led up to the six-car garage on the right edge of the main house. The ranch consisted of a large horse farm surrounded by neat white wooden fencing, with several new red-and-white barns sprawled across the acreage. The main house was elevated on a hill overlooking two lakes.

Sighing, Mack rubbed his eyes and opened the curtain separating the cargo area from the driver's compartment to look outside through the front windshield. The sun was just dipping below the horizon. Mack figured there would be no action until after dark, but he still had his doubts about parking the van in the driveway of the main house. The white Ford E250 surveillance van resembled a contractor's service van, with a red fiberglass ladder resting on the rack on top. So that the surveillance van didn't stick out, they had another white box van parked directly in front of their own, and a grey sedan parked next to that.

The surveillance van was parked on the outside of the driveway. On its right side was a steep, graded hill that led to the first of two lakes–large ponds, really. To the left was an expansive yard sprawling in front of the main house.

Mack glanced over at the two LCD monitors mounted on the desk built into the cargo wall. Each monitor had two video camera feeds, so the screens were split into equal halves to show two images each.

"I'm not feeling too good about this," he muttered to Caroline.

"We're in a good spot. Don't worry."

Using a joystick control, Mack rotated the roof camera toward the lake. "I wonder if anyone has ever had a little too much to drink and driven off into the lake."

Caroline, taking a seat next to Mack, grinned. "Falling off that little cliff would sober someone up real fast."

Mack laughed, then suddenly turned serious. "You need to put on your vest."

"Relax. This van is a tank. We can't be shot, and no one can get in."

He opened the curtain separating the cargo area from the driver's compartment and pointed at the windshield.

She replied, "What of it? That windshield is layered with polycarbonate and is completely bulletproof."

"Famous last words," Mack said. "And who was it that badgered me for years about my vest until it finally saved my life?"

"Fine," she said.

Mack scowled skeptically.

"I said I'll put it on."

He smiled, then opened the curtain and looked out the windshield again.

He looked at his watch: 12:05 AM. He squeezed a blue racquetball to help maintain his alertness.

Caroline reached across him to grab a pencil off the desk, leaving sweet jasmine smell of her perfume in her wake. The last six hours had been torture, as she moved around him in the confined space, and he fought the urge to kiss her.

"You're looking tired," she said, opening a crossword puzzle book. "Go ahead and take a nap."

"I guess one of us has to be first to get some sleep." He shifted in his chair, trying to get comfortable.

The monitor light flickered before Caroline's face, drawing Mack's attention to it. A man dressed in dark clothes stood in front of the van.

Mack lunged toward the driver's compartment and yanked open the curtain. Gabriel's eyes widened as they peered at Mack through the windshield. Mack froze as he stared at two handguns as big as cannons that he hadn't noticed on the video feed–pointed toward his head.

The guns flashed bright as twin bullets simultaneously exploded toward Mack. The polycarbonate-layered windshield spider-webbed but remained intact.

Gabriel dropped down, invisible behind the van hood, but as quick as he disappeared, he had jumped up onto the hood of the van and swung a huge ax into the windshield.

The ax blade cut a massive gash into the glass.

He hopped off the hood with tremendous speed, and when he landed, he had thrown the ax aside and had redrawn his two hand cannons.

"Say hello to God for me," Gabriel slurred through a wicked grin.

Frozen in terror, Mack focused on Gabriel's hands as he pulled the trigger.

94

Bic lay on the soft penthouse lawn next to the pool, dressed in green fatigues.

He had been lying there for hours. Deeds hadn't been in his penthouse since 6:00 PM. He was an avid fan of *Saturday Night Live*, according to the intel, and almost never missed an episode. Deeds was evidently a man of habit, too–like most of these men were–and he always sat in the big leather chair in the center of the media room facing a massive wall-mounted plasma TV.

Bic shifted his position slightly. The shot would be good, clean. With the bullets he was using, the penthouse's glass wall wouldn't be a factor.

Bic checked his watch–11:30 PM–maybe Frank wouldn't be watching his favorite show tonight. Bic felt a faint thrill of relief at the idea of not having to kill this man. But the soldier in him, who was trained to kill, knew he had to carry out his mission, or there were going to be consequences.

A sudden flare of light caught Bic's eyes through his scope. He looked. The plasma was on now. He could see the top of Deeds's shoulders and the back of his bald head over the chair.

Bic used the spotting scope to scan the room for any visitors. Deeds, a divorcee, usually slept alone–except for the occasional twenty-something showgirl. But there was no one else to deal with.

Bic reengaged his rifle. Peering steadily through his scope, he zeroed in on the back of Frank Deeds' head. And with a shallow breath, silently, he squeezed the trigger. Deeds's body pitched forward. His blood painted the television.

Number eight, crossed off the list. Deeds was dead.

Bic grabbed his rifle, rising quickly. The shot he had just fired was like the shot fired at the start of a race. This death was no accident, and so the clock was ticking. Sometime, hopefully no earlier than tomorrow, Deeds' body would be discovered, and there would be a manhunt for his killer.

Within minutes, Bic had put his Black Magic disguise back on and disassembled his sniper rifle. Within the next 24 hours, he would drive to Palo Alto to take out number nine, and then it was up to Seattle to finish the list.

And though he dismissed it, that thought, too, gave him an unwelcome thrill of relief.

95

Caroline yelled for Mack to get out of the way, before ramming him away with her shoulder.

Before Gabriel could fire again, she opened fire with an MP5 submachine gun seated against her shoulder. The gun spat fire, sounding like a hundred cannons exploding in the tight confines of the cargo box. The rapid stream of lead smashed the already-battered windshield into ruin, sending a fountain of safety glass and bullets spraying out into the darkness.

She ceased firing, keeping the gun at the ready.

"The safety door," Caroline yelled as she pointed the MP5, ready to fire if Gabriel reappeared.

Mack sprang into action as he lunged forward and pulled the metal door shut.

He looked back at Caroline. "I froze *again*," he said.

"I had your back this time," she said.

"I felt the heat of that bullet as it zinged past my head. If you hadn't pushed me–Jesus, my ears are ringing." Mack looked at the door he had just shut. "I'm not sure we should have locked ourselves inside this box."

Caroline straightened slowly and looked at the monitors. Everything appeared surreally peaceful, as it had only moments ago, only the intense reek of gunfire betrayed that serenity. What the monitors didn't show was their assailant. He might be dead just beside the truck. Or he might not be dead at all.

"You think you hit him?" Mack asked.

"Ordinarily, I'd say yes. But the SOB's pretty wily."

"My ears are still messed up. Can you hear any movement outside?"

She shook her head. "I can hardly hear anything."

"We have to go out and deal with this."

Caroline nodded. As she reached for another clip for the MP5, she stopped, and her fearful expression drew Mack's eyes to what she saw.

In the monitor. Gabriel had reappeared in front of the van. He paused, then threw a Molotov cocktail through the shattered windshield.

The bottle tumbled end over end like a flaming baton landing in the front section of the van. A solid thud against the steel partition door was followed immediately by the unmistakable roar of an explosion.

Half of the monitor screen went fuzzy.

Mack jumped back into the chair in front of the computer and grabbed the roof camera joystick. Caroline called 911, letting them know they were trapped in a burning vehicle, and a homicidal maniac was trying to coax them out.

Mack rotated the roof camera, trying to ignore the fiery hell outside as he attempted to locate Gabriel. "Hold still, you bastard!"

"The closest fire truck is fifteen minutes," said Caroline.

"How about the closest morgue?"

"We have two ways out," Caroline said, eyeing the van's back doors doubtfully.

"He's probably waiting for us to come out that way, plus it's locked on the outside with a padlock."

Caroline touched the steel partition door at the van's front, but pulled her fingers away quickly. "*Ouch, hot!* Well, no way we're going through that door."

"Think we can wait it out until the fire department gets here?"

"We'll be baked alive in minutes–" Caroline coughed, "or choked to death even faster."

The heat was climbing rapidly as a fine gray haze, and an awful burning plastic smell thickened in the van. Mack pointed the MP5 at the rear door. "Cover your ears."

He was on the verge of squeezing the trigger when a voice spoke through the walkie-talkie, they had set up with the Shepards. "Are you guys alright? The whole front of your van's on fire!"

Mack grabbed the two-way radio from the desk. "Mr. Shepard, this is Agent Maddox. Gabriel is still on the loose. Do not come out of your safe room."

The billionaire answered urgently, "He's just shoved a piece of cloth into the gas tank and is trying to light it."

Mack pointed the MP5 at where he thought Gabriel was standing outside the van, and fired four quick shots. The bullets clanked right through the sheet metal.

He picked up the radio. "Can you still see him?"

"He backed away real fast."

Three shots clanked into the rear of the van. Mack and Caroline dropped to the floor for cover.

"Is he shooting at us?" Mack asked

"No," Shepard said. "He just ducked, then ran."

"Police?"

"*The cloth is lit! It's going to blow! Get the hell outta there!*" Shepard yelled.

Suddenly a new voice came over the two-way radio. "Hang on, rookies."

"Moretto!" Mack shouted. "Where are you?"

"Coming down this long-ass driveway."

"Just step on it, will you? This maniac just shoved a cloth fuse into our gas tank and lit it."

"Relax, kid, the van's not gonna blow up."

"Thank God."

"At least I'm 75% sure it won't."

"*Seventy-five percent?*"

"Oh, sweet Jesus," Mack heard Moretto say, just as a thud sounded against the rear door of the van. Given the explosion that immediately followed, Mack knew Gabriel had just hit the back of the van with another Molotov cocktail. Flames began to lick through the bullet holes in the sheet metal.

Parts of the interior near the bullet holes caught fire immediately. Cursing, Mack and Caroline grabbed whatever they could to smother the flames. They succeeded, but the cargo area had filled with acrid smoke.

96

"They're gonna be burned alive in that holocaust," Moretto growled, as he turned sharply to the left, off the driveway and onto the front yard, in a military-style Hummer.

TJ, his 9mm ready, scanned for Gabriel out his open passenger window. Moretto broke sharply, almost spinning the Hummer out before stopping about thirty yards from the burning van.

"Kid, hang tight, I'm gonna push you into the lake," Moretto shouted into his two-way radio.

Mack didn't respond. The van was engulfed in flames.

"I got you covered," TJ said, as he jumped out of the Hummer and took up position behind the vehicle. Moretto hit the gas hard and closed the gap rapidly between his Hummer and the driver's side of van.

Despite the size of his vehicle, the heavy, parked armored van didn't move easily. Moretto cursed and fought with his truck to get the van to move.

Taking this time was making him a sitting duck, so Moretto reached for the gun he had put on the seat beside him. *Oh no! Where the heck was it?* It must have been tossed onto the floorboards during the collision. He didn't see TJ or Gabriel anywhere, but knew both were playing cat and mouse too close to his vehicle.

The flames from the van now consumed the front end of the Hummer.

With the accelerator pedal buried, he continued to push. The Hummer hadn't been designed as a bulldozer, but it was doing a fine job. Soon the van began to slide down the hill toward the lake. When the grade grew steep enough, the van tipped and began to roll into the water.

The flaming van tumbled down the hill out of sight and into the water with a splash. Satisfied, Moretto scanned the floorboard frantically, but couldn't see his gun.

He checked his perimeter. Neither Gabriel or TJ were in sight. He felt around in earnest for his gun, reaching deep into the floorboard areas of both the driver's and passenger's sides. Then he heard two shots fired, and TJ screamed his name.

Moretto sat up and looked out the driver's side window. Gabriel was standing fifteen feet away from the Hummer, engaged in a firefight with TJ, who was pinned down in front of the second van.

Gabriel must have had eyes in the back of his head, Moretto thought, because the instant his head rose above the window frame, Gabriel extended his other arm behind him and loosed several bullets in Moretto's direction.

Moretto reacted quickly, jamming the Hummer into reverse and hitting the gas as Gabriel fired. The bullets cracked through the window. Two zinged by Moretto, but a third caught him in the left arm. Cursing, he put the Hummer in drive.

As he drove, Moretto turned left to get a bead on Gabriel.

Moretto then turned back to the right. If he didn't have a gun, he would have to use the only weapon he had to smash the psychotic scumbag.

Moretto crashed the flaming front end of the Hummer into the gray sedan in the last spot he saw Gabriel. Metal scrunched sickeningly as the Hummer lurched to a dead stop.

97

The surveillance van lay on its passenger side at the bottom of the lake. Small streams of water came through several bullet holes, but flowed heavily through a one-inch gap in the front steel partition door. Mack's greater concern was Caroline. She had hit her head during the fall and was now unconscious.

The crash had also warped the partition door frame, preventing escape in that direction. The cargo area was already half-full of water. Mack stood holding Caroline. He wasn't sure what happened; all he could recall was their mingled screams as they were tossed around like rag dolls while the van tumbled down the hill.

She was breathing normally, which was good. And at least one of them was conscious. Mack had attempted to open the rear doors, but they were too damaged to open easily.

Mack vacillated, in a panic. He needed all his strength to break through the rear doors, but he couldn't let go of Caroline. If he did to force the doors open, she would drown. "I can't make that choice," he whispered quietly, looking down at her. "I promise, I will never let you go."

"I hope I smashed your ugly head into a million pieces!" Moretto screamed into the wall of flames, seconds after he had crashed the Hummer into the side of the gray sedan.

He thought for an instant he'd crushed the bastard, then thought blood loss was causing him to hallucinate. Gabriel flew from the roof of the sedan through the flames onto the hood of his Hummer. Blue-white flashes emerged from the 9mm in Gabriel's right hand, which was pointed in the direction Moretto had last seen TJ. Gabriel wasn't looking in that direction, though. He was looking directly at Moretto— down the barrel of his other 9mm.

The detective stared into the black-eyed snake gaze as Gabriel mouthed *"It's time to fly away, little birdie."*

The gun in Gabriel's left hand flashed twice, and Moretto went numb as two hollow-point bullets ripped through the windshield and into his chest. A sudden, thick gout of blood spurted out the side of Moretto's mouth. He struggled to say something, curse out this killer who had murdered him, but his lips only twitched silently as Gabriel sprang off the Hummer hood, both guns blazing.

98

"Moretto!" TJ watched Gabriel fire two shots into the Hummer's windshield through the wall of flames. He erupted out of a squatting position, like a sprinter at the starting gun, behind the second van and charged toward the fire, unloading his clip at the assassin.

The last shot hit Gabriel in the left shoulder, knocking him off his feet and onto his back. TJ jumped headfirst at him.

He straddled Gabriel's chest. The man had lost both of his guns in the skirmish.

Gabriel thrust his arms at TJ's midsection, trying to throw him off. An All-American wrestler, TJ knew there was no way Gabriel was getting him off as he centered his two-hundred-pound frame right on the bastard's chest.

"I'll gonna *kill you!*" TJ screamed, raining down a flurry of lefts and rights onto Gabriel's face. This assassin wasn't leaving Shepard Ranch in cuffs, he was leaving in a body bag.

TJ swung with such force he tore the skin off his knuckles as he landed blows. Gabriel's skull recoiled repeatedly off the ground.

Loud horns and flashing red-and-white lights appeared out of nowhere. Squad cars and fire trucks raced down the long driveway.

Something tore into his midsection with searing pain. Instinctively, he grabbed for the blade with both hands, stopping the cold steel from plunging past his thick stomach muscles. TJ groaned as he fought to not let the knife go in any deeper.

Gabriel pushed harder, fighting TJ's strength and the lack of leverage from being pinned.

He needed to disengage, but found himself trapped—he had been paying attention only to the hand with the knife, but in the confusion,

Gabriel had gotten him in half-guard with one leg. If the bastard was able to wrap his second leg around him, he would gain the leverage needed to bury the blade in his stomach.

TJ yelled as Gabriel twisted the knife in his guts. He clenched Gabriel's wrist with all his might, fighting furiously not to allow him to sink the blade in any further. The pain in his midsection flared like a bolt of lightning, threatening to sear away his consciousness.

Through a haze of agony, he saw that his opponent had freed his other leg and had it wrapped around him.

Quickly, TJ released his right grip and buried his thumb inside the bullet wound on Gabriel's shoulder.

Gabriel howled something unintelligible as his body recoiled from the pain. TJ pulled himself off and rolled rapidly across the ground away from him.

Two firemen quickly ran up to him. One dragged him about twenty feet away from the burning vehicles, while the other threw a heavy silver blanket over his legs. It was only then that TJ realized that his lower half was on fire. He pointed to the Hummer, and screamed at the firemen to save Moretto.

The firefighters rushed to the burning vehicle and pulled Moretto out. The instant TJ saw the dangling, lifeless arms, he knew his partner was dead, and his rage suddenly reignited. He kicked the blanket off and stood. Ignoring the stench of his own burnt flesh, looking around for a gun.

He had only one thought in his head: he was going to put a bullet right in the middle of his head.

"Where's that bastard who was trying to kill me?" he yelled to the three officers who emerged from the other side of the Hummer.

"He's gone," one of the officers replied.

"Someone give me a weapon," TJ demanded as he flashed his badge at the three officers. "He couldn't have gone too far."

One of the three officers reached down to his ankle and pulled out his backup gun, extending the butt toward TJ.

"Hey," one of the firemen yelled at TJ as he stalked off, checking his weapon for ammo, "the 911 call was from two people trapped inside a burning van!"

99

Mack wasn't sure if his foot was broken yet from repeatedly slamming it against the rear doors of the van. He was still holding up Caroline, but it didn't seem to matter–the doors wouldn't budge.

He shined his flashlight and saw there was only about a foot of air left in the top of the cargo area of the van. He was doing his best to hold Caroline's mouth above the waterline. She was still unconscious, and Mack was about to suffer a fate worse than death right before he died: he would have to watch her drown.

Mack held her close and whispered into her ear, "I'm not afraid anymore. I'm done suppressing my feelings to protect myself–you're perfect, and I don't care if one day you might leave me. I'm madly in love with you. I need you to know that." As Mack finished, he gave her a gentle goodbye kiss on the lips.

Caroline's eyes fluttered open. The instant Mack saw their fiery green color, his energy returned a hundred-fold.

"I'm guessing we're not doing too well here," she muttered, her eyes darting in several directions.

With the waterline up to both of their chins, she closed the gap and kissed Mack. The deep, quick kiss was filled with a passion that Mack had never felt before.

"Thank you," she said at last.

"Get ready–when the door opens, we'll instantly flood."

She nodded.

He sucked in the biggest breath he could and went under. The van was almost completely flooded now, the pressure between outside and inside would be almost equalized.

Mack positioned himself horizontally in the water. He grabbed onto the desk with both hands. He then thrust both legs into the rear door. He repeated the thrust several times, but the door didn't budge.

Mack came up for air and spoke to Caroline. "I'm going to kick the door. As I do, you need to pull the handle."

"Got it," she replied.

They both took a couple of deep breaths and went under the water together. Mack wedged himself between the desk and the rear door. He gave Caroline the thumbs-up and she pulled on the door handle.

Mack thrust his legs into the door with everything he had. A dull thud echoed from his feet at impact. The door still didn't budge.

With his shoulders and back now wedged against the desk, he pushed against the door with all his strength. The veins in his neck popped out like steel cables. With his strength almost gone, he gave a final push. The door popped open about two inches, and a crushing tide rushed into the van.

Caroline tried to push the door open further, but she couldn't. Nearly out of breath, Mack swam up to the door and saw, through the crack, that the padlock was still intact. With his lungs tightening and his brain screaming at him for oxygen, he feverously pushed and pounded at the door.

This reckless action wasted what little oxygen he had left. Feeling as if he were about to slide into unconsciousness, he looked to Caroline for his last conscious thought.

She had retrieved the MP5 off the floor and was headed his way. Pushing past him, she wedged the barrel of gun into the two-inch gap between the two doors, and they both pushed, using the weapon as a crowbar.

The barrel bent as they pushed so intensely, but the doors only moved another inch.

Suddenly, they both stopped trying. They locked hands and gazed into one another's eyes to embrace the end.

Death was coming, and all he wanted to do now was tell her he was sorry he had brought it to her.

She pulled her Glock 17 from her underarm holster, put the end of the barrel flush against the shackle toe of the padlock and fired.

The report sent its shockwave slamming against his eardrums.

Mack threw his shoulder into the door with all he had, and it swung open.

100

At 8:36 AM on Sunday morning, Bic cruised by the Spanish-style mansion of Guy and Lindsey Braddick in Palo Alto, California. The sprawling two-story house, with its red-tile roof, was served with a patterned-brick horseshoe-shaped drive with a massive stone fountain centered in the middle. To Bic's surprise, there were no signs of extra protection anywhere around: no squads in the driveway, no suspicious vehicles on the street or in any neighboring driveways. Unless the FBI had set the perfect trap, number nine had no idea he was coming.

Unlike everyone else on the list, Braddick was young, only thirty-seven years old. Despite his youth, Guy Braddick had founded the largest social media company in the world. After successfully navigating his company for the last fifteen years, he had been rewarded with an $82 billion net worth.

Comfortable with what he had observed, Bic was in position ten minutes later. A row of bushes that ran along the side of the house up to the first of six garage doors provided perfect cover. With the Braddick's home spread over five or six lots, he wasn't worried about the neighbors seeing him.

Bic knew from his intel that Guy and Lindsey went to church every Sunday morning, leaving their house around 8:45AM. He watched through the hedge as, right on schedule, the leftmost garage door slid silently upward.

He heard car doors shutting. Not wanting the vehicle to back out, Bic sprung out from behind the bushes and ducked under the rising door into the garage.

Bic could see both Guy and Lindsey were in the car. He tapped on the driver's side window with the silencer on his Glock to get Guy

Braddick's attention.

The man looked up in utter disbelief. Bic couldn't tell if he was scared, or just shocked that someone had had the nerve to come into his garage with a gun.

"*Roll down your window,*" Bic rasped.

The man did so calmly, which was strange enough. Stranger still were the actions of the man's wife, who made a reaching motion toward the back seat.

He was about to squeeze the trigger when a sight made him freeze.

Guy Braddick's wife was reaching for her children. It had been a reflexive act. The unthinking motion of a mother's instinct.

Bic's mind reeled. His intel hadn't said anything about kids. Since everyone else on his list was above fifty-five, kids had not been an issue.

With the gun still pointed at Guy's head, Bic peered into the back of the vehicle to see a little dark-haired boy–about ten–and his blonde-haired, blue-eyed little sister. Rage flowed up Bic as he wondered why his employers' intel hadn't told him about the kids. What the hell did they expect him to do?

"Please don't hurt my babies," Lindsey pleaded, with tears welling in her eyes. Bic looked at the woman, recalling the thump, and then the iron pan hitting his mom in the face. He couldn't leave these kids like he had been left.

He took a deep breath as he looked toward the open garage door. The quiet tranquility outside seemed so peaceful–to walk out of this garage, let these good people live, might just be his only chance at redemption.

But then he thought of Gracie. He might never be free of this employer, but regardless, he had to finish his job.

He said carefully, "I'm not going to hurt your children if you do exactly as I say."

A couple of minutes later, the crying kids were locked in the theater room, the young boy pounded on the door screaming out for his parents. Bic led Guy and Lindsey to the opposite side of the house, where they sat together on a couch.

He tried to harness the rage from his father to finish this job, but he couldn't. Even fifty years of fury couldn't justify this hit. He pointed the gun steadily at Guy Braddick's head as his eyes burned under the cover of his dark sunglasses.

"I'm sorry," Bic said softly as he squeezed the trigger twice. They died no differently than any of the others. But Bic was now a maker of orphans.

For the first time, he truly felt like Clarence Green. For the first time, he felt like a monster.

101

Caroline woke around 9:00 AM. "What happened?" she groaned.

"You don't remember?" Mack asked, rising from the comfy chair in the corner of the single-occupant hospital room.

He leaned over her. "Welcome to the concussion club. We're having buttons made."

"How long was I out?"

"About eight hours, give or take."

Her eyes searched the room, as if answers to shadowed areas lay there somewhere hidden. "You alright?"

"I'm fine, knock wood. A couple of bruises and scrapes. I've sustained worse on the court."

She looked at him then, and there was a smile in her eyes. It was the glint of shared intimacy. She remembered. Thank God, *she remembered that kiss.*

The door opened, and Bender entered the room.

Mack stood up quickly.

"Well, look who's up," said Bender.

"Not one for clichés, are you?" said Caroline.

"And I hear *you're* in pretty good shape," he said to Mack.

"Could be worse."

"I've already visited TJ," said Bender.

"TJ's here too?" said Caroline.

"He and Moretto came in like SEAL Team Six," said Mack. "TJ's got third-degree burns on his legs and a stab wound."

"Moretto?" she asked.

Mack looked to Bender, who shook his head slowly. "He didn't make it."

297

A heavy silence overtook the room.

"Dammit," Caroline said softly.

Bender put a hand to his forehead. "And I hate to be the one to compound bad news, but about twenty minutes ago, agents discovered Guy and Lindsay Braddick dead in their home."

Mack was speechless for a moment. "Hold on... what are you saying? Gabriel made it all the way to Cali from Denver? I mean, after the display we saw last night, I wouldn't have doubted anything about that man. But that kind of speed is just impossible. Am I wrong?"

"Apparently so. Or we're looking for someone else."

"Or we have a copycat," said Caroline.

"What about Ralston Templeton?" Mack asked quietly.

"Interesting you should ask."

"Not him, too."

"No, he's fine. I spoke to him personally this morning. Formally requested he let us take him and his family into protective custody. He refused, of course. He said, and I quote, 'No one can force me to leave my own home.'"

"Who does he think he is? Davy Crockett?"

"He said he's hired a professional security team to protect his family."

"He obviously doesn't realize who's coming after him. Gabriel will tear through any rent-a-cops like wet paper towels."

"Assuming Gabriel's actually gunning for him," said Bender. "At any rate, he's hired an elite team of ex-military special forces. They're probably already on site."

Mack shook his head. "This is bad."

Bender nodded in agreement. "Templeton's living up to his reputation as a control freak. It took me five minutes for him to agree to let even *one* FBI agent come assist with his protection."

"Well, he's a fool if he thinks–"

"You're the one he agreed to."

Mack looked at Caroline, who shrugged her shoulders. "I'm sorry, sir, I may have damaged an eardrum underwater. Come again? He wants me?"

"He knows you've encountered Gabriel twice now–and of all the agents in this investigation, you're still standing. No offense, Caroline."

Caroline held up her hands in absolution.

"I assured him that you'd be an asset to his team." Bender looked at his watch. "A car's waiting for you outside, Mack. You have a flight in forty minutes to Seattle. A chopper will then take you from the airport to Templeton's estate."

"Sir, I appreciate this, but I—"

"I'll want a full briefing when you arrive," Bender said, then exited the room.

102

Once Bender was out of the room, Mack plopped back down into the chair and slumped.

"I can't do this," he said to the ceiling.

"Do what?"

"I'm a fraud."

She paused. "Mack, what the hell are you talking about?"

He looked at her. "Come on. You know I froze up in the van. If you hadn't pushed me out of the way, I would have taken a bullet in the head."

"It all happened so fast. You can't fault yourself for that."

Mack shook his head in disgust. "You don't understand, Caroline. I choked when I saw him on the sidewalk, too. I had the draw on him, but I hesitated. Just long enough for him to turn around and shoot me."

Caroline looked at him sympathetically. "Mack, I know I'm one to talk, but you can't dwell on the past."

"It's not just the past," he said, looking away. "I'm... *broken*. Just like my father."

"You're nothing like your father," Caroline said definitively, sitting up. "You're just human. We all have issues, and we all fail." Caroline looked back over her shoulder. "Trust me, you can't let your failures define who you are. It will ruin you." She paused, as if the weight of what she'd just said was now crushing her.

"Samantha?"

She nodded. "Mm hm. It was a sex trafficking case. One of our wealthiest existing clients was accused. Samantha was his accuser. I'd convinced myself she was just some spoiled little brat with a predilection for bad choices. And we spun it that she knew what she was getting herself into. So, I defended the guy under the pretext that I was protecting the firm's billable hours. I was good, Mack. We got him off."

"You did what you thought was right," he said, feeling instantly ashamed for so trite a sentiment.

She shook her head. "I should have known. Samantha was the daughter of a family friend, a little girl I knew for—" It took a moment for Caroline to collect herself. "Anyway, her sister confronted me outside the courtroom after I won the case. The awful things she called me. After the trial, I did a little digging and found out that I'd set a monster free. He'd done this to a bunch of girls. Used them up, sold them. He wound up killing one of them."

Something was tugging at the corners of her mouth. She fought it by pursing her lips. "They found Samantha hanging in her closet." She wiped her eyes with the back of her hand. "After that, I quit practicing law and joined the FBI, determined to save the world in a day. You know?"

"I think sometimes you're driven to try and save *everyone*," he offered.

Caroline gazed into his eyes. "Right. But I realize something now. After meeting April. I understand the patience it takes, and how rewarding it is, if you can help one person. Anyway, the point is, nothing can change our mistakes, but our failures can change us for the better. They make us stronger, more capable, more determined to make things right."

"If I choke again, more people could die."

Caroline reached for him, locked eyes, "The man I know as my partner, the man I—" here she paused. "I *believe* in, won't."

He went to her and gave her a gentle hug, then kissed her cracked lips.

103

Bic boarded the Lear jet his employer had arranged for him to fly to Seattle. He was a soulless zombie, a preprogrammed killing machine. No control, no agency. Completely locked in. In order to save Gracie, he had to keep killing until he finished the list.

All he had left was Number Ten. After Number Ten was done, he wouldn't kill again. Somehow, after Number Ten, he would try to make right all the evil he had done.

How had this happened? Was it the Braddick family?

Was it the sight of those kids munching snacks and watching movies? Or the look in Guy and Lindsay's eyes when they turned away from their children for the last time?

What would his Mama think of him?

The hand of the devil was what he was. He knew that now. So perhaps he did have some agency. This is what he was at his core. His father's fault or not, the second he had made a choice to kill innocent people was the second he became a doer of evil. He wasn't just created by his father, he *was* his father. Evil in his heart, nudging him toward a dark desire that needed to be satisfied. After this job was done and Gracie was safe, he would find the next excuse to continue to kill.

A tingling numbness walked down his spine as his subconscious blurted out a question that echoed though his mind: *Am I a serial killer for hire?*

He drove through steady rain in downtown Seattle, the Templetons' home address punched into the car's navigation system. He had a wrapped pork chop lying on the passenger's seat. He could smell the thing, growing more rancid by the minute. It made him want to bring up his lunch.

Just get through the next couple of hours, and then this thing, whatever it was, would be over.

His burner phone rang unexpectedly. He kicked himself. He had forgotten to call Gracie back.

"Yo, Bic, it's Hawk. I'm in Chicago."

Bic's breath grew ragged. If his employers had hurt Gracie or kidnapped her or added her to the list, he would kill all of them in the most violent and gruesome ways he could imagine.

"Gracie okay?"

"She's fine, buddy, relax. I've got some news for you, and I didn't know how you would react, so I wanted to be in Chicago before I gave it to you. I found him."

Bic almost crashed the car upon hearing this. His temples throbbed. He could feel the rage coursing through him like lava.

"Where?" was all Bic could ask.

"New Orleans."

To New Orleans, thought Bic, and straight on through to Hell.

104

At 1:45 PM, the chopper descended toward the landing platform of Ralston Templeton's estate. Mack had figured Templeton's house was going to be enormous, but he hadn't expected the property to resemble a small college campus. More than one roofline popped out of the dense pine cover blanketing the lakefront lot.

He analyzed the area. All these beautiful landscaping features were bad news when you're trying to protect someone from being attacked. This wasn't going to be easy.

The property rose about ten feet above the lake. Dark, unworked rock lined the shore, and the ten-foot wall of jagged stone created hundreds of good hiding spots. That area would be impossible to survey from land, so someone would need to regularly inspect it by boat. Then you had to deal with the multitude of trees and shrubbery. An experienced sniper would be all but impossible to find in this environment. If he had to, he would be able to wait for days, undetected, until he got his shot. And then there was the sheer scale of the estate. If a man wanted to get lost on these sprawling acres, he could.

When the chopper landed, he was met by a fiftyish man dressed in green fatigues and holding an M-16.

"Sir, can I see your credentials for verification?"

Mack handed the man his ID.

"Agent Maddox, I'll need your weapons."

"Excuse me?"

"Sergeant's orders. No one on the premises except security will be armed."

"I can't have a weapon?"

"You're here as a consultant, sir. You'll need to leave the fighting to us."

Mack handed the man his 9mm. "I just had it cleaned."

Ten minutes later, Mack was taken to the five-bedroom guest house on the south end of the estate to meet with Sergeant Keith O'Donnell. The guesthouse was detached from the main house, which was located north and slightly west of their position. To the east was the lake. The sergeant and his men had already converted the guest house into military barracks. The great room had been turned into a sophisticated surveillance center, full of communications equipment and flat-screen monitors. The perimeter of the estate had already been salted with sophisticated sensors and video surveillance cameras. All the windows had been blacked out to prevent sniper fire. The dining and living rooms had been converted into supply rooms storing an array of impressive weapons, combat gear for both land and water use. They even had a fire-retardant bomb suit hanging from one wall.

Mack's talk with Sergeant O'Donnell was short and to the point: the sergeant made it clear Mack was there to provide real-time, FBI-vetted intelligence, period. If he or his superiors didn't like the arrangement, they were more than welcome to leave. Mack's phone rang as he concluded the short, harsh instruction.

"Mack, it's Tom," Walton said.

"Yeah, Tom. Find anything good?"

"I can't talk long right now, but wanted to let you know I found a lot of good information on where to go hiking in Utah."

"Utah?"

"Yeah, Utah, remember? You asked me to find the best spots for hiking. I did, but they're not cheap."

"Right, but you found some—good. I'll talk to you later."

Mack hung up, his mind troubled. Tom had found a match on Phil Utah for the insider trading.

And Utah was an old buddy of Bender's.

105

The Big Easy, the Birthplace of Jazz, the City that Care Forgot—just the things that would have drawn his father to New Orleans. Bic stood in front of rustic, white-washed St. Augustine Catholic Church in the Tremé neighborhood. A fat, full moon, still low in the sky, threw his shadow over the church doors. He rechecked the text message to make sure he hadn't given the cab driver the wrong address.

This was the place.

His mind wandered as he stood before the church doors, but what drew him back to focus were quick, vivid flashes of his father bashing his mother's skull in with that hot iron skillet. Swing after swing, thud after thud, he once again watched that murdering bastard end his mother's life.

Then he remembered *his* turn, and felt a cold chill squeeze his neck as the evil man choked him, while shaking him so hard the back of his head smacked repeatedly against the concrete floor.

With the phrase his father had given him ringing through his thoughts, he kicked the large wooden church door open, knocking it off its hinges.

He marched into the church, the fury completely consuming his mind as he screamed, "Clarence Green, it's pork chop-eatin' time!"

For a long, quiet moment, there was no response.

His breath rasped from his chest. The silence of the place enveloped him totally as he darted several glances around. Tears were flowing down his cheeks.

Behind the altar on the back wall, a single light shone on a simple crucifix. The eyes of Jesus Christ captured him.

God Himself was telling him it was time to forgive.

"I don't think I can," Bic mumbled.

The eyes drew him in, and Bic suddenly found himself kneeling in front of the altar, his arms extended like the arms of the Lord.

An elderly black man with a fringe of gray hair appeared. Bic hopped to his feet, his tranquility replaced with a surge of adrenaline.

"Is it you?" Bic's voice shook with a deep anger as he took several steps forward. "Is it you?"

The old man didn't answer. Bic reached out with his massive hands to grab hold of him. The stiff white clerical collar on the man's neck stopped him.

"You're a priest?" Bic asked numbly. As his vision cleared he began to realize that rage had superimposed his father's face over this priest's.

The man nodded, the quickened breath of panic coming from his nose. His trusting light brown eyes never looked away. Bic now saw this man was in his fifties–not in his eighties, as his father would have been.

"I'm sorry, Father." Bic let go of the man, reached into his pocket, and brought out a bundle of hundreds. "I'll pay for the damage."

The priest shook his head. "I'm not happy about the door, but I understand." The priest extended his arm and guided Bic to the front pew. Bic hesitated, then sat, and the priest joined him.

"I've been expecting you, Bic Green." The priest's face lit up when he saw Bic's reaction. With a calming smile, he said, "I knew you would come looking for your father someday, as did he."

His confused numbness turned to red-hot fury at the priest's words. "Where is he?"

"I'll show you in a moment," the priest said. "But would you indulge me first?"

Bic rose to his feet, "No. I won't let him get away."

"He has nowhere to go, Bic. Please, you'll have your way."

Bic stood, his rage muddled by the priest's tranquility.

"Bic, you came here to kill the man who took your mother's life. I can understand your anger, but what would killing him accomplish?"

"It would–" Bic began to say, but faltered. He had never thought past the act itself. It had shaped him, forged him. For his entire life, he had lingered in that precise moment, never venturing beyond. "It would help me," he said at last. "Because I *need* it." He almost blushed at how childish and hollow it sounded.

The old man looked at him, compassion in his eyes. "You need it only to feed the darkness."

At an intellectual level, Bic knew the priest was right, but what did the darkness know about payback? He owed his father something, and he was going to give it to him in grand fashion.

The priest took a deep breath. "But I won't break through to you, will I? You were born in the darkness, and you'll die in the darkness as well. Come, I'll take you to your father."

"I'm not leaving this church until I see the priest holes."

The priest became enamored a bit, "You did your homework."

"A church this old, there's bound to be one."

"You're right, but there's nothing to find."

"Show me."

"Fair enough," the priest walked behind the altar and pulled up the green linen cloth to expose a metal trap door built into the floor.

Bic bent down and opened it. He illuminated the light from his phone to reveal a small empty room made out of brick.

"You ready now for me to take you to him?"

The priest led Bic out a door at the end of the south transept.

A moment later, Bic stood over a small headstone, and shined his flashlight to expose his father's name scratched into it. The writing appeared to have been done by a child still learning to write.

He regarded all the shabby homemade headstones and artifacts scattered throughout the graveyard. This was a poorhouse for the dead. Coffins jutted up from the ground in all directions like weeds.

"When did he die?" Bic asked hollowly.

"A couple of months ago."

Bic shook his head. He didn't know if he was going to walk away, or start digging up his father's grave with his bare hands.

The priest touched his arm. "Bic, I knew your father for six years. I realize this may not make a difference, but the man I knew was much different from the man you knew."

Bic looked at the priest, silently urging him to tell him more.

"When he came to our doorstep, he was nothing more than a scared little man at the end of a life filled with terrible sin. We got him off drugs, and he gained clarity on the man he wanted to become, and he gave himself to Jesus. Bic, I swear to you in this holy place that there wasn't a single day I knew him that he didn't regret what he had done to you and your mother."

Bic stared. His tears had stopped, clogged up by something–rage? Pity?

"Do you know what I've done because of that man?" he said.

"I couldn't even begin to guess," the priest said sadly. He pulled a folded piece of paper from his pocket and handed it to Bic. "Take this and read it. It's from your father. For you."

Bic unfolded the paper and shined the flashlight on the spidery scrawl.

Dear Son:

I know I changed the course of your life in the worst way on that horrible day, and for that I am sorry. I don't want to insult you by asking for your forgiveness. Instead all that I ask is you forgive yourself for the sins you have committed. If I can teach you just one thing as your father, the most important thing, it's never too late to place yourself in the hands of the Lord.

IT WASN'T TOO LATE FOR ME – IT'S NOT FOR YOU!

CLARENCE

He folded the letter carefully and put it in his front pants pocket. "Why didn't he find me to tell me this? The terrible things I've done… if only…"

"Would you have forgiven? He talked about your forgiveness every single day I knew him, from the first day he showed up right up until the day he died. You came here for blood and broke my church door. Those who dwell in darkness seek refuge in self-deception. You're no different."

Bic turned and walked out of the cemetery, feeling lightheaded. His mind raced out of control.

He needed to speak to Gracie. She could soothe his aching soul.

When he opened his phone, he saw he had an email from his employer.

Attached was a graphic of a map. Pinpointed was the location where Hawk was safe-keeping Gracie. It read, simply:

The job will be completed within twenty-four hours, or Gracie will substitute.

Crazy thoughts flashed into his head, destructive and self-destructive.

106

ongressman John Alfred Tidwell sat in his office at nine in the evening, highly agitated, waiting for a response from his hired killer. He had sent him several emails over the past nine hours, ever since he had received intelligence from his people that the assassin had unexpectedly flown to New Orleans.

Tidwell looked at the numbers on the list he had written down. With nine people crossed off the list, they were at a little over $200 billion in additional death-tax revenues for next year. But they had to hit $250 billion. Without half of Ralston Templeton's $120 billion-empire, Tidwell's bill would never pass, and the joint venture with Russia to harvest the world's largest oil and gas reserves wouldn't happen.

Thinking of what Parelli had said—about what the Russian mobsters would do to him if he wasn't able to get Templeton killed in the next couple of days—every passing minute without a response made Tidwell more certain the sonofagun had gone AWOL. With two days left, he couldn't afford to waste another hour.

Tidwell grabbed a pay-by-the-minute cell phone and placed a call.

"This is Jones," Parelli answered.

"Mr. Jones, this is—"

Parelli cut him off. "Where's our fundraiser?"

"Our main fundraiser, I believe, has left our campaign and unexpectedly gone to New Orleans."

"I'm going to pretend you just didn't say that. You just didn't tell me that, correct?"

"We can fix this."

"Would you mind telling me why on earth he did that?"

"My best guess is family business."

There was a frustrated exhalation on the other end. "I don't suppose he said anything about this to you."

"No. But he sent emails to a PI he hired where he mentioned looking for his father."

"What a cluster," Parelli muttered.

"Since he hasn't communicated with me, and considering our current time crunch, I think we need to move to Plan B for our final fundraiser."

"We'll send the guy who ran Chicago and Denver to take care of business."

"That's what I thought." said Tidwell.

"You have a problem with that?"

"No problem at all."

"On a related note," said Parelli, "my guys tell me there are some pretty heavy hitters running the campaign for the opposition in Seattle."

Tidwell shuddered as he pictured the impending standoff at the Templeton complex. "Yes. There's a group of highly trained professionals there."

"How many cats we talkin' about?"

"Six to eight. I don't have an exact number."

"I think we need to bring another player into the mix."

"Who?" Tidwell asked.

"Our guy from Chicago and Denver has an older countryman whose skills are equal, if not better. The guy's a tornado. Completely destructive."

Tidwell grinned. "He sounds perfect for a final campaign."

"We'll need your Salt Lake City contact to bring the new guy into the country."

"I'll take care of it," Tidwell replied.

107

Mack had spent the last six hours going over every aspect of the case. He had been assigned to one of the five guesthouse bedrooms by Sergeant O'Donnell, as a means of keeping the agent out of his hair. Mack had strict orders not to bring any "civilian drama" into the war room unless it was specifically requested.

At first, he'd chafed at this shabby treatment, but he quickly realized the necessity of an all-business approach. The contract Templeton had instructed his attorney to draft was an all-or-nothing proposition. The only upfront compensation for these men were living and operating expenses. Payment would be commensurate with performance. In other words, if Templeton, his wife, and his child were still alive a year from now, each man would be paid $10 million. If anyone in his family was killed, they'd get nothing.

Mack's case notes were spread out all over the bed. The room was large, furnished with a stylish king-size platform bed with matching dressers and nightstands, a daybed, and a luxury sofa. The only thing missing was a desk, which Mack would have greatly appreciated.

He reviewed every aspect of the case, trying to determine if he had one perp here or two. The DNA extracted from the sunflower seeds in Chicago was a perfect match to the traces of blood on TJ's shirt.

He flipped to a clean page on his yellow legal pad and wrote down a single question: *Why didn't Gabriel kill Colin Shepard?* He clearly had the opportunity to do so, but he hadn't. Instead, the little savage had focused solely on the FBI agents.

He put the Chicago and Denver files on one side of the bed, knowing for sure those were Gabriel's work. *Two killers,* he thought. *There's gotta be...*

He looked at the stack of twenty-two unsolved assassinations over the last three decades, all of which were tied together by a pork chop left at the scene and a peculiar array of killing techniques.

There was one immutable fact here. Gabriel would have been a kid when the first of the pork chop murders took place. This killer was probably in his mid- to late-fifties.

He grabbed his cell phone and called Caroline to see if she'd uncovered anything.

"Mack! Where are you?"

"I'm at Ralston Templeton's estate. How's your head?"

"Fine. I left the hospital an hour ago."

"I thought you were told to stay overnight. Are you at home?"

A long, silent moment passed. "No."

"Where are you going at this time of night?" He glanced at his watch.

"Look, you're not going to understand this," she began, "so I'm just going to lay it out for you. I got a call from Freddie. Something came up and I need to see him."

Mack felt something in his chest snap like a broken guitar string. "You're right," he said finally. "I'm not sure I understand."

"He called me about April. I'm going to meet him at the facility. Plus, it gives me a chance to end our relationship in person. After everything he's done for April, I owe him at least that. Please understand."

End our relationship? Mack's heart leapt in his throat at what those words meant to him. He tried to keep his head on straight. The call waiting prompt came over the line.

"Uh, listen, I have to go. Tom Walton's calling. Good luck with everything."

"Yeah, I'll talk to you tomorrow."

Mack clicked over to the incoming call. "Talk to me, my man, I need you to throw me a bone."

"Oh, I have a sauropod humerus for you!"

"I like the sound of that."

"The LLC JFT. Enterprise was established in 1972 in Switzerland. This particular LLC only has a twelve-digit number in the bank's digital records."

"What's that mean?"

"As far as the bank's concerned, the owner of this account is the twelve-digit number. If you have the account number and the password, you own the account. That's the Swiss for you, my friend. The only information on who owns this kind of account is kept on paper in a vault, with each account having its original paperwork in a safe deposit box only the bank president himself has access to."

Mack hesitated for a moment, thinking rapidly, then said, "I asked for a bone and you gave me chicken fat. Thanks for your help."

Tom laughed, "Oh, my friend, they haven't beaten me yet. The games have only just begun."

"How's that?"

"The *who* is still a blank, but not the *what*. I've started to track the in- and out-flows of money from this account. Over the last thirty days, it's been as active as a volcano. I'm trying to track down a couple of the transactions that were routed to banks in the Caribbean."

"I misjudged you, buddy. I owe you one."

"Listen, Mack, this is much more stimulating than I'd anticipated. Oh, hey, I almost forgot. I got some skinny on your Utah friend."

Mack felt his heart rate pick up. "Please tell me he shorted Incubus."

"No, but he bought a thousand put options on Texas Computer Corporation. Would you like to know when?"

"When?"

"One, count it, *one* day before Henry Barron was killed."

"No way. And you said a thousand!"

"Correctamundo. The stock dropped twelve dollars a share the morning after Barron was killed."

"I can't do that kind of math in my head. How much did he make?"

"One point two mil."

"Smoking gun. What now?"

"That's for you to decide, partner. What I did with the computer systems doesn't exist. My boss is very clear: no rogue projects without his knowledge."

Mack nodded. "This never happened."

"I'll call you once I nail down those transactions."

"Appreciate it." Mack started to hang up, but held off as he glanced down at the questions on his legal pad. "Wait, Tom, one more thing. Can you do some research and tell me what makes Colin

Shepard different from all the billionaires who were killed?"

"Um, I guess? Can you give me a hint what you're looking for?"

"A perp had a chance to kill him, but didn't." He quickly recounted the events of the last few days, ending with, "I'm not sure why Gabriel was even there to begin with."

"I'll check into his financials and let you know."

After the call ended, Mack took moment to think. Perhaps it was laying out the scenario for Tom in detail like that, but the reality grabbed his throat and squeezed.

This guy almost killed you twice...

He couldn't bring himself to finish the superstitious thought.

108

She couldn't tell Mack the truth about Freddie. It was killing her, but she just couldn't.

They'd shared a couple of kisses. That was all. And they'd weathered some storms together. And he knew her secrets and understood her and–yes, perhaps he loved her. And still she couldn't bring herself to tell him.

She took a left onto some side streets. She needed some time. It was ridiculous. She was only prolonging the inevitable with Freddie.

And what about *him*? She felt foolish, like a teenager trying to decide which pop star she wanted to date.

Caroline slowed the car to a crawl. She then stopped it altogether and got out. The air was sweet and Spring-like. She filled her lungs with it.

It was true what she had told Mack, that Freddie was good with April. But she hadn't told him everything–

Dammit! Why did that keep coming back to her?

"This is ridiculous," she said aloud, and got back into the car.

When she got to their agreed location–the parking lot of the rehabilitation center–before opening hours–Freddie was already there waiting for her.

Congressman John Alfred "Freddie" Tidwell opened the door to his limo and welcomed her in with a smile.

"Come here often?" he said playfully. His expression changed. "Hey. What's wrong?"

"We need to talk," she said, about to close the limo door.

An assault rifle appeared in the crack.

"Just come out quietly, Congressman. You too, missy."

319

The black van had pulled up next to the building with the stealth of a panther. Three figures in fatigues and balaclavas had crept up and now surrounded the limo.

"What is this?" said Tidwell.

A massive arm appeared alongside the rifle and grabbed Caroline.

"Ow! Let go of me!"

The voice behind the assault rifle spoke in calm, even tones. "We'll paint this parking lot with you if you don't shut up and come along quietly. Both of you. Let's go."

The partition separating the passenger area from the driver's cabin slid down, revealing a driver with a malevolent smile on his face. "Go now, Mr. Congressman," he said in a thick Russian accent. He yelled something to the commandos in his native tongue. One of them reached in, grabbed Tidwell by the shoulders, and pulled him out effortlessly.

"I'm coming!" Tidwell said. "Ease up!"

"We have no time for stupid games," said the driver. He addressed the commando holding Caroline: "What took you so long?"

"The dame took a detour," he answered.

A chill ran down her spine.

One of the commandos shut the limo door and patted the roof. The black van sped up, and the side doors slid open. Caroline and the congressmen were pushed in, followed by the three commandos.

They rode with guns trained on them.

There were no windows. They had no idea where they were headed.

109

"Sergeant," Mack called as he entered the great room.

The sergeant was seated at one of the folding tables his team had set up, consulting with one of his men. Both were dressed in fatigues. They appeared to be studying the building plans of the main house, along with diagrams of the grounds and surrounding areas.

"Agent Maddox. I can see you're ready to go this morning," said the sergeant, glaring disapprovingly at Mack's wrinkled clothes.

"Sorry, sir, I was up all night working on my assignment."

"Tell me what you have."

Mack talked quickly. "I have identified two assassins. One is in his mid-to-late fifties. He's highly skilled in multiple methods of killing, and he has sniper capabilities. This killer is patient and will use intelligence to outflank or outsmart us for an easy kill. I can't confirm his appearance, but I suspect we're looking for an African American male–according to an eyewitness–of above average height.

"The second assassin is Gabriel Hernandez." Mack pulled out his photo and handed it to the Sergeant. "He's in his late thirties and is also a highly-trained killer. He's taken a bullet to the left shoulder in the last couple of days. He's wily and *will* attack with intense firepower. In the past, he's used a rocket launcher and other explosives effectively, and was able to eliminate an entire SWAT team. He's a highly skilled sniper, able to achieve kill shots from over a thousand yards away."

Mack looked at the sergeant, who was scribbling intensely on a legal pad. When he was done, the sergeant looked up at Mack. "You have any other intelligence?"

"I'm not sure if it counts as intelligence, but I can offer a warning:

do not permit DEA agents in, especially senior officials who are operating out of their jurisdiction."

"I don't understand."

"Let's just say the DEA has an interest in gaining the upper hand in this case and have been duly admonished *not* to stick their snouts in our case."

The sergeant's face didn't express nearly the amount of surprise Mack had expected as he picked up his two-way radio and clicked the side button. "Gino, do not allow any DEA agents onto the premises. Or other government agents onto the premises without Agent Maddox's clearance."

"Yessir," Gino replied.

The sergeant cocked an eyebrow at Mack. "Anything else?"

"Not at this time, sir, but I have some inside people working on a couple of leads."

"Good. Makes me happy when my decisions are right. I noticed in your file you finished top in your class in sniper training."

"Yes, sir."

"If I need a spotter for one of my snipers, can you handle that assignment?"

Mack rubbed the top of his disheveled head. "Crack this entire case on no sleep *and* enter into combat duty? Sure, why not."

"Good. Now, go take a shower."

110

Driving north on I-5, Phil Utah was pleased to see the sign for the Oregon border looming ahead. The last fourteen hours had been long and tense. He had agreed to pick up the new "fundraiser" named Publio and deliver him personally to his Seattle target late that afternoon. With his high-level clearance, Utah had no trouble in ferrying him across the border.

He hadn't wanted to bring this lunatic into the country, but what choice did he have? He wasn't knee-deep in this manure, he was neck-deep. For the thousandth time, he glanced in the rear-view mirror at Publio, who lounged in the back seat. The Mexican's mean-looking face was set in a square Frankenstein skull. His dark eyes were set close together and topped by a shaggy, thick unibrow.

Since Utah had picked the man up, the Mexican hadn't said a single word the whole trip. He had nodded yes or no to every question Utah had asked him, but that was all. The only comfort Utah had was the unmarked Crown Victoria he was driving. Meant to carry dangerous criminals, the car was equipped with a protective Plexi shield separating the front and back seats. Utah was quite aware this animal might try to kill him. He had no assurance he was back in Tidwell's favor.

With a fourth of a tank and a full bladder, he pulled off at the next exit. His cell phone ring startled him, but not nearly as much as who was calling him.

"Utah here."

"Phil, my friend," Parelli replied. "I need to talk to Publio,"

"For what?" Phil scowled.

"Phil, I'm not asking."

"He doesn't speak a lick of English."

"*Hablo español, idiota.*" Parelli said fluently.

"Ah, hell." Utah pulled over to the side of the road. With nothing but pine trees and bushes in every direction, he could take a leak on the side of the road while Parelli talked to Publio.

Agitated, Utah opened his door and motioned for Publio to do the same. In a loud, slow voice, Utah said, "Here. Someone wants to talk to you."

Publio nodded and reached for the cell phone.

Utah handed him the phone and, wasting no time, took a few steps away from the car to urinate into a bush.

"I understand," Publio said.

Utah, still urinating, was dumbfounded by Publio's crisp, perfect English. An alarm went off in Utah's head at the sound of a spring-trigger release, followed by the sound of metal sliding against metal.

Before Utah could even finish, Publio had plunged the large blade that had sprung out from under his shirtsleeve deep into his side and twisted it a quick ninety degrees.

Utah fell to his knees, paralyzed by the single blow.

Publio violently pulled the massive blade out of Utah's body. He then grabbed the bleeding man by the hair and put the phone to his ear.

"We all get what's comin' to us," Parelli said. "Have fun burning in Hell, traitor. Oh, and about your little plan to screw us all? We hacked your computers two months ago. There won't be a single word sent out to anyone."

As Publio dragged Utah further into the forest, the agent had time to reflect on how much sustenance his body would provide the local scavengers.

111

Mack sat at the kitchen table of the guesthouse with Corporal Tim Riggs. The youthful-looking and square-jawed soldier was actually over fifty. His most telling features were his cauliflower ears that he'd acquired, according to Riggs, from his early years wrestling. Riggs always kept an eye on Sergeant O'Donnell, looking for any indication the sergeant might need assistance. O'Donnell was energetic and relentless. Mack had yet to see the sergeant go off to sleep.

Corporal Riggs explained to Mack the structure of the Marine fire-team. Each fire team had four men. One was the team leader, or corporal. In the Marines, five teams made up a rifle squad. For this operation, the sergeant had assembled two fire teams. All eight men had arrived and were ready for action, but so far there had been no sign of Gabriel or the other assassin.

Corporal Riggs and his team had the responsibility of maintaining the immediate perimeter around Templeton's main house. The second fire team, led by Corporal Crooker, was responsible for the outer perimeter–a much tougher job, as they had to cover the lakefront and all the surrounding forest. Mack hated to think that when one or both of these killers made their move against Templeton, some of these men wouldn't make it.

"Have you guys been working together since your service in the military?"

"The sergeant and I have. The other guys here served in the military around the same time we did, but not with us. Well, I'll be damned!"

A large black man still wearing his sunglasses walked into the room. Sergeant O'Donnell embraced him.

"Now, that man we *did* fight with in 'Nam," said Riggs, standing to embrace the man himself.

"Mack," the sergeant said, "meet your new best friend. Mack Maddox, this is Corporal Bic Green. He's going to snipe for us, and you're going to spot for him." The sergeant patted the large man on the back. "We haven't worked together since '75, but this time I figured I had ten million reasons to get this recluse to come out of hiding and finally join us for a job."

"Good to meet you, Mack." A massive hand thrust out to greet him.

Mack shook it. "Corporal."

"Call me Bic. If you're going to be my spotter, we need to be on a first-name basis."

"Bic, it is."

"Here's the contract with Templeton," O'Donnell said, holding out a document. "It's pretty standard, but I need you to sign it so we can get started."

Bic removed his shades to read the document.

Something about the man's eyes. They were like an albino's eyes. The irises seemed to glow red, surrounding pupils the size of pinheads. Mack felt that if Bic looked up from the contract and met his gaze, his stare would pierce him to his soul.

"Well, listen," said Mack, "There's a turkey sandwich with my name on it. I'm gonna grab some lunch. Meet back here?"

"Be ready in thirty minutes," said Bic, his eyes still on the contract. "I want to have our ghillie suits ready before dusk."

"Yessir."

A couple minutes later, Riggs joined Mack at the kitchen table for lunch. He caught Mack glancing over at Bic and said in a calm, soft voice, "If you know what's good for you, don't ask him."

"Hm?"

"His eyes," said Riggs. "Don't ask him about his eyes."

"Well, I didn't plan on it, but thanks for the warning."

"I'm serious, Mack. I'll tell you a story, then drop it if you know what's good for you."

Mack nodded.

"It was on one godawful rainy night back in 'Nam, and we were tracking across an open field toward a part of the jungle with a double canopy of trees, looking for a dry place to sleep for the night.

Suddenly, a bunch of VC start pouring in out of nowhere, like they were coming from the ground like ants." Riggs's jaw tensed as he continued. "We were caught in a crossfire. About fifty of them had the twelve of us pinned down in an open field with little cover." Riggs shook his head. "They were picking us off like tin cans in target practice.

"I was scared stiff. All I could do was lie there in the wet grass with enemy fire coming from both directions, listening to the sounds of bullets whizzing by and snapping into or through everything around me, including my friends.

"About five feet from me, I heard an awful scream. It was Bic Green. In the dark, with the wet grass cover, I couldn't tell where he was shot. As I got up the nerve to try to move to him and not get shot myself, he screamed louder." Riggs's eyes suddenly moistened, and hands started to tremble.

"I looked and I saw his eyes, glowing red, like he was possessed or something. I swear I thought I was seeing things. Then, from his knees, he jumped to his feet. Bullets were zippin' by, but he just stood there, calm, like he knew he couldn't be shot.

"He took off into a dead sprint toward Charlie and yelled so loud it was like a god was roaring through him. 'It's pork chop-eatin' time!' he says."

The hair on Mack's arms stood straight up as Riggs continued.

"I never saw anything like it in my life. The bullets lit up the air all around him, but they couldn't hit him. He took out one gook after the other with his M-16. He must have killed at least ten of them by the time he made it to the tree line. They were missing him from ten feet away.

"In the tree line, he popped in and out from behind trees as he massacred one after another.

"They scrambled like mice as they yelled to one another, '*NÓ LÀ MA ĐEN, NÓ LÀ MA ĐEN, NÓ LÀ MA ĐEN*.' Seconds after that they were gone, and all but four of us made it out alive, thanks to Bic."

Riggs seemed lost in a distant, terrible memory. Mack put a hand on the man's shoulder and gave a soft shake. "Hey, you alright?"

"Yeah, yes," Riggs replied. "Those times… they never come back easy. And it's just bad form to ask a man about the things that drive him crazy on the battlefield. Understand?"

"Yes," said Mack. "Just curious though, what does *nó là ma đen* mean?"

"It means 'It's a black ghost.'"

112

"You ready?"

Mack almost jumped out of his shoes as he turned to see Bic standing in the entryway, his massive shoulders spanning the width of the door frame.

"Uh, sure, yeah." Mack tried to answer calmly, but a rush of fear deadened his voice.

"You okay?"

"Yeah, I'm fine," he said, suppressing a tremor of fear. He realized he could never tell Sergeant O'Donnell and Corporal Riggs what he suspected about Bic. This man had saved their lives in 'Nam. They were beholden to him. To sway them, he would need a little more evidence than something the guy said forty years ago.

Bic tossed him his BDUs. "I want to have our suits field-ready by dark."

For the next hour, he and Bic worked on making ghillie suits by cutting brown and dark-green strips of burlap and tying them to the square netting attached to their jungle-pattern BDUs.

Bic unzipped the long black bag at his side and pulled out an M24-A2 Sniper Weapon System. Mack noted the rifle was field-ready, with camo tape on the barrel and stock, and mesh netting over the scope to cut down on reflections. Seeing the ten-round magazine in Bic's hand sent electric chills through Mack. Did one of those bullets have Ralston Templeton's name on it? Or his?

One thing he knew for sure: he couldn't do anything unarmed. They had taken his weapon when he arrived.

Bic holstered a sidearm, then wordlessly gave Mack a Leupold spotting scope.

The cloudless night was cool, sprinkled with bright stars and lit by a full moon. The moonlight reflected off the still waters of the lake, providing ample light to see by. For the past two hours, Mack had been lying on the forest floor, peering through his spotter scope, checking in all directions for anything suspicious. The hundred-yard stretch of dense trees between the main house–where Templeton was located–and the guest house seemed to be the most strategic location, so they had taken up station there. Mack worried about Gabriel and his love of Molotovs, but the location had a clear view of the main house to the north and the lake to the east, and it allowed them both cover and the chance to flee to other cover quickly if compromised.

He considered just shooting Bic right then and there. He'd justify it to the higher ups somehow.

"Mack," Bic said calmly.

Mack looked toward him. Bic was so well-camouflaged that he couldn't make him out, even from only two feet away.

"Look down at the lake. Under the boat dock, the middle extension."

Mack turned his high-powered scope on the target. The main dock stretched west about fifty feet into the lake, branching out into shorter side docks.

"Keep your focus," Bic continued. "If he's there, he'll make a move to get to the boat house next."

"What if he's already behind the boat house?"

"Already on it." Bic picked up his two-way radio and thumbed the side-switch. "Sarge, get a couple of men to sweep the boat dock area. I may have seen something, not confirmed."

Moments later, two figures armed with M-16s glided from the rear of the main house toward the boat house. Mack watched them disappear behind it. The next thirty seconds felt like minutes.

"I can't see them," Mack rasped.

"Confirm the dock area's all clear," Bic said into his radio.

Ten seconds passed with no response.

O'Donnell's voice piped in. "Men, confirm all clear."

Another silent ten seconds passed.

"Code red." The sergeant's voice, filtered through the two-way, was curiously devoid of emotion. The two men were probably dead, or lying somewhere mortally wounded.

With two of their group of ten already down in the first minute, Mack had to make a choice: shoot Bic now and deal with Gabriel, or... wait and see what came next.

What came next was a lit Molotov cocktail, thrown from the back side of the gabled roof of the boat house. The thing tumbled through the air like a flaming circus baton, heading straight for a large pine just fifty yards away.

113

Several hours had passed. Caroline was unsure how many. They were in the middle of a big waiting game, but the question was, for what?

Both she and Tidwell were seated in matching Queen Anne chairs, zip-tied at their wrists and ankles and bound to the chairs. The fine art in the study had been stripped from the walls, and almost all the furniture removed from the room. A single unshaded floor lamp provided light.

Caroline looked at Tidwell. The powerful, confident, well-spoken man she had been so attracted to ever since she first met him—when he came back to speak to her law class at Stanford—had just about broken. He looked like he might start to cry and beg these men for his life. She didn't have the heart to tell him not to bother, that begging wouldn't change a thing.

"We have to escape," she whispered.

He looked at her, his eyes worn. "They'll kill us."

"Right," she said, a current of rage growing in her gut. "Let's go."

He attempted to move his arms, which were zip-tied to each side of the chair's back. "I can offer them money," he pleaded.

"Money's not going to work,"

"Then we'll just have to give them whatever they want."

Caroline looked at the man, realizing how worlds apart they really were.

It was just her now.

She awkwardly stood, still tied to the chair, and with small quick shuffles, backpedaled rapidly until she crashed into a nearby wall, shattering the hundred-year-old chair upon impact.

Scrambling on the floor to free her hands, she heard quick,

charging footsteps. A man then snatched her to her feet.

Caroline struck the man in the side of the head with a piece of the chair. He stumbled backwards, dazed. She swung again.

The man recovered quicker than she had anticipated and caught the club in his hand.

He struck Caroline in the ribs with a vicious blow. She gasped for air, but quickly kicked the man in his midsection, then bashed him in the chin with an uppercut.

The man flew backward.

A bullet snapped into the floor inches from her feet.

"Enough," another man yelled, pointing his gun at her.

"Come get some," Caroline said, tears and sweat pouring down her face.

"How 'bout I shoot you in the head if you don't put that club down."

"How 'bout you go screw yourself."

The third man reappeared in the room, aimed, and shot a dart into Caroline's leg. She screamed as a jolt of pain coursed through her.

"You cowards," she said as her senses went muggy.

She tried to charge at the two men. She went five steps and collapsed.

114

The lit bottle smacked against the tree and shattered. With a huge roar, the flames wrapped around both sides of the tree. The flames engulfed a soldier lying within its path. From a half a football field away, Mack watched as the man rolled on the ground furiously, shrieking like a banshee, fire and smoke all over him until, mercifully, his screams and movements ceased.

Already, three down.

Mack looked to Bic for direction, but the big man was gone. His worst fear had just come to fruition. He squeezed the MP5 desperately and took cover behind a tree, flipping the gun's safety switch. He wasn't sure, but he assumed Bic had just begun his run to go kill Ralston Templeton. Added to that, without Bic, Mack was cut off from radio communication with the team. Even if he wanted to warn O'Donnell about Bic, he couldn't.

Fully automatic weapon fire ripped through the silence. For a moment, Mack considered retreating deep into the forest and escaping with his life. Dressed as he was in heavy camouflage, he could make it. But he was there to do a job: to protect Ralston Templeton and bring down two killers.

He dropped and belly-crawled toward the main house. The shooting continued uninterrupted. Mack held his fire, reluctant to compromise his position, especially as he had no idea where the perp was situated. Or anyone else, for that matter.

He stopped at the edge of the dense forest, about twenty yards from the side of the main house. Rapid blue-white flashes of light were stabbing into the dark from nearly every direction. He couldn't tell who was shooting at who. The estate had become pure chaos.

He peered through his scope, focusing on the shots fired from the boat house, and spotted a man firing an automatic weapon from that location. The gunman looked Hispanic, all right, but this man was at least fifty.

The cold steel of a large-bore pistol barrel pressed against his head.

"Hello, my little bullet-dodger," said Gabriel.

Bic had taken his ghillie suit off, and was dressed now in BDU pants and a black T-shirt. He had entered Templeton's house through the south wing, and was cautiously making his way deeper into the mansion. He wasn't sure exactly what he was going to do. All he could think about was his little Gracie. But when this was all done, he was going to hunt down his employer and kill him. That dirty snake had crossed the line, and he would die for it.

He savored the coming slaughter like a long-awaited meal.

115

"*Shhhhhhh,*" Gabriel whispered excitedly into Mack's ear. "The wolf's about to kill the chickens in the hen house," he slurred, holding Mack from behind with one arm pulled behind his back, and the pistol jammed into his side.

Mack, now a human shield, felt confident he could escape Gabriel's lax grip, but he couldn't escape the gun.

Entering through a busted window on the first floor, Gabriel half-pushed, half-dragged Mack through the eerily-silent main house. The Templeton mansion was essentially a vast maze composed of a few open living areas and a warren of private rooms. Mack had studied the schematics and knew the plan. They would have to go upstairs or use an elevator to get to where the Templetons were nestled on the second floor.

Gabriel squeezed Mack's arm as he yanked him from the hallway into a huge study. "Not a noise or I'll make a tunnel out of your head right here," he commanded as he threw Mack into the front corner of the room. "On your knees, hands on your head, pig."

Mack did as he was told. Rapid fire exchanges still stuttered on from outside, initially more than half a dozen weapons fired, but these had diminished to two or three pops now.

Gabriel retreated from the doorway and positioned himself along the wall by the door. His whole body coiled as he prepared to strike. Seconds later, a line of at least twenty bullets shot from the hallway popped through the wall and into the study. A priceless oil painting sprang off the wall and crashed to the floor, and several bullets snapped into the large mahogany desk before angling up into the oversized flat-screen monitor on top of it, shattering it completely.

Gabriel dropped to the floor and bear-crawled behind the heavy desk. As he did, he looked to Mack with his weapon pointed at him, making sure he understood that if he moved, he would die.

Mack, still at the front corner of the room, wasn't sure how he had avoided being shot, but he was glad he was no longer directly behind Gabriel, who had disappeared from view except for the heel of his left shoe, which poked out from behind the desk. He was half-thinking of making a run for the doorway—hoping whoever was on the other side of the wall would recognize him instantly and not fill him full of lead—when he heard a distinct sound. A heavy metallic object had rolled fast into the room across the hardwood floor.

"You *putas*," Gabriel spat, diving under the desk.

Just then, the world's biggest giant roared, and everything went white.

He'd instinctively balled himself up when he saw the grenade roll in.

After the explosion, he opened his eyes, astonished not to be blind. When Mack felt heavy footsteps thudding across the floor, he looked up to see Bic charging into the room, spraying the desk with M-16 fire. Like a football player hitting a blocking sled, Bic dropped the rifle and pushed the massive wooden object across the floor. He didn't stop until the desk was flush against the back wall of the room, trapping Gabriel underneath it.

Bic retrieved his M-16 off the floor, then contemptuously removed his sunglasses, tossing them aside.

Time seemed to slow to a crawl as Gabriel, from underneath the desk, unloaded his clip in a random pattern in a last-ditch effort to hit Bic. Mesmerized by Bic's glowing red eyes, Mack watched as Bic returned fire. Flashes spat from the end of the gun barrel, wooden splinters erupting in all directions as the bullets snapped into the desk.

A solid thump thrummed faintly through the floor from under the desk. At first Mack assumed it was Gabriel's head hitting the floor, but he knew better.

"He has grenades!" Mack screamed.

116

A thunderous explosion shook the eight-hundred square foot master bedroom. Sergeant O'Donnell had heard this destructive sound many times before. He looked down grimly.

Ralston Templeton's face was a mask of pure terror. O'Donnell had seen this look many times, too–the realization that money couldn't always buy one out of bad situations.

"Riggs, give me a status report," the sergeant snapped.

Corporal Riggs, peering out the master bedroom window with night-vision goggles, turned toward the sergeant. "It looks like all our men have been taken out." He said, pushing his goggles up to his forehead "It's possible we're all that's left." Riggs tossed the goggles onto a nearby Louis Quatorze chair, and picked up his M-16.

O'Donnell turned back to Templeton, his wife, and their ten-year-old son, who were all standing in the doorway of the bedroom closet. The woman was an intelligent-looking blonde, and the boy looked like a miniature version of his father: slim build, a narrow face with quick, clever eyes, and shaggy brown hair. Templeton glanced from the boy to O'Donnell, his eyes filled with desperation–the type of fear the sergeant had seen before when men came to the realization they weren't going to make it.

Templeton found his voice. "Sergeant, if you get my family though the night, I'll pay your team a billion dollars."

"That's not necessary."

He saw the look in Templeton's eye. The rich man knew his money wasn't worth dirt here. It was his last hope.

Templeton wrapped his arms around his wife and son.

"Riggs, go hunt that varmint down."

"Yes, sir," Riggs said firmly, and exited the master bedroom.

O'Donnell looked at Templeton. "Now, sir, take your family into the closet, and don't come out until I come get you. Understand?"

Templeton nodded.

"Make sure everyone stays behind the Kevlar panel at all times." The sergeant pointed to the four-by-four panel in the back corner of the closet, then hustled the three inside, shut the door, and locked the complex array of bolts he and his team had added over the last few days. Then he barricaded the closet door with a massive ornate armoire that was probably worth more than he made in a year. Once that was done, he positioned himself in the opposite corner of the room behind the long dresser. With an M-16 equipped with a rocket launcher and enough ammo to hold off a small army, Sergeant O'Donnell waited.

War would come to him.

117

John Alfred Tidwell glanced at the clock on the wall. 10:49 PM. By now, hopefully, the Templetons were dead and the list had been completed. He was sick of sitting here tied to a chair and acting like a wimp. He gave one of his hired mercenaries, the one who Caroline had cracked in the head, a discrete sign to drag him out of the study so he could get an update.

"That's it," the henchman said, glaring at Caroline, who was not only tied down in the chair next to Tidwell's, but duct taped as well. "It's time to show you we mean business." He gestured to his associates. "Take her crybaby boyfriend and bloody him up a little."

The other two went to Tidwell, untied him, then dragged him out of the room."

Immediately after the doors to the study were closed, Tidwell stretched in an exaggerated manner, then took a few steps into the library adjacent to the study and phoned Parelli.

"Is it done?

"Oh, it's done," Parelli growled. "Gabriel, Publio, and the Black Ghost have all gone radio silent!"

Tidwell felt like a firecracker had just exploded in his stomach. "Wait a second. What?"

"They're either dead or they all quit, Mr. Congressman." A sigh echoed down the line. "It's over. They won."

"It can't be," Tidwell said after a moment. "We still have until tomorrow morning. As a backup, I've arranged for a demolition expert who can blow the hell out of wherever they take Templeton. He costs ten million. I think I can come up with at least half. How much can you wire me tonight?"

"John, let's not sink any more dough into this deal. It's cooked."

Tidwell paused–in quiet realization and dread. His face grew hot. "It's not done! Are you aware of what the Russians will do to us? They won't let us off this easily. You set this whole thing up! You're not quitting now!"

Parelli gave a small laugh.

"You lifeless whore," Tidwell hissed. "What the hell do you think you're doing here?"

"Me? Why, I'm just returning the favor, Mr. Congressman. One family to another."

"What's that supposed to mean?"

"Your grandfather sold mine down the river, Johnny. The man who gave me everything as a kid spent the last sixteen years of his life rotting in prison because of your greedy fat rat of a grandfather."

Tidwell remembered the name of the man his grandfather had railroaded into oblivion. "Giovanni Franconni?"

"*Mi Papa*. My ma's dad."

"What does that have to do with us?"

"Sins of the father, Johnny. And as a gift to *mi papa*, I'm going to railroad you into the fiery depths of Hell. See you there someday, Mr. Congressman."

118

Mack wasn't sure if a portion of the house had collapsed on him, or if it was only Bic.

Bic stirred with a groan, then he pushed himself up and rolled to his feet. Mack coughed hard, his lungs choked by all the smoke and dust lingering in the air from the explosion.

Bic extended his hand and helped the agent to his feet.

"Thanks," Mack said, dusting himself off.

Bic nodded.

The study was gone. Gabriel and the desk had been vaporized.

Mack regarded Bic, who dove on top of him right before the blast. He had taken the brunt of the concussive force of the explosion.

Bic drew the black 9mm pistol tucked in his pants and calmly handed it to Mack. He then pulled a massive combat knife from the side holster on his hip.

Bic's eyes burned a violent red as he turned and walked down the hall toward the north end of the house.

"Mr. Templeton and his family are on the other side of the house," he said as Mack followed. "If I know Publio, he'll come right in the front door, guns blazing."

Mack took dead aim at the middle of Bic's back. "How do you know that, Bic?"

Bic turned and faced the barrel of the gun he had just given to Mack. He calmly raised his hands in the air, as if he had just been caught at something. "Mack, I just saved your life."

Mack's trigger finger was tense. "I know who you are," he said. He looked directly into the blazing red eyes. "Pork chop left at the scene, twenty-two unsolved murders over the last thirty years, sound familiar?"

Bic didn't respond.

Mack had to take control of this situation and fast, or he would wind up dead. He jerked the gun downward, and for the first time in his life Mack Maddox shot another human being. The round caught Bic square in the knee in a spray of crimson.

Bic growled and did a strange half-rotation, then regained his stance with all his weight on his remaining leg. The teeth bared. The eyes glowed. The Black Ghost moved toward Mack.

Mack backed up quickly. "Freeze, or I'll shoot!"

Bic ignored him. Nostrils flaring like a bull's, he continued forward.

Mack's index finger tingled as he pulled the trigger. The shot popped into Bic's chest, leaving a wide red splotch.

The impact of the bullet made Bic take a step back. He almost lost his balance, but somehow stayed on his feet. He looked down at his chest, then his gaze sprang back up, the reddish blaze suggesting that Mack had just made a terrible mistake.

Mack fired three more rounds in a tight circle around the man's heart.

Bic's eyes rolled backward, and he collapsed face first to the floor.

At that moment, a swarm of bullets buzzed over Mack's head and he hit the floor.

119

Tidwell leaned back in his leather chair in shock. He stared at the framed picture of his grandfather on his desk. He hadn't seen this curveball coming. He needed to act fast or he was going to wind up in prison. Or worse.

His original plan had been to use Caroline as a witness to him being brutally beaten—a perfect alibi, and from an FBI agent, no less. But now he needed to take this thing to a whole new level, the one contingency plan he'd hoped he'd never have to use.

In the basement of the house was a cadaver on ice. He would have the man's body burnt beyond recognition. With the $20,000 he had spent to have the cadaver's jaw and teeth redone, the burnt body would match his dental records perfectly. He would then live on his estate in Morocco, under a new identity.

He knew what he had to do next. His hands trembling, he placed a call to Mikhail Petrov, the man in charge of the Ministry of Fuel and Energy of the Russian Federation.

"Mikhail, it's John Tidwell. I have some additional information on our bill."

"Ah, I was hoping you would," returned the minister. "I was disappointed when the bill did not make it through your Congress."

"Please, just hear me out. I've been working very hard to make it happen, but my partner on the other side has abandoned me."

Tidwell waited for his response, knowing that just as he was involved with partners on the "other side," mainly Parelli, Mikhail was dealing with the Russian mob. Finally, Mikhail said slowly, "That is most unfortunate."

"Listen, Mikhail, I'm not insinuating that there's anything wrong on your side. I just want to confirm that the money end of the deal is still good. I know you're a man of your word. If you give it, it will be good enough for me."

"You have my word," the man said slowly.

Tidwell released a held breath. "This is good news. I will proceed."

"Good. I will talk to you soon, my friend."

Tidwell hung up the phone with renewed focus. Screw Parelli. It was now time to cross number ten off the list, in a style that would make his grandfather proud.

120

Mack had hit the deck just in time as a cluster of bullets destroyed an antique grandfather clock against the hallway wall.

Lying on his belly behind Bic, he took dead aim at the corner wall down the hall, where the shots had come from.

He'd fired five rounds into Bic and only had a couple left. He had no choice but to stay put and force the other man to charge.

He winced as automatic gunfire ensued. To his surprise and relief, someone was shooting at Publio, flushing the man into the hallway. He turned the corner towards Mack to use the wall as cover from the incoming rounds. Drywall chunks and splinters of wood flew into the hall as heavy gunfire pinned Publio down.

The ugly Mexican screamed profanities in his native tongue as he returned fire. Completely consumed by the firefight, he didn't notice Mack on the hall floor thirty feet away from him. Mack rose to one knee, formed a solid triangle with his arms fully extended, and took aim.

With the clean shot, his mind screamed to squeeze the trigger, but in that moment he again froze.

Publio saw him, and screaming something in Spanish, swung his M-16 around, spraying a sweep of gunfire destroyed everything in a left to right beeline toward him.

In the split second just before Publio's bullets reached him, Mack stared down death. And unafraid, he fired his last three shots. All three plunged into Publio's midsection. Publio dropped to the floor like a puppet with his strings cut.

Corporal Riggs charged into the hallway, sweeping the area with his M-16.

Spotting Mack, he asked, "All clear?"

"Clear," said Mack, wearily getting to his feet.

Riggs bent down to check Publio's body. "He's gone."

Mack glanced toward Bic. "So is he."

Riggs regarded the large man, a grimace on his face. "Dammit." He unclipped his two-way radio from his belt and said, "Sarge, it's over, we got him. Mack and I are safe."

"Good work," O'Donnell replied. "The Medevac chopper has already landed on the premises. So far they haven't found any survivors from the team."

"Bic's gone, too," said Riggs.

"Are you sure?" the sergeant asked.

Riggs bent down and checked for a pulse again. "Yeah, he's gone."

The radio fell silent for a moment, then O'Donnell ordered, "You and Mack sweep the house and make sure we're all clear to get the Templetons to the chopper. After the Medevac team rounds up all the bodies, we have another chopper on its way to transport us out."

"Yes, sir."

Mack didn't know what to say or what to think. Lots of lives had been taken tonight, but at least the killing was over.

121

One of the men using Caroline's phone called Mack.

Mack's voice sounded full of joy. "It's over! We did it!"

She did not reply.

"Caroline, you there?"

The man holding the phone, on speaker for all to hear, said, "You have three seconds."

"Caroline, who was that? What's going on?"

Caroline looked at the man with a stone face, so like the face of the murderer she had once helped go free—that guilt had never left her, but she wouldn't compound it. She wasn't going to help these men carry out their murderous plot in any way.

The man smiled as he said, "Now!"

The door opened, and Tidwell was dragged into the threshold. He stared at the floor. He looked broken.

The man holding the .357 walked over to him, aimed at his face, and pulled the trigger. The body was instantly flung out of her field of vision, and she heard the sickening thud as it hit the hardwood floor.

"Caroline!" Mack screamed.

With a mad rage, Caroline looked at the man holding the phone, not saying a word as Mack frantically called for her to answer him.

The man pushed the index card in her face, urging her to read it, as the other pointed the gun at her head. Staring down the barrel of the gun, she already knew that just like Tidwell, she was dead no matter what she did. The terror of the moment suddenly turned surreal as she harnessed the power from her life experiences, turning her guilt into empowerment and strength.

Caroline looked the man dead in the eyes and smirked.

"You feisty spitfire," the man finally said. He smacked her in the face, then put the phone to his own ear.

"What's it going to be?"

"Mack," she called out, "don't listen to a word he's saying, they're going to kill me no matter what! I've seen–"

There was another slap to her face, and the man said into the phone, "Tell me now if you're as stubborn as her. I'll put a bullet in this hussy's head and we'll call it a day."

"Don't lay another hand on her," Mack hissed.

"I just set a timer for sixty seconds. You have exactly that amount of time to kill two people, or I'll kill one."

"Mack, don't do it!"

"Thirty seconds."

"I'll be okay!"

"Ten seconds."

"Mack! Can you hear me? You're not that little boy frozen in terror anymore! Do you hear me? You're stronger now. You're better. I love you!"

"Say goodbye–in three, two..."

Mack closed his eyes.

"One."

Tidwell's ear still rang, despite his earplugs. And the left side of his face was still stinging from the blood-filled squib that exploded just as the blank-filled gun went off.

His head ached. His mind reeled. And he watched the entire phone conversation on the video monitor from within his library.

"One."

"Wait," Mack's tinny voice gasped, "I'll do it. I just need more time."

"You have five seconds," the man said. "When I get to zero, put one in her head. Five, four–"

"I said, I'll do it! The Templetons are locked in a safe room. They are not going to be let out until morning as a safety precaution. Then they're being transported to a safe house. I will take them out tomorrow at 8:00 AM."

Tidwell looked at his watch. Then he spoke to the man talking to

Mack through his radio earpiece. "Tell him he has eight hours. If we don't receive the video of a double murder on her phone, then she's dead."

122

"Mack," Sergeant O'Donnell said as he waved for him to come into the room and meet the Templeton family. "Mack, you okay?"

An image flashed nauseatingly across Mack's mind: that of Caroline's brains coming out her skull from a bullet wound to the head. He forced instead other, better images. Her gleaming smile; those deep, intelligent green eyes; the feel of their lips meeting for the first time, and then the second, as they stared death in the face together in the submerged van. He had no doubt in that moment that he was about to lose his soulmate. And he knew that in this twisted game called life, when he was in the depths of his depression, he would blame himself, as if he had pulled the trigger. If he couldn't save Caroline, he would be handed a life sentence in a prison of inescapable guilt.

"Mack," Riggs asked, moving toward him. "You all right?"

Mack snapped to. "Back in a sec."

Sprinting back toward the guest house, he dialed Walton's cell. The Medevac team had already gathered all the bodies and left the premises. The night had become quiet again, except for a subtle breeze gently disturbing the treetops.

Tom answered on the first ring. "Mack, I was just about to call you."

"Tom, I need you to find someone for me," he nearly pleaded. It might be one in a million, but his Langley ally might be Caroline's only chance.

"Who?"

"My partner Caroline Foxx is being held hostage. I have just under eight hours to find her, or she's dead."

"What do you need?"

"I need you to go back to the office and get some information for me."

"I never left. I've been working your case all night."

"Her phone records–see who she called in the Bay Area. The guy she went to see, his first name is Freddie. Look for any contact. Fred, Frederick, Winifred..."

There was a pounding of computer keys coming from the other end of the line, then a pause, and Tom said slowly, "Oh man, you're not going to believe whose number she's been calling in the Bay Area over and over lately."

"Whose?"

"Congressman John Tidwell's."

Mack shook his head. "Any other calls to the Bay Area?"

"None in the last month."

He thought for a moment. "That's it! John *Alfred* Tidwell, Listen, Tom, can you verify if the last call made from her phone came from this congressman's address?"

Moments later, Tom reported: "I'm 99% sure her phone is at his address."

"Text me his coordinates, will you?"

"How are you going to get to San Fran in eight hours? You need to call Bender for help."

"How do I know Bender's not involved? He was tight with Utah."

A sudden howling gust of wind from outside caught his attention.

Mack looked outside. "Tom, just text me the address."

He left the guest house. The helicopter meant to transport Templeton and his family to safety was landing on the helipad fifty yards away, toward the lake. Mack jogged toward the chopper, with each step becoming increasingly certain of what he needed to do. The wind from the rotors whipped dirt, leaves, and pebbles into his face as he approached. He quickly assessed the twin-engine chopper. It appeared to be equipped for six passengers. It would do. He banged on the cockpit door.

The pilot unbuttoned the hatch. He was dressed in a gray jumpsuit, with his flight helmet still on, and to Mack's relief he was unarmed. He scowled as Mack pushed his way into the chopper, waving a badge in his face. "FBI. Change in plans. You're taking me to the San Francisco Bay Area. I'll have an address for you shortly."

"I'll need to get authorization for that," the man said uncertainly.

Exasperated, Mack pulled out his pistol and aimed it at the man's head. "Here it is. Now fly this bird."

123

Running on fumes, the chopper landed in the backyard of Tidwell's sprawling estate at 7:52 AM. The perfectly-manicured grass leading up to the white stone mansion reminded Mack more of a golf fairway than a yard. The helicopter almost certainly botched any chance at surprise, and he had a long stretch of grass to cross before entering the house.

He hadn't been contacted by Caroline since the call he had received demanding he kill the Templetons. There were at least two men inside, and in his haste, he hadn't bothered to grab an automatic weapon before leaving Seattle. Riggs had given him two clips when they had swept the Templeton estate. Two clips and a 9mm. That was all.

He did a full sprint across the open grass, jinking back and forth. If he could just make it into the bushes on the side of the house without being picked off...

But no one fired on him.

Maybe the house was so big no one inside had even heard the chopper land–doubtful. Or maybe they had watched him run across the yard, and were just waiting for him to try and gain entry somehow–slightly less doubtful.

He found a basement window along the east side of the house toward the back. He kicked it in and shimmied inside, leading with his weapon. He was in a wine cellar. He swept his gun across the room, examining the impressive rows of full wine racks.

Mack made his way toward the exit. The door was unlocked, so he opened it. Almost instantly a thick smell rolled over him, so overwhelming he could almost taste it. In one breath, the unknown stink went from sweet to so foul it made him want to puke.

With no exterior windows in the room, a thin arc of light from the wine cellar cast Mack's shadow into the large rectangular room beyond. Weapon extended, he swept the room from right to left. He stopped and took aim at what appeared to be the outline of a body across the room at the base of a flight of stairs.

The body lay very still, and though it was too far away and too dark in the room to tell much, its posture and smell revealed it to be a burned human corpse.

Mack rushed toward the body, heedless of danger, praying desperately he wasn't too late; that this wasn't Caroline. He chanced to see a light switch on the wall, and turned it on.

What he saw in the light made him fall to his knees.

124

The severely-burnt corpse lay on the floor with its mouth frozen wide open in a silent scream. The expression, hideous and unnatural, was what had softened his legs. The body glistened weirdly, as if the fire had been put out by an extinguisher. The faint smoldering and the strong smell suggested the body had burned within the last couple of hours, if not more recently, but Mack's revulsion turned to a strange relief as he bent to examine the corpse. It was burnt beyond recognition and wizened hideously, but by height alone he could see it wasn't Caroline. Was it Tidwell?

A loud bang came from upstairs. The noise didn't sound like gunfire, more like a wrecking ball blasting through a wall. He hurried up the steps, heart thumping in his chest.

He moved quietly, staying low. The difference between being shot or not would depend on his approach. Burned bodies, strange, violent sounds—he was preparing himself for anything.

From a crouched position, he took hold of the knob on the door at the top of the stairs. The adrenaline in his veins made his hands tremble. He swung the door open, and recoiled against the wall, away from possible gunfire.

Nothing. No gunfire, no voices, no alarm—only silence. Fearing it was a trap, but with no other choice, he moved forward. He sprang into the room and looked around frantically. To his left was the grand living room, with massive arched windows giving way to a storybook view of the property behind the house. He spotted another body on the floor in the far-right corner, halfway in the room and halfway in an adjoining hallway. It looked to Mack as if he was killed in the process of either entering or leaving. The man had a military bearing. Tall, with a fit build and close-cropped hair.

Keeping his back to the wall, Mack made his way to the body. He swung his gun frantically as he crept, trying to cover all the points of possible attack.

The man's head was turned over his shoulder at an unnatural angle. His neck had clearly been snapped, the head nearly detached from the neck. Mack reached out and touched the man's skin. Killed just moments ago. The violence of this death horrified him, with his hope of finding Caroline alive motivating him onward, however dimly the possibility now seemed to be. He stood quickly and entered the hallway leading toward the front of the house.

Immediately to his left, he cleared the dining room. Loose plaster fragments scattered across the Oriental rug caught his attention. The plaster fragments were concentrated in an area on the far side of a wide china cabinet, which partially obscured them. He stepped deeper into the room to investigate.

The sight he saw on the other side of that cabinet once again left him weak in the knees. A man's bloody, misshapen head protruded from the wall beside it. It had been rammed through from the other side. *The wrecking ball,* Mack thought crazily.

A sound of struggling from the adjoining hallway. He left the dining room and cautiously peered around the corner.

Having prepared himself for anything, he found now that his imagination had come up short. Before him was a sight to him as shocking as the second coming of Jesus. He felt weak, giddy, and found he had to grip the wall over the impossibility that now confronted him.

When you shot people, they were supposed to stay dead.

The fiery red eyes pierced deep into his soul.

125

Bic Green stood in the hallway of the congressman's mansion, holding a smaller man by the neck in his massive right hand. The man dangled bonelessly, like dead prey in a falcon's talon.

"Freeze!" said Mack, feeling as if it were useless to even suggest such a thing.

Bic let go of the man's neck. The body hit the floor with a thud.

"You don't belong here."

"Yeah? Look who's talking. I saw you die with my own eyes."

Bic's eyes became even more intense. "This doesn't concern you."

Mack awkwardly glanced at the dead man at Bic's feet, then toward the other, whose body still dangled from a bloody hole in the wall.

"I told you. It's not your conc—"

"Put your hands on your head!"

Bic ignored the command, saying, "There's a girl here. You need to get her out, both of you need to get out." Bic's expression turned impatient. "Or do you want to try me again?"

"Where is she?"

Bic gestured to the door on his left.

"I can't just let you go." Mack tensed his jaw as he said, "You have to go down for what you did."

"I already have."

"You don't look so dead."

Bic took a step toward Mack.

Mack held his ground and began to squeeze his trigger finger.

Bic pulled down the collar of his black V-neck T-shirt to expose his chest. In the middle was a light patch of salt-and-pepper hair, but not a single scratch. "I'm not dead," he said quietly. "I'm not even real."

Mack shook his head in disbelief, knowing two things *were* real: he had shot Bic in the chest, and he was positive Bic hadn't been wearing a vest when he did it.

Bic took another step toward him. "John Alfred Tidwell, the man you saw burned alive in the basement, is the mastermind behind this whole thing."

"What whole thing?"

"All of it. The billionaires."

"Lies," said Mack. "He can't possibly benefit from these deaths."

"You're not looking in the right place."

"Stop right there, Bic! I mean it!"

"It's over now. I'm dead. Everyone is dead. This case is solved." Bic turned away. "Now, go save the girl. You won't have much time. Tidwell had allies. I'll keep them busy until you go."

"Why would you do that?"

"You killed me," said Bic darkly. He turned back and glanced at the agent. "It's the least I can do to repay you."

He turned at last and started down the hall. With each step Bic took, Mack considered a thousand different scenarios. The Black Ghost had been stopped, the Black Ghost hadn't been stopped, the Black Ghost had to be stopped–but then Mack glanced at the other room, thought he heard the faint thrum of helicopter rotors, and concluded that yes, the Black Ghost would have to be stopped.

Soon. Not today. But soon.

He stood and watched as Bic walked down the hall and disappeared into the darkness. Mack took two quick steps the opposite way and threw open the door to the study.

He ran to Caroline, whose eyes grew wide when she saw him. She was bound to a chair with duct tape over her mouth. He carefully peeled the tape back.

"I knew you wouldn't fail."

"I couldn't," he said, as he gently cupped her face with his hands and then pressed his lips against hers. Mack drank in the moment, magical, powerful. "I won't ever let you down," he said at last. "I will never let you go."

126

"There was only one glaring difference between Colin Shepard and all of the other billionaires," Mack said to Bender. "Shepard had all his money going to a foundation he set up a few years back."

"All of it?" said Bender.

"*All* his money. It was a tax haven. Not one cent for Uncle Sam. If money was the motive behind these murders, the only logical reason for killing the other billionaires and not Shepard would be to generate revenue for the government in the form of estate death taxes."

Bender sat, lips pursed in deep thought for a moment. "Do you know what this means?"

"Oh, I sure do," said Mack. "It means Tidwell had quite the little operation going."

"It means," said Caroline, standing in the doorway to Bender's office, "that this is a government conspiracy that makes Watergate look like a party game." She was battered and bruised, but there was a strength in her gleaming green eyes that could not be extinguished for anything.

"That's one way to put it," said Mack, rising. He walked over to her, looked into her eyes, and embraced her.

"Welcome home, Agent Foxx," said Bender, a glisten in his eye. "You and Mack have done some outstanding work together."

Mack turned back to Bender. "Caroline's right, though. This thing is bigger than we think. Somebody high up in the government needed to generate revenue, and fast. They hired an assassin to kill the wealthiest people in America. The death taxes would then be used to fund their project."

"About this project," said Bender.

"A Siberian pipeline. In a nutshell, Tidwell killed a bunch of innocent people for oil money."

"I guess oil is as good a motive for murder as any other."

"Sadly, yes," said Mack.

127

For Mack and Caroline, the next day was complete chaos. Details about Tidwell's scheme were leaked to the press before they even turned in their completed reports, and the media had a field day with the story. As one pundit put it, the facts were too outrageous to be anything but true.

Mack became the country's golden boy. He had solved the case and taken down two assassins. Hijacking a chopper to Tidwell's mansion was met with mixed reviews, but the hunch had paid off. Mack had dealt with a mansion's worth of mercenaries, whose deaths he couldn't explain, and thankfully in the wave of praise, he didn't have to. Of course, in none of his press conferences and interviews did he mention the fact that Bic Green was still alive and at large–if, in fact, he really was. What he did mention was how he only had saved Caroline's life one time, but she had saved his three times in the last couple of weeks. And he was quick to give her equal credit for solving the case.

Early in the morning on the second day after the showdown, Mack woke suddenly. It was a little after four in the morning. Caroline, who had spent the night, was on her side, sound asleep. Mack stared at her long, toned legs poking out from under the white sheets. He smiled widely, recalling the things she had done to him the night before, and imagining how he would return the favor.

As he tried to go back to sleep and forget about Bic, the information he had received late the previous day wouldn't allow him to. He tried to take it at face value and just accept what had happened–to forget about Bic. But come on, all the men who had been killed at Ralston Templeton's estate, including Bic and Publio, had supposedly been cremated the day after they were killed, before anyone from any reputable government agency saw or confirmed the dead bodies, of course. What really set Mack off was the sham story they'd used to burn the bodies right away: Corporal Crooker, one of the dead men, had allegedly come directly from an area in Africa where there had been an outbreak of the Marburg virus. How Mack would love to get his hands on the postmortem blood report that supposedly confirmed the presence of the virus. All this just screamed conspiracy.

He quietly crawled out of bed and went into his kitchenette for a glass of water. A week's worth of mail, which Caroline had stacked neatly on the kitchen table, caught his attention. Perhaps some return to normalcy would settle his muddled mind. He began thumbing through the mail. A direct mail postcard from a local paintball field caught his eye. All those colorful splats on the shirts in the postcard.

Red splats, like blood.

That dirty dog, he thought, and the light of pure reason suddenly blazed in his brain.

I shot Bic with the weapon he gave me.

128

He sprang from the kitchen table to the three-drawer hutch up against the wall in the living room. In the top drawer was the 9mm he'd used to shoot Bic.

He released the magazine and pushed the top bullet out into his palm.

The bullet sure *seemed* real. It had to be.

He pushed a second bullet out of the magazine. This one was different than the first. He looked at the first bullet more closely. On the casing was a deep scratch.

He went back to the drawer and grabbed a pair of pliers. Very carefully, he pulled the first bullet from its casing. The casing was empty. Devoid of propellant. He thanked God he hadn't tried to shoot Bic at Tidwell's house. One jammed bullet later and Mack too would have dangled like a dead chicken in Bic's massive choking hands.

Corporal Riggs, he thought.

He remembered Riggs asking him if he was low on ammo and offering to trade him the new magazines for the one he had used to shoot Bic and Publio. He'd asked Mack if he was *low on* ammo, not *out of* ammo.

Mack's entire body went cold. Riggs had carried a shiny silver .357 as his sidearm. *Why the hell would the corporal just happen to have two clips for a 9mm?*

He rehashed what had happened at the Templeton mansion. The first two men who were killed, Anderson and Stevens, had run behind the boat house. He hadn't actually seen what had happened to them. From the radio silence, he had assumed they were dead. Next, there was the kid burned alive by Gabriel's Molotov. That wasn't fake.

But then he remembered seeing a fire-retardant suit in the supply room. The kid could easily have put on the suit while Mack was in the forest with Bic setting up watch.

The more he thought about it, the more it made sense. He hadn't actually seen the other four men in the team get killed. He'd just heard Riggs report to O'Donnell that they were dead. That left Gabriel, Publio, and Bic.

He had no doubt that Gabriel was dead. He had seen Bic pump at least twenty M-16 rounds into the desk Gabriel was underneath, and the grenade made short work of the rest.

Bic had survived point-blank fire from his weapon, so he could only assume that Publio had as well. As Mack thought about shooting Bic, he realized he didn't remember seeing any blood pooling on the floor. Mack glanced at the colorful paintball postcard. Could he have shot some type of high-tech paint bullets, and been so overwhelmed by the intensity of the situation he didn't even know it?

He felt the rush of adrenaline as he thought about what he would say to A.D. Bender. That none of the bad guys were dead, except maybe Gabriel, Tidwell, and his thugs? Well, where was the proof?

Really, all he had was a bullet without any gunpowder. All the fallen were confirmed dead, then *cremated*.

Easy out, there.

Everything else lined up perfectly with the story he had given. The media had received an audio tape of Tidwell talking to Jones and Utah, basically outlining the whole plot. So, the media was taken care of.

He walked back into the bedroom, sat down at Caroline's feet, and rubbed the back of his neck. He looked over. She was watching him.

"You alright?" she cooed.

"For now, yes."

She sat up slightly, a small smile on her face. "What's that look for?"

"Lots of things," he said, touching her nose. "Let's go to sleep. I'll tell you some other time."

He kissed her once, then walked around to the other side of the bed and got in. He spooned her, took in the smell of her hair and noticed he was smiling.

At least *this* case was closed.

129

John Tidwell lay on a hard, cool surface in the dark with his wrists tied together, listening to what he thought were seagulls cackling. Given the subtle rocking motions he felt, he suspected that he'd just awoken inside the hull of a boat. He was still groggy, but recalled a searing needle-like stab, as if from a tiny bullet or dart, and then blackness. He had no idea how long he had been unconscious. Hours, maybe days.

A deep voice startled him. "You're off the coast of South Africa."

"Who's there?"

A man with exceptional strength grabbed Tidwell by the ropes around his wrists and pulled him to his feet. The man then dragged him up two steps and opened a door. Bright afternoon sunlight spilled into a cabin richly paneled in African mahogany, stabbing Tidwell's eyes and making him nauseous. He couldn't see well enough yet to identify the man dragging him along, but he knew who it was. He recalled seeing a reflection of the man in his living room window, aiming his rifle, and those eyes, glowing hot red–before the tranq dart hit him.

"Listen, I can explain," Tidwell said, forcing himself to look into the man's dark sunglasses.

The big man stood silently on deck, his expression cold, inhuman. He took off his sunglasses, and his red eyes confirmed for John Alfred Tidwell, for the first and last time in his life, the reality of the Black Ghost.

"I'll give you millions," he pleaded, as Bic reached into a compartment to retrieve what looked like a ski rope.

Those red eyes blazed in fury. "You shouldn't have blackmailed me with Gracie's life."

To his own amazement, Tidwell's fear was suddenly usurped by a spasm of anger. "We had a contract," he spat, "and you broke it. I'm the one who should be upset."

The large man attached the end of the ski rope to the thick rope shackling Tidwell's wrists together. He then picked Tidwell up and threw him overboard. The shock of the icy cold water nearly stopped his heart. As he sank, panic overwhelmed him, and he began to kick his legs. He had difficulty swimming upward with his hands tied together, but after a few moments, he broke the surface.

He gasped and spat. *"I'm a U.S. Congressman!"*

Tidwell continued to kick to keep his head above water. He looked around. To the east, a couple of hundred yards away, he saw a rocky island spotted with... something... *seals?* In all other directions, there was only dark blue ocean as far as he could see.

The boat engine started and drove away slowly. Tidwell's efforts to free himself redoubled as he saw the slack on the rope begin to go.

Tidwell was dragged through the water. It stung as it rushed in thick slices against his face. He tried to scream as his body scudded along the top of the water like a fishing lure. The rushing tide rushed into his nose and mouth.

After dragging him for three or four hundred yards around the rocky seal roost, Bic turned the boat around and drove up alongside Tidwell.

"What do you want from me?" he screamed with a shred of breath as he treaded water.

Bic bent down out of Tidwell's field of view for a moment. When he reappeared, he tossed something in the air–something the size of a large rock. The thing plopped into the water next to Tidwell's face.

"It's pork chop eatin' time."

Bic disappeared into the cockpit. The boat accelerated for another pass alongside the island of seals

As the slack in the rope tightened, Tidwell looked across the long stretch of dark blue water, knowing he was going to be trolled across as bait. The rope pulled at his wrists, propelling him forward along the surface. He pleaded with himself to stay calm. Nothing was going to happen. This man was an assassin, for God's sake, a whore with a gun. He couldn't say no to money.

Through the foam, he caught sight of a swirl of shadows beneath him. He screamed for Bic to get him out of the water. He knew, in the back of his mind, that the combination of his panic and his rushing heartbeat was like a ringing dinner bell.

He was right.

130

The 4,000-pound dark gray torpedo hit the congressman from below. Within a split second, his body shot up ten feet above the surface, his midsection inside the jaws of a seventeen-foot great white shark.

The enormous shark's thrust peaked with its body completely out of the water. The scene was surprisingly beautiful, despite—or perhaps *because of*—the screaming man thrashing inside the shark's mouth.

Shark and man disappeared below the surface, which, seconds later, was skimmed with a greasy slick of blood.

Bic stared out at John Alfred Tidwell's final resting place. Funny what came to mind at times like this.

Back in 'Nam, he and his buddies had passed jokes back and forth to kill the time on patrol, and one day Riggs had asked him, more than a little bitterly, "Why don't sharks eat politicians?"

"Hell, I don't know," Bic had replied after a moment's thought.

"Professional courtesy."

Almost forty years along, Bic shook his head and muttered, "Bastard. Ruined a perfectly good joke."

He untied the ski rope and threw it into the water. Then he entered the cockpit, knowing he had one final call to make before he left this life and started a new one. Bic picked up a satellite phone and dialed the private number of the man who had been his agent in the world of hits, brokering and arranging payment for all the deals right from the beginning, when he had needed the $100,000 to try to save Gracie's mom from cancer. He had never forgotten how Tony had arranged for him to get paid up front before he went to Colombia to do the hit, just in case he didn't come back.

"It's done," he said.

"Fantastic, my friend!"

Bic paused.

"You there, Bic?"

"Yeah. Tony, I want you to know, I appreciate everything you've done for me and my family over the years, especially making sure Gracie and Hawk made it out okay."

"Anything for a brother in arms."

"But this life is over, man."

"I understand," Tony said solemnly.

Anthony Parelli was a man who wouldn't hesitate to call him again if he needed a special "favor." In his world, a true friend meant someone you could always call upon for a favor.

"Just so we're clear," said Bic. "I mean, I'm done doing jobs. I thought it didn't matter. I thought I'd killed so many people there was no saving me. But my father got a second chance in life, and so I have hope I can make things right, too."

"I can respect that, my friend. May God bless you." After a brief silence, Parelli said hesitantly, "You know, it's not a good idea to come back to the States."

"I figured as much."

"The other guys are gonna buy a resort in Fiji. You're more than welcome there."

For an instant, Bic considered spending time with his old 'Nam buddies. Besides Gracie and Hawk, O'Donnell and Riggs were the closest thing he had to family. But Bic knew that even with all the money they had just made, that group was bound to find more trouble. "Yeah, but I'm thinking more of staying in Africa."

"I respect that. Take care, my friend. I hope you find what you're looking for."

Bic disconnected the call. He knew Parelli wasn't a good man, but he was like family, and had been there for Bic in 'Nam, and other times after.

Bic stood out on the bow of the boat, taking in the majestic view over the ocean. *I could just stay here a while,* he thought, enjoying a rare moment of peace. Bic imagined his beautiful mother standing in their rundown apartment and singing with that angelic voice of hers. *I love you, mama,* he thought.

Then it all became a hellish torment. Bic reached for his side, eyes bulging in agony. The pain was sharp and deep. It quickly intensified, dropping him to his knees, as it felt like someone was squeezing his kidneys with a vice grip. Without warning, Bic spit up a mouthful of dark red blood.

Bic Green collapsed onto the deck, unconscious.

As Bic was dragging Tidwell to his death, smoke was curling up from the stack of a small, dilapidated wooden shack deep in the bayou outside of New Orleans.

Inside, a very old black man, with cryptic runes smeared in white paint across his face and body, held a large needle over the flame of a black candle inscribed all over with serpents, before a makeshift altar. The square table was covered in ritual rattles, thunderstones imbued with supernatural powers, necklaces, jars of poisons, and several statues of dark spirits. All were intertwined around the axis, a wooden center post with the serpent gods carved into its sides.

The iron of the needle glowed bright red. Satisfied, the man retrieved a black voodoo doll from an iron pot. He then raised up the doll and chanted a spell in an ancient language.

The man's eyes rolled back into his head as he jabbed the needle into the doll's side. Smoke came from the doll as the red-hot needle burned it from the inside.

As the flame reflected in his chalky white eyes, the man hissed in a deep, dark voice, "I'll see you in Hell, my son."

The man then twisted the needle deeper before dropping the doll back into the black pot. As he covered the pot with the intentions of locking this cursed spell of agonizing pain for eternity, he said, "It's pork chop-eatin' time!"

THE END

Acknowledgments

Writing this series has been over a decade long journey that I have truly enjoyed. I owe an enormous debt of gratitude to my great family, incredible friends and the skilled professionals I have worked with along the way.

To my wife, Jennifer, from reading the very first words to building the website all while taking care of our wonderful children. Without you there would be no novels, movies or songs. You are an amazing wife, mom, friend and person.

To my mom, your wisdom and our facetime laughs together is what I cherish the most. Even though you are the smartest person I know, you are always understanding and take the time to dumb it down for me. Thank you for always being there for my family.

To my sister, Nina Hunter, thank you for not only reading everything, but being there to lend your creative talent in whatever way I need.

To my sister, Gia Hughes, you have always been there with unconditional support, this book is no exception. My brother in Law, Tim Hughes, I can always count on you to come up with something creative for any of my projects when I need expertise in the medical field.

To all the talented professionals who helped sculpt this novel to its polished finish. The team of awesome editors I worked with over the many revisions: Floyd Largent, Keith Olexa, Brian T. Schmidt, Emmett Haq, Paul Lorello, Isabel Penraeth and Peter J. Wacks. Each of your knowledge and expertise in the craft of writing not only grew this novel into something I am truly proud of but were an integral part of my growth as a writer. I am grateful to have worked with such skilled and great individuals.

Special thanks to Peter J. Wacks for helping me with the final polish on the book and giving me the confidence to know that it is ready to share with the world.

Sincere praise to Erik Gevers for the impeccable formatting and to Dane Low of ebooklaunch.com for the great cover art.

Thank you to the awesome team at Next Step PR. Kiki, Colleen, Kristina, Darlene, Athena, Jill and Megan. You have done an amazing job helping me get my book out there for people to discover and I truly appreciate your dedication and guidance.

Also, sincere appreciation to all of my beta reading friends, Jeff Burtis, Bradford O'Neil, Dan Galligan, Al Sicard, Joanna Wilson and Linck Bascomb. No one ever truly knows how powerful a little positive feedback can be to energize the creative drive to the finish line. Gratitude to each of you for playing this critical role in this journey. Thank you.

A special thank you from Jennifer to Mia Sheridan and Alessandra Torre. For two of her favorite authors to give sincere advice has been a true blessing, thank you.

"A reader lives a thousand lives before he dies..."
George R.R. Martin

I want to take a moment and say thank you for reading Black Ghost, I hope you enjoyed it! I am honored that you trusted me to take the journey with the story and characters.

Black Ghost was written over many years, the first draft finished in 2008 was over 107,000 words. The final draft you've just read was just over 80,000. The process of shrinking 37,000 words happened over seven complete rewrites. During this time, I also learned how to write movie scripts, which I believe had a huge influence on the pacing of my writing. I went from long chapters to short meaningful dense chapters. I hope it was a page turner for you.

With all that cutting some really fun chapters were either substantially condensed or completely taken out. I put together a fifty-one-page deleted/altered chapter PDF that I'd like to send you as a thank you. You can either reach out to me directly at freddie@freddievillacci.com or go to my website at freddievillacci.com and sign up for the newsletter. If you enjoyed the book, these deleted or condensed chapters will be a fun read.

Any feedback or questions feel free to email me at freddie@freddievillacci.com, I'd love to hear from you.

I am truly honored that you lived another life through reading the first book in the Black Ghost series.

Sincerely,

Freddie Villacci

Also, please review the book on Amazon if you liked it ☺. Reviews are like gold to an author and I would truly appreciate it.

About the Author

Freddie Villacci, Jr. was born and raised in Wood Dale, Illinois. He earned a degree in marketing from Berry College, while playing baseball. At the age of nineteen he began to invest in the stock market and continued on with a career in the insurance and financial services industry.

In his first published Novel, Black Ghost, he has used his professional background to give depth and credibility to the plot centering around the estate death tax laws.

Besides books, he also fuels his creativity writing movie scripts and songs. FACELESS, an independent movie is due out in 2021.

Freddie loves being out in the sun, especially playing baseball and golf with his daughter and twin boys. He and his wife, Jennifer, have a passion for supporting charities that help children.

Freddie would love to connect with his readers at
www.freddievillacci.com

THE CURE

A
BLACK GHOST
THRILLER

FREDDIE VILLACCI, JR.

Here is a look at what is coming next for Bic Green. The Cure, book two in the Black Ghost thriller series, is sure to keep you on the edge of your seat!

She could save millions of lives. But now she's fighting for her own.

On the brink of completing her lifelong mission and discovering a cure for cancer, Gracie Green is eager to advance to human trials and share her findings with the world. But top executives within the FDA, backed by the world's largest cancer drug company, have other ideas. Determined to stop her cure from ever seeing the light of day, they enlist the help of Ex-CIA operative Jaco Ivanov. He has one mission – to wipe Greentech from the face of the earth.

Hunted by an expert killer and framed for a terrible crime she didn't commit, Gracie finds herself on the run and struggling to stay one step ahead of Jaco and his minions. In way over her head and surrounded by a murky world of shadow governments, intelligence agencies, and illegal dealings, her future hangs in the balance. There's only one thing Jaco didn't account for – the Black Ghost.

But even with the infamous hitman's help, Gracie will need more than luck to find the truth and bring her cure to the world. Can she hope to survive against such powerful enemies? Or will the Black Ghost finally have met his match?

CPSIA information can be obtained
at www.ICGtesting.com
Printed in the USA
LVHW090100090322
712998LV00017B/289/J